BRIDGET WALSH

Daughters in Exile

A story of the Irish Famine: Transportation and Emigration. 1846-47.

First edition

ISBN: 978-1-7396885-2-3

Editing by Nancy Carnell
Cover art by Latte Goldstein

This book was professionally typeset on Reedsy.
Find out more at reedsy.com

With love and thanks

To my team:
Nancy Carnell, my daughter and copy editor.
Fran Carey, my daughter and book-seller in Ireland.
Charlotte Walsh, my daughter-in-law and marketing editor.
To my family for reading my pages, and their love and support.

To my Open University Masters Workshop readers and
commentators
Many thanks.

This book is written in memory of all those who suffered, and
those who were forced to leave Ireland during and after the
Famine years.

Cast of Characters

New York
Annie Power. Born February 1829 (17 in Sept 1846)
Finn Power. Annie's brother, born September 1832 (14 in Sept 1846)
Katty Power. Annie's sister, born May 1837 (9 in Sept 1846)
Bridie Foley. The aunt, born in Waterford, 1805. Emigrated in 1823
Pat Brady. Chairman of the Aid for Ireland Committee

Historical characters in New York
Bishop Hughes
Sister Mary Angela. Sisters of Charity

Girls in Annie's Refuge
Colleen O'Brien from Cork
Niamh and Deirdre O'Hara from Tipperary
Roisin, Clodagh and Christine, from Sligo
Jeannie Sullivan from Tralee

Melbourne, New South Wales, Australia.
Jane Keating, born September 1830 (16 in October 1846). Goes by the name Jane Annie Power. Jane took Annie's place in prison and was transported to New South Wales
Sergeant Owen Doran, a British solder, and Irishman.

Colonel Johns. Jane's employer

The newspapermen. Harold and Andrew Stephenson, father and son

Jane's Aboriginal friends: Jimmy, his mother, Sally, and her mother, Grandmother

Historical characters in New South Wales

Caroline Chisholm. Philanthropist

Charles La Trobe. Superintendent of New South Wales

William Thomas, Assistant Protector of the Aborigines, served under George Robinson, the Chief Protector.

"as late as June 1846, La Trobe ordered Thomas to burn the camps of the Boon wurrung and the Woi Wurrung to force them to move on (from Melbourne)." (p186,) Boyce, James (2012). *1835: The Founding of Melbourne & the Conquest of Australia.*

Gaelic phrases

Cead Mille Failte. A hundred thousand welcomes.

Go raibh maith agat. Thank you.

Gaelic endearments.

A stor. Star

Mo chroi my heart

1

Jane Keating: June 1846. The Atlantic Ocean

Locked in the hull of the King Henry, Jane Keating's stomach turned as the ship heaved its way out of the River Liffey and into St George's Channel. The slap of the crew's bare feet on the deck above and the clatter of chains mingled with the cries of the other imprisoned women and the shouts of their children. Some of the convicts had been allowed to bring their children with them. Boys and girls skittered around the steerage and called out to each other until quietened by sharp comments from green-faced women on their bunks. A few of the women had babies in their arms, wrapped in shawls, kept close to their chests. Jane swallowed down another dry wretch, trying not to smell the sweat and urine that mingling with the stench of her fellow sufferers' vomit.

Most of the convicts were young, in their twenties. One of the older women, Lizzie Connors, in the next bunk, told Jane that she had been arrested for larceny. 'Not my first time, girl. I think they must have got tired of arresting me.'

It was after supper, and they had been at sea for several hours. Lizzie was stretched out on her bunk, her arms behind her head. She was a stocky woman, in spite of all the hunger there was in Dublin.

Lizzie must have been successful at the stealing, for a while there, at least, Jane thought, and dozed, exhausted from the idea of leaving Ireland. Her mind froze at the thought she might never walk on Irish soil again. 'No,' she murmured. 'No.' She would come back, somehow. She had no regrets about what she had done. None.

By eight o'clock that evening, the prisoners had quietened down and most lay on their beds. The children, too, had stopped racing around, and huddled beside their mothers.

The light through the hatches had dimmed in the enclosed cabin that was their prison. Low sounds filtered down from the upper deck; the ship's bell rang eight times, distant voices of the crew, answering and calling; the slap of water against the outside of the hull. Jane was in a cocoon, deep in the ship.

* * *

The creak of the prison door opening woke Jane from her doze. A tall man, formally dressed in a black suit walked into the prison. He was accompanied by a young, dark-haired soldier, in a red and black uniform. Neither spoke, they just walked through the length of the hull, checked the bunks, looked into the water closets, then left, locking the prison door behind them. Soon after, the hatches in the ceiling were covered and darkness fell over the sleeping convicts. Jane still had her chains on, and whatever way she turned, the sores on her wrists and ankles burned.

Seven years. The words hummed through her mind as the ship rolled out into deeper water and further away from Ireland. She'd be twenty-two by the end of her sentence, a woman, not a girl.

The sleepless night gave Jane time to reconsider her actions. Did she do the right thing by taking her dear friend Annie's place to serve her sentence for her? She had been so sure at the time. Annie had her brother and sister to care for, while Jane had no-one to leave behind.

It had been easy to do, for the two girls were both about the same height and build. Jane had walked into the prison, disguised as the young man, Jack, to say goodbye to Annie. Their friend, Speranza, paid the jailer to leave for five minutes. The two girls exchanged clothes. Annie then walked out to freedom, and left Jane behind in Kilmainham Gaol, facing transportation to New South Wales.

But here and now? In this stifling cabin with fifty other convicts. Seven years. What would she look like at twenty-two? Would she survive this transportation to the end of the world? Would she ever see Ireland again? The questions shivered their way through her mind. The night passed while she counted the ship's bells every half hour.

* * *

It was their second day at sea. The gratings in the low ceiling opened and a faint light shone on the curved walls of the hull and woke the chained women.

Two crewmen came into the prison, and each carried a hammer. They began to remove the chains, and a cheer went up. The crewman on Jane's side of the compartment had rough-cut hair and he was missing several teeth, his lips were wet and loose around his mouth. Jane held her breath to avoid the stink of sweat off his sailcloth trousers and filthy shirt. He struck the shackles on Jane's ankles and she breathed a sigh of thanks. But he didn't stop there. He wrapped his calloused fingers around her left ankle, just where the skin had chafed from the restraints, and inspected her foot. He moved closer, and sniffed the sole and her toes. His hot breath stank of brandy and his dark beard bristled like a scrubbing brush against the tender skin, she felt the slobbery tip of his hot tongue lick her instep.

She pulled her foot away and shifted back against the hull of the ship. 'Let go!' she said, then raised her other foot as if to kick him.

The crewman laughed. 'Ooh, a temper! I like that in a young'un.' He winked as if it was just a game, then let her foot drop onto the mattress.

Lizzie, in the next bunk, saw what happened and shouted 'Get off her, *ya eejit!*'

He turned to take Lizzie's chains off, but she was ready for him. He didn't attempt to sniff or lick any part of her.

The two men gathered the chains and manacles into a box and left.

'Lizzie, you saw what he did?' Jane tried to still her breathing and blew out through her mouth. Her heart-beat skittered in her chest.

Lizzie nodded. 'He's a dirty *divil* that one. Watch yourself, girl, or he'll have you for his supper!'

'What do you mean?' Jane asked her.

'They're all the same. You be nice to them, and in return

4

they'll give you some extra food or favours. They have plenty of brandy.'

'Not me. I'll tell them I'm promised back home and my sweetheart is waiting for me.'

The older woman chuckled at the obvious lie and shook her head. Her voice was cracked and slightly hoarse. 'Well, aren't you just blessed, darlin'? Those crewmen don't mind about sweethearts or husbands for that matter, and the soldiers'll come sniffing around too, just you wait.'

'How do you know all this?'

'They're men, aren't they? No other women on board, only us, their prisoners. And you, a fine girl, with those grey eyes and black hair. A bit on the thin side, but then we're all half-starved, and that's the truth of it.' Lizzie lay back on her narrow bunk and closed her eyes.

She may be right, but they'll not have me, Jane decided, and rubbed the chafed skin on her wrists and ankles. She looked around the hulk of her moving prison, and the women, all clad in the same convict uniform of a drab grey skirt and blouse, topped with a ragged shawl. Most were older than Jane. At fifteen, she was one of the youngest to be transported, apart from the babies and children.

Here, in place of her friend, Annie Power, she passed for seventeen. She would try to keep her first name, Jane, somehow. No-one would know she was a Keating.

She spent some time that morning on the hunt for a weapon; something she could use to protect herself, if that seaman, or anyone else, came at her. A floorboard under her bunk was cracked and she pulled away a long splinter of wood. That would have to do.

* * *

Later that day, all the prisoners were taken up on deck by their guards and assembled in front of the captain. The deck rocked beneath Jane's feet and she, and many of her convict ship-mates, struggled to keep their balance. Brilliant beams of light reflected off the canvas sails and the water. Jane squinted after coming up from the dim light of the steerage. Creaking spars and cracking sails merged with shouts from crew high up in the topsails. Her ears rang.

She shaded her eyes with her hand and looked up at the two huge sails almost ready to burst with the force of the wind as it blew horizontally across the ship's deck. For just a moment, Jane was thrilled to stand there and let the wind whip her hair, now damp from the spray, around her face; her skirt pressed tight against her legs by the sharp ocean breeze. Then she shuddered, as a trill of fear ran up the back of her neck. Above her head, the sky was full of great white cloud-sacks in furious motion battling each other, with only a distant glimmer of blue beyond. She looked out across miles of dark green ocean. The surface of the sea moved and the ship rose and fell, and she with it. She swallowed down a sudden nausea.

Ireland was now far behind them. If she had wings like the sea birds circling the masts, she'd take off right there and then and fly back home. But there's no family left there for me, only Father Hanrahan. He helped me before, he might help again, she thought. Even the workhouse in Galway would be better than here. She pressed her lips together. No, not the workhouse. Not the way of her mother and brothers.

* * *

The captain came up on deck with the soldier and the tall man who had inspected them the previous night. Jane and the other women all waited to hear what next there was in store for them. How long were they to be on the ship for? Where in the world were they? Would the chains go back on?

The captain was a short, energetic man, got up in a navy blue jacket with gold epaulets that dazzled in the sunshine. His tricorn hat was jammed on his head, and had matching gold braid. All his trimmings fluttered around his head and shoulders. Jane hid a smile, for he looked just like a puffed up pigeon. His voice was a deep baritone that somehow didn't match his small, round body. Even so, he needed to shout to be heard above the wind, the straining sails and the creaking spars.

'My mission is to get all of you to Melbourne with no mishaps or injuries along the way. We have a surgeon-superintendent here, Mr Blake, who will be in charge of you on the journey.' The captain's companion, a long, angular person, dressed in a tight-fitting black jacket and trousers, nodded and tipped his hat to the women.

The captain continued. 'You'll have fresh air every day and there's plenty of food for the journey. We'll dock in Cape Town to pick up supplies of fresh water and food, about three or four weeks from now. Then we'll resume our journey to New South Wales. Once there, you'll serve out your sentence. Now, I'll hand you over to Mr Blake.'

It was a relief to think she'd be fed every day; more than she'd had since their potato crop failed last year. If it wasn't such a sad thing, Jane might have laughed to hear that she'd be better fed and taken care of as a convict than a free person in Ireland - who could easily starve to death or die of fever, and no-one give them, or their children, a second glance.

The surgeon-superintendent, Mr Blake, stood with his back to the ship's railings. His tall hat seemed likely to fly away in the wind, so he took it off and held it under his arm. His thick dark hair blew around his face, and he smoothed it with his free hand.

The young soldier beside him had no such problem, for a strap under his chin held his uniform shako in place and he stood to attention beside the surgeon. The two men's silhouettes were outlined against the deep green sea. The moving horizon merged with the pale sky in the far distance. Jane swallowed hard and blew out a breath.

'Good morning to you. The deck is dry, so sit down while I tell you how we'll manage on this journey.' Mr Blake waited while the women arranged themselves, then nodded and continued to speak.

'This is my third time on a transport ship to New South Wales. I have not yet lost a prisoner to sickness and I don't intend to lose any of you. You have all been passed as fit and we need to work together to keep you that way. We'll be on this ship for at least three months, and maybe more, a journey of fourteen thousand miles. Now listen to me closely.' He paused to get their full attention. 'I have three rules you must always follow. The first is cleanliness. The second, no fighting. The third, no talking to the crew. You must all follow the rules to the letter. If you break the rules, you will be punished.' He looked at the women for a moment, then his face lit up with a thin smile. 'However, if you follow the rules, you will be rewarded.'

'Sergeant Doran here, will put you into groups of ten, a mess; and you'll choose a mess leader from the group. He'll explain how that works when you go back down below deck.' Mr Blake looked at the soldier beside him. 'Sergeant, I'll let you get on with it. And don't forget explain the rules.' Mr Blake put his hat back on and left.

The rest of the morning was spent going through the arrangements for their living space. Mess leaders were chosen and Lizzie put herself forward as the leader of Jane's mess. They would all take turns to help Lizzie with the work to keep their space in good order by emptying the slop buckets, and ensuring laundry was done. Sergeant Doran emphasised that cleanliness was paramount. He arranged for two of the women to teach the children each morning and he provided books and slates for the school.

* * *

The days on board the ship settled into a routine of work and play. Lizzie organised the women in her mess to help her with the tasks; to empty the slop buckets, tidy the bunks and sweep the floor. She inspected all them to make sure they were clean and tidy before the breakfast of porridge was brought to the prison. The best-kept messes were given prizes for cleanliness. One of the prizes was a small notebook and pencil won by Lizzie, who had no use for it, and gave it to Jane. She began, that day, to keep a diary of the journey.

Most days, when the weather was fine and the work was done, the convicts were allowed up on deck to sit and chat. Mr Blake set up a portable table and chair in a corner of the deck to see any who felt the need to report sick. One or two of the prisoners complained of sea-sickness, or diarrhoea, but the majority were in good health.

Mr Blake had a supply of wool and needles for those who knitted, and several of the women began to work on jumpers, blankets and scarves. Jane had never learned to knit. When she finished school at twelve years old, all her time was spent outside working with her father. Instead, she worked with Lizzie on the cleaning jobs; sweeping and scraping the floorboards in their mess, and doing the washing once a week. And so the days passed on their journey south.

Back home, Jane had often stood and looked out over the ever-changing ocean that filled Galway Bay, and the sky at the limits of the horizon. Now, here she was, on the Atlantic Ocean, beyond those limits, where each day brought her further and further away from home.

She found her sea-legs after a week and enjoyed the work she did with Lizzie. It kept her from thinking about her troubles. She felt she'd put some weight on, her face felt less tight and angular, her hip bones less sharp.

* * *

But the nights were the worst. After the Superintendent finished his rounds at nine o'clock, she would lie on her bunk and wait for sleep to come. Her mind roamed constantly from her present situation, forward to when she would turn sixteen in October, when the ship would be almost in New South Wales. This time last year, she'd had her mother, father and brothers, with no forewarning of the potato blight that would destroy their food crop for the winter. Then, just six months ago, suddenly, she was the last of her family and had set out to walk the road from Galway to Waterford. She dressed as a boy for safety and called herself Jack Keating.

It was a miracle that she met Annie Power in the market place in Waterford. Annie had taken Jane home with her. Annie's father, had made her welcome and had laughed when she told him that she really was a girl.

All that was gone now, leaving both Jane and Annie orphaned by the potato blight.

She knew what her father would say. 'Come on, Janey, we've work to do!' If only he was still alive and she could hear his voice and kiss his face. She shook her head. That would never happen again in this life, but she made a promise to herself. She'd go back to Ireland one day and kneel by his grave, to show him that his daughter, Jane Keating, had survived.

* * *

Two weeks into their journey, and it was before dawn. The convict quarters were quiet, apart from the creaking movement of the ship and the slap of the waves against the outside of the hull. It was still dark, most of the women were asleep, when Jane woke suddenly, at the clink of metal on metal; a key, as it turned in a lock. Silence, then the steerage door creaked.

Jane turned her head to see the door open. The bearded crewman from before, who had licked her foot, sneaked in and closed the door behind him. She smelt him, caught her breath and shuddered. Somehow, she knew instantly, he had come back for her. She reached under the bolster and put her hand around the weapon she had made out of the splinter of wood that was nearly a foot long. She had wrapped a piece of rag around one end for a handle, and left the other end with its broken, jagged edges. She lay still on her bunk, not breathing. Her heart hammered in her chest, and she watched the crewman creep over towards her. He reached out with his calloused hand and grabbed her leg. She kicked him and shouted. 'Don't touch me!'

If he was surprised, he took no notice, and ran one hand up to the top of her leg, while the other hand covered her mouth and pushed her head back on the bunk. The pressure eased off her face as he used one hand to haul at her drawers, and Jane bit down on the palm of his stinking, scaly hand. Then she lifted the splinter and stabbed him in the arm with all her might. 'Go on, Jane!' A hot surge of triumph flooded through her for a split second.

Her attacker roared in pain and pulled his hand away from her teeth. Jane saw the bones in his knuckles whiten, then felt her nose crack as he punched her in the face. Her head bounced off the mattress, her vision blurred and a white hot pain pierced through her nose and eyes right into her brain.

By this time, the whole place was awake. Some of the women ran around, half-naked in just their shifts, screaming for help, while others banged on the prison door. Lizzie came to her aid and held Jane close as the crewman swore and tried to pull the weapon out of his arm.

After a few moments, the prison door burst open. Sergeant Doran and another soldier raced in, their pistols held up, ready to fire.

In the light from the open door, Jane saw her attacker had managed to get the splinter out, leaving a dark bloody mess near his shoulder. She forced herself to sit up. Her head was still dizzy from the punch, and she swung her legs off the bunk. 'Help me! He tried to rape me!'

The crewman staggered upright and waved the bloody splinter. 'That bitch stabbed me!' He yelled to anyone who could hear in the uproar.

The two soldiers caught hold of the crewman and dragged him out. A couple of minutes later the sergeant came back in, to check on Jane. 'What's your name?' he asked.

'Jack,' she said, and shook her head. 'No, Jane Keating, no, Power.' Jane found it difficult to speak as blood flowed from the back of her nose into her mouth and both eyes had swollen almost shut. She had absolutely no idea who she was supposed to be at that moment.

'Come with me, Jane,' he said. 'I'll get the surgeon to look at you.' She staggered upright and caught his arm to stop herself from falling.

'Listen to me. Pull a skirt up and put your boots on. It's wet and windy on deck.'

She dressed quickly and wrapped her shawl around her. They left the women and children to settle themselves down and try to get back to sleep.

* * *

Jane and the sergeant climbed the ladder to the deck. Jane went first and held on tight to the railings going up the steps. Her head ached and she was still dizzy from the punch. The movement of the ship threatened to unbalance her. She stopped when she reached the deck and waited for her escort to join her. She looked up at the silver crescent of the moon. Stars glistened like ice crystals across the black night sky. The rain fell on her face and together with the cold air, cooled the pain in her nose. She took a deep breath. The sergeant held his arm out. 'Keep hold of me, so you don't slip. The surgeon's cabin is not far.'

They walked across the deck, wet and glistening from sea spray, past two sailors on duty on the main wheel. Up ahead, on the quarterdeck, Jane saw the outline of an officer on watch, wrapped up against the wind and rain, a hat jammed on his head.

They went through a covered companionway to another set of stairs, this time, more like a steep ladder, leading down below the deck. Sergeant Doran went first this time, and Jane followed him into a long compartment, almost half the length of the ship. They passed hammocks slung from beams overhead. Each hammock swung slowly to and fro with the rise and fall of the ship, and the place was silent apart from the low snores of sleeping sailors wrapped up in their canvas cocoons. At the end of the compartment, Jane's guide stopped at the surgeon's quarters and knocked.

After a few minutes, the surgeon put his tousled, sleepy head around the door and listened to the soldier's report. He made them wait while he dressed, then invited them into his cabin. One side of the cabin had a bunk and a desk and the other was set up for use as a dispensary in the daytime. In one corner, a swinging lamp was suspended from a low beam overhead and spilled an orange glow across the room.

Jane swayed with the rise and fall of the ship until the surgeon indicated for her to sit at a small table. 'Tell me your name, then I'll look at your injuries.'

'Annie Jane Power. But call me Jane,' she said.

He nodded, then sponged her face clean of the blood, examined her cheekbones for fractures and declared them sound. He used some form of manipulation in an attempt to fix her nose. The pain from that was worse than the original punch. Jane's eyes watered and she groaned in pain, until he gave up. 'You'll have a crooked nose, I'm afraid,' he said, and wiped her face again, this time to dry her tears. 'You're fortunate your teeth are all still in your head. Now, tell me, Jane. Have you spoken to the sailor before now? Did you encourage him to come and visit you?'

Jane shook her head and winced at more pain. 'No. But two weeks ago, when he took my chains off, he licked my foot. Lizzie saw him do it.' Once started, her tears seemed to keep falling, she brushed them away.

The surgeon sighed. 'The captain may want to talk to you tomorrow. Go and get some sleep.'

Sergeant Doran escorted Jane back to the prison. Before he unlocked the door, he turned to her. 'You'll be safe for now, Jane or Jack Keating, or whatever name you're going by.' Then he lowered his voice to whisper. 'You need to get your name right.' She could see, and hear, that he was Irish, from his accent and narrow, dark looks.

Jane risked confiding in him and whispered back. 'My real name is Jane Keating. Here, I'm Annie Jane Power. What's your name?'

'Owen Doran,' he replied, and gave her a curious look. 'I heard you say, Jack.' Then he waited for her to go inside. She stepped into the prison compartment, and the key turned in the door behind her.

* * *

Lizzie, her neighbour, was still awake, but the rest of the

women were asleep. It was almost dawn and the ship's bell had just rung for the change of watch.

'He got what he deserved,' Lizzie said. 'I'd say he'll make himself scarce for a while. Are you all right, girl?'

'*Go raith math agut.*' Jane thanked her in Irish. 'I'm sore, and my nose pains, but I'm still in one piece.' She smiled at the woman through swollen eyes, the skin around her nose and cheeks already tender to the touch. 'And I'll need another stick, I left that one in his arm.'

Jane sat on the bunk and leaned back against the planks of the hull. The air was heavy in the dark space of the convict quarters. At night the smells from the water closets, a combination of blood, shit and piss, overlaid the odour of sweat and stale breath. The air was so thick and soupy that she could almost catch it in her hand. It reminded her of the smells from the butcher's stall beside the market place in Galway. But there, the sea breeze from the bay made sure to clean away the miasma before morning came. Unlike here.

'What did you do to get sent away from home? You don't look like a criminal to me.' Lizzie said.

Jane thought Lizzie had gone back to sleep but saw her dark eyes showing above her grey blanket.

'It was a mix-up.' Jane brushed her hair away from her face. The least said, she thought.

'And what of your family, do you have anyone back home?' Lizzie persisted.

'No. They got sick and died. The fever.'

'Sure, God love you, you're all alone in the world.' Lizzie shook her head. 'It's hard times we're living in, Jane. You know, I think but for the potato blight, half the women on this ship would still be at home, minding their children.'

16

'I'll go home one day, when I've served my sentence,' Jane said.

'Please God, we'll both get back. I have two small grand-children I want to see again before I die.'

'Lizzie, that's a shame. Ah, but you must miss them.'

'They have a good father in my son. He'll look after them. His poor wife died on their third child, may she and the child rest in peace.' Lizzie's hand reached out from under the blanket and she crossed herself, then closed her eyes.

'Then we both have something to look forward to,' Jane said. She slid down in the bunk and pulled her blanket up around her. The pain in her face ran through her head every time she moved. A thought scuttled through her mind. How in God's name was she to get back to Ireland from the other side of the world? She dismissed it, but the echo of the thought remained, and burrowed in.

* * *

After breakfast the next morning, Sergeant Doran came to take Jane to the captain's cabin. Lizzie caught the sergeant's arm as he waited for Jane to tie her boots. 'Listen here to me. You tell the captain, I saw that ruffian come in last night and try to have his way with Jane. And she no more than a girl. Disgraceful, so it is.' Several women nearby whispered and watched.

He nodded. 'I'll do that, Missus. I expect when he sees Jane's face, the captain will not be pleased.'

The captain didn't take much persuading as to who was in the right of the situation. 'My crew member said you had asked him to come and see you last night. According to his account, you changed your mind, and stabbed him with a piece of wood.'

Jane stood before his desk and shook her head. 'Captain, he's a liar. My neighbour, Lizzie was awake and she'll tell you. He crept in. Sure, t'was the middle of the night! When he took the manacles off, a while ago, he licked my foot and made out it was a joke. That's why I had the piece of wood, in case he came back.'

She saw the captain's face wrinkle in disgust. Would he believe her?

Sergeant Doran shifted over towards Jane. 'I can fetch Lizzie if you want to question her, Sir.'

'No, there's no need for it. It's a tall tale to think you'd ask him to come and see you in the prison. He could easily have let you out and the two of you gone up on deck. Which, I'll have you know, is forbidden on this ship!'

Jane endured his gaze on her swollen nose and bruised cheekbones. She gritted her teeth to stop herself from asking. 'And what'll you do about it, Captain?'

As if he heard her unspoken question, he said. 'He won't come near you again. I'll see to that.'

The captain was true to his word. Later that morning, the crewman was brought on deck and strapped to one of the masts where he endured twenty-five lashes with a cat o'nine tails. Crew and prisoners were lined up to witness the punishment. A bucket of salt water was thrown over his back to wash off the blood and he was taken below decks.

Jane was only sorry she wasn't asked to help dish out the punishment.

18

2

Annie Power: August 1846.
Manhattan, New York

A nnie recognised her mother's sister as soon as the door to the apartment building opened. Their aunt, Bridie Foley, opened her arms to Annie, Katty and Finn, and the first words she spoke were the Irish welcome. *'Cead Mille Failte.'* They hugged and kissed and cried together in the doorway. At long last!

Bridie was the picture of Annie's late mother, Caitrín. Dressed in black, of wiry build and whippet-thin. Her auburn hair, showing only a few streaks of grey, and was tied back in a bun. Tears shone in her lively blue eyes when she saw her sister's children had arrived. Bridie had emigrated to New York when she was a girl of Annie's age. Now she worked as a nurse at the infirmary on Water Street. A widow, she lived alone.

They followed their aunt up two flights of stairs to the third floor, and their new home. The apartment had three rooms: a bedroom off the narrow hall, a kitchen and a parlour. The shared privies were outside in the yard. She took them into the tidy kitchen. A glass-globed oil lamp was placed in the centre of the table that was just big enough to seat four. A framed daguerreotype of Bridie and her late husband, Kevin, hung on the wall beside the table.

'Give me that bag and take your coats off. Now, sit down there, you must be starving. Tell me about your journey, while I get you some supper.' Bridie put the coats and Annie's cloak away in the parlour, came back, and poured cups of tea for them. She looked at her sister's three children and blessed herself. 'Thanks be to God and his Blessed Mother!'

Her smile turned to a look of horror when she heard the account of Katty's abduction at the docks. She sat herself in the chair by the stove. 'Them devils should be hung! Come here to me, Katty. Here, sit on my knee and let me look at you.'

Nine-year-old Katty did as she was bid and Annie saw a tiny smile appear on her sister's face as soon as Bridie's arms went around her. 'Why, you're as light as a feather, sweetheart.'

'He was a bad man, auntie Bridie. Look, he pulled my arm.' Katty pulled her sleeve up and showed the bruising on her forearm.

'Sure, darlin' girl! Let me kiss it. There now, that'll be better soon.' Bridie glanced at Finn and Annie, but said no more. After a few minutes she lifted Katty up and put her down on Annie's knee. 'Sit there, while I get you something to eat. It's a blessed day to have you here. I'm only sorry your poor mother and father couldn't be here with you. May they rest in peace.' Bridie stood and peered at Finn. 'Now then, Finn, you look like you could eat a dish of bacon stew? I've had this pot on the go for a week now, waiting for you. And another one last week. But sure, it's all the better for the cooking.' She took out four bowls, filled them with the stew and sliced a loaf of bread onto a plate in the middle of the table. She handed out spoons. 'There, eat your fill. And it's most welcome you are.'

After the supper, Bridie showed them where they would sleep. Katty would share Bridie's double bed. Annie and Finn would sleep in the parlour. Bridie had bought two roll-up mattresses, blankets and pillows and she showed them how to make up their beds. She shifted the two wooden armchairs and the small side table to one side, and they unrolled the mattresses over the multicoloured rag rug on the floor. It was a squeeze, but the mattresses fitted.

'Bridie, this is wonderful,' Annie said. 'Thank you. And thank you for the money and clothes you sent to us. You saved us when we had nothing left.'

Katty was exhausted after her experience that day. Her eyes closed, and her head drooped, and she was soon tucked up, fast asleep in Bridie's warm bed.

Annie, Finn and Bridie, sat in the kitchen and talked about the journey and the man who had tried to take Katty.

'I read about them criminals in the newspaper,' Bridie said. 'They prey on new arrivals like wolves. It said there's a superintendent for immigration, but he can't seem to get anything done to stop it. I'm just so relieved you're here, and safe. Sure, I've spent the last two weeks running to every knock at the door. Please God, Katty will be fine in a day or two.'

Annie's eyes started to close. 'I'm tired too, Bridie. I think I need to lie down.'

'Well then, your beds are ready for you. There's a chamber pot under the table in the parlour to save you going outside at night. Here, girl, bring in a jug of hot water with you and get a little wash before you lie down.'

Bridie filled the jug from the kettle on the hob and handed it to Annie.

'Good night, Bridie, and thank you. Don't be long, Finn. You must be tired, too.'

In the quiet parlour, Annie undressed to her shift, used the chamber pot, and washed her hands and face. She let her hair down and shook it out, and tried to push away the thought of the man at the docks. She prayed she'd not see him again.

Back home, in their small cabin, they had all lived together in the one room. It was always warm from the fire, kept going day and night, and she was never alone. Her father's loving presence had filled their home, right up to the day he died. Annie looked at the four walls around her, at the statue of the Sacred Heart on the side table and the empty fireplace. She nodded. She could be lonely here, but she'd be fed and, please God, safe. 'We got here, Da,' she whispered, as if in prayer.

Like Katty, as soon as she lay her head on the pillow, she fell into a deep, dreamless sleep. She didn't hear Finn come in a few minutes later.

Their new life had begun.

3

Annie Power: August 1846. East Broadway

The next morning, Annie was still tired after the long journey, and the shock of Katty's abduction, but she had promised herself she would hunt for a job the first chance she got, so after breakfast she set out to do just that. Bridie was on a late shift that day, and would spend the morning getting to know Katty and Finn.

'You want to see Sister Mary Angela. She has the new Sisters of Charity novitiate and orphanage on East Broadway.' Bridie said at breakfast. 'I'll write you a letter to bring with you. There'll be work there, and she knows me from St Patrick's Cathedral. She'll put you right.'

Annie's head cleared a little as she walked along the sidewalk. It was early morning, and the rising sun was still low in the sky, creating lines of pinks and reds above the rooftops. Then she turned the corner onto a main street, into a cacophony of shouted accents from street sellers. It was a street market, with dozens of hucksters lined up along the sidewalk in front of shops and apartments. The road was filling up rapidly with traffic. Horses neighed and carts and cabs clattered along the main street, and jostled for space.

People bumped Annie's shoulders as they rushed past, and she had to brace herself to stay upright. She checked where she was; it wouldn't do to get lost here. Then she followed her aunt's directions and walked east, along the main street. The further along she went, she had to watch her step, for the sidewalks were filthy and muddy. The roadway was clogged with foul-smelling lumps of excrement and yellow-brown streams of piss deposited by the horses, mules and oxen, pulling carts and wagons. Annie passed one man who stood on the sidewalk and pissed out over the road, with no shame at all. 'Jesus, Mary and Joseph!' She looked away, and continued to walk along East Broadway.

After a while, she came to a building with a large wooden crucifix above the door, and blew out a breath. 'Yes, this is it.' She lifted her hand and knocked, unsure suddenly.

'I've come to see Sister Mary Angela,' Annie explained to the young nun who answered the door. 'I have a letter here from my aunt.' Her fingers trembled as she handed over the letter. 'Dear Lord,' she prayed, 'let them help me.'

The nun took the letter and showed Annie to a bench in the wide hallway. The nun went off down the hall, her light footsteps tapped on the gleaming dark red floor tiles. Annie watched her disappear around a corner, then smoothed her hair back from her face. She placed her hands together in her lap, closed her eyes and breathed the prayer again.

Her prayer must have worked, for Sister Mary Angela herself came to greet Annie. She was a compact woman of middle age, and her soft face sparkled with shrewd brown eyes. '*Dia dhuit.* God be with you,' the nun said.

'*Dia is Mhuire dhuit.* God and Mary be with you,' Annie replied. She breathed easier to hear the blessed Irish words of welcome. The Sister led the way along the corridor, and spoke over her shoulder.

'I remember your aunt Bridie. Give her my best wishes, won't you? She's a great woman for her work in the infirmary. Now tell me, did you manage to find us easily?'

'Bridie told me how to get here,' Annie replied with a smile. 'She knows everything about the Sisters of Charity.'

'That's good to hear. Come with me. We'll get a cup of tea and we can talk.'

In the kitchen, Sister Mary Angela took off her bonnet, and set about making a pot of tea. She pointed to one of the benches on either side of a wide oak table in the centre of the room. 'Have a seat.'

Annie sat and looked around her while the nun made the tea. Steam rose silkily from the spout of the black kettle boiling away on the hob, on the wall opposite. She guessed the kettle held enough water to make tea for at least twenty.

Late summer sunlight streamed through the window and reflected off the same red floor tiles she had seen in the hall. The walls were whitewashed, and behind her, iron pots hung above a scrubbed sideboard with a wide set of drawers and cupboards. An open door in the corner led into a pantry where Annie saw shelves loaded with labelled jars of preserved tomatoes, peaches and pickles. Her mouth watered at the sight of such riches. Through the window, several nuns in their black habits and white aprons worked on vegetable plots to harvest the last of the crops. She closed her eyes. Back home, the land and their only food crop, potatoes, were still poisoned by blight. There was none of this bounty anywhere to be found.

'Tell me about your journey here, my child.' The nun said, as she poured the tea.

Annie shook her head. 'It was a hard journey, Sister.' Her eyes suddenly brimmed with tears. She remembered how sick and afraid she had been by the time they reached Quebec. And her poor sister, Katty. 'I'm sorry. It makes me cry to think of it.' A smile trembled on her lips. 'But we're here now, thank God.'

The nun nodded her understanding and sat down across the table from Annie. 'It's time to look forward.'

Annie sipped the tea. 'I need to get my brother and sister into school, and I have to get a job. Bridie said you might be able to advise me.'

'Your aunt lives close to the cathedral, I think?'

'Yes, on Princes Street. She has offered us a home with her.'

'So, your brother and sister, how old are they? Have they been in school in Ireland?'

'Oh, yes. They can read and write very well in both Irish and English, and they have studied geography and mathematics, too. Finn is thirteen, no, he'll be fourteen this month, and Katty is nine.'

The nun nodded. 'There's a Catholic school near Lafayette Street - St Paul's. You'll get them in there. It's run by the Sisters of Mercy. They take pupils up to fourteen, so your brother can maybe go there too, for a while.'

'Ah, thank you Sister. I made a promise to my late father they'd finish their education.'

Annie took a sip of the hot black tea. It was strong and bitter and spurred her on. 'And I need to find work, Sister. I want to pay for our food and board with Aunt Bridie. We'll not be a burden on her.'

Sister Mary Angela looked at Annie for a moment, narrowed her eyes and pressed her lips together. 'So, tell me then, what work have you done in Ireland?'

Annie opened her bag and took out her references. 'I worked as a teaching assistant for almost three years at the school on the estate where we lived. I have a reference here from Miss Nagel, the teacher. And I write poems. I've had three of my poems published in The Nation newspaper in Dublin.'

'Well! I'm impressed, Annie. A published poet, no less.' Sister Mary Angela opened and read the letters. 'These are very good. But our nuns do all the teaching. We don't need to employ teachers.'

Annie's heart seemed to miss a beat. 'There's no work for me here?'

'No, I'm sorry. At least, not for teaching.'

Annie closed her eyes to stop the tears and pressed her lips together to stop them trembling.

The nun sipped her tea again. 'However, there might be something,' she added.

Annie glanced across the table. She saw a look of compassion on the nun's face.

'At the orphanage, Sister?'

'Yes.' The nun handed a small cotton handkerchief to Annie. 'Here, dry your eyes and let me think about it, I'll speak to my Sister and see if there are any other jobs. It's hard work, mind; the place is already full with orphans. Most are the sons and daughters of immigrants. Their parents are either dead or have abandoned them.'

'I'll take anything. I can work hard and turn my hand to

most things,' Annie said, and felt the pressure in her head ease a little.

'Sister Fidelma is in charge. Let me have a word with her first. Then call in to the orphanage when you have your brother and sister settled in school. She'll be expecting you.' The nun paused, tilted her head like a small blackbird to look again at Annie, then said, 'I tell you what. Why don't I take you to have a look at the orphanage? It's only next door, then you'll have a good idea if it would suit you.'

'Thank you, Sister. I'd like that.' Annie smiled. She put her cup down and stood. 'Now?'

'Yes. Come with me, there's a door from here through to the chapel and the school is on the other side.' The nun walked briskly to the end of the hall, opened a heavy door and Annie followed her into the Convent chapel. They both genuflected in front of the altar, left the chapel and stepped into the lobby of the orphanage and school.

At the end of the lobby, Annie and Sister Angela walked past a large dining hall. High-pitched sounds of children's voices echoed out, for it was now mid-day and dinner time. The room held ten or more refectory tables. The benches on the long sides of the table were filled; some with boys, and some with girls, all intent on their bowls of steaming broth.

One child, a fair-haired girl, about fourteen years old, glanced up, and her blue eyes focused on Annie. For some reason, the girl's hand holding the spoon stopped, halfway to her mouth. Time seemed to pause for a few seconds. Annie and the girl looked at each other. The sounds in the room faded. The girl didn't speak, but somehow, Annie heard her unspoken words. 'I'm here. You found me.'

Instantly, Annie recalled the legend of the Children of

28

Lir. Their father, a King, had married again and their new stepmother was jealous of his love for his children. The Queen cast a spell on the young princes and princesses, turned them into swans and exiled them for three hundred years. For just that moment, Annie saw this girl was one of Lir's precious daughters, cast out, an exile, like Annie. The girl blinked, looked away and continued to eat her broth.

Annie shook her head. 'Who is that girl, there? The older girl with the dark hair, on the end of the second table.'

'I don't know her name. Why do you want to know?'

'Is she an orphan?'

'I expect so, Annie. Although a few are here because their parents are sick or can't feed them. She's an older girl, so most likely an orphan.'

'My God, these poor *crathurs*,' Annie murmured. 'To have come all this way for a bowl of soup.'

'These are the lucky ones, don't forget,' the nun said. 'They're fed and have a roof over their heads, as well as their schooling.'

An hour later, Annie said goodbye to Sister Mary Angela and walked back along East Street to her new home.

* * *

It was easy to get lost in New York, but Annie had begun to find her way. The sidewalks were filled with barrows and stalls and there was just room for pedestrians to pass between the stalls and the road. The hucksters shouted about their bargains so much that their voices melded into one stream of sound. Annie couldn't comprehend much of it, but some, at least, sounded like American English. She browsed as she walked and stopped at one stall that was loaded with clothes, all second hand. Most looked to be working clothes made of heavy, dark material; wool or fustian. One half of the stall displayed men's trousers, shirts and jackets, while the other half was piled with layers of women's skirts, linen blouses, boots, shoes and coats. Annie noticed a flash of colour in amongst the dull fabrics. As soon as she slowed, the stallholder moved to stand next to her and pulled out the rest of the piece. It was a hand-knitted shawl. 'It's a beautiful piece of work, Miss. Will you try it?'

Annie smiled and noted the woman was warmly wrapped in a similar shawl. 'It is beautiful, but I'm just looking, thank you.' Even as she spoke, Annie's hand reached out to touch the shawl. It was of the softest wool and had been knitted in three colours; rose pink, pale grey and a dark purple-heather. There was a bit of weight to it, so it would keep the wearer warm. She recognised the Aran blackberry stitches around the edges and the honeycomb stitches at the centre. She was sure an Irishwoman had knitted this.

The woman held it. Annie took her cloak off and turned to let the woman drape the shawl around her shoulders. She took the two ends and wrapped them around her waist. It was such a fine shawl.

She didn't ask how much it cost for she had no money to buy anything. 'I'm sorry, it's beautiful, but I can't buy it.' The woman held a mirror up in front of Annie.

This was the first time Annie had looked at her reflection since she'd left Dublin, all those months ago. Then, her hair had been tied up in a black, silk scarf and she had worn men's clothes to make her escape from Kilmainham Gaol. Here, she saw herself wrapped in the rose shawl, but she almost didn't recognise the face reflected back to her. She was at her thinnest, her face looked haggard. She had tied her hair back that morning, and in the daylight, saw it had lost its copper lustre. Her skin was waxy, the colour of a burnt out candle, and her hollowed out cheeks emphasised the dark rings under her eyes.

But the shawl glowed, and she felt its warmth. She looked away from the mirror, then took the shawl off and handed it back to the vendor, who shrugged and put it back on the stall.

Annie walked on past stalls and barrows. 'I'll come back for that shawl, as soon as I earn some money,' she promised herself.

As she walked, she kept seeing the reflection of her face in the mirror. Why did she look so old and unhappy? She had achieved her aim of getting herself, Katty and Finn to safety. Was this the end then, and not a beginning for her?

The answer came to her, like a bell had rung in her mind. It must be a beginning. She must take this chance to accomplish something in her new life. Straight away, she knew where to start. She walked back to the orphanage, to find that Princess, the daughter of King Lir. Annie wanted to know how she came to be there.

* * *

The nun who answered the door recognised Annie, and agreed to her request. She brought Annie through to the dining room. It was surely meant to be, for the girl was there, helping to clear the tables. The nun showed the two of them into an empty classroom, and left them to talk.

'I came back to find you. I think I know you. Where are

you from?' Annie asked the girl.

'Yes. I remember you. I was on the same ferry to New York, the Oswego Chief. Your name is Annie Power, and you were with your brother and sister.'

'That's right. But we didn't speak?'

'No, you had a friend with you, but I spoke to Finn and Katty.'

'John was the friend. We came over on the same ship to Quebec. He got off the ferry at Albany to go on to Boston. Who did you travel with?' Annie asked.

'No-one. Just me.'

'You travelled alone? But sure you're just a girl!'

'I'm fourteen. I came here to find a job and send money home to my family. I met Sister Fidelma at the Port and she brought me here to the orphanage, two days ago. But I'm not an orphan. And I can read and write. I just need a job, but I don't know how to go about it. The nuns said they'll help me, but I feel as if I'm stuck here. They're all so busy.' The girl was as tall as Annie, and thin to the point of emaciation.

'I'll help you,' Annie heard herself say. A feeling of relief settled around her. 'I've got a few things to do first, then I'll come and help you. Give me a week, and I'll come back.'

The girl's face brightened. 'Thank you, Annie.'

'What's your name?'

'Joanne Hayden.'

'I won't forget you, Joanne. Here, give me a hug.' Annie had made a promise and she would keep it. She had her mission.

4

Jane Keating: August 1846. Cape Town

The King Henry made good progress on the journey, and by the middle of August, the ship was nearing the Cape of Good Hope. They were in sight of land, when disaster struck. It was early morning, before breakfast, and the first indication was a cracking noise from the hull as if the ship had collided with something below the water. The second indication was a hard judder from the impact.

In the convict quarters, anyone standing, was thrown against the side of the hull or their bunks, as a section of the wooden hull imploded. Streams of seawater poured in. The women nearest the ruptured wall were drenched with icy water. Instantly, there was pandemonium. All the women shrieked for help. Jane was soaked through and Lizzie fell and banged her head against the side of her bunk. Seawater slopped around the floor. Jane assisted Lizzie to get back on her bunk, then sat with her until a gang of crew came in and hurried them all up on deck.

More seamen raced past them down the gangway to repair

the hole in the ship's hull. On deck, the Captain, hastily dressed and without his gold studded uniform, shouted orders to take down the sails. The ship wallowed in the water, and the main mast was at an angle to the surrounding sea with the sails and rigging touching the water. Some of the women were crying, while others tried to comfort them. Jane watched the crew, who looked to be well trained and competent. She only began to worry when the captain ordered the ship's two tenders to be lowered over the side of the ship.

Even Jane could tell the numbers of crew and all the convicts wouldn't fit in the two small boats if they had to abandon ship. She thought about who would be left behind, and looked out across the sea. The Cape of Good Hope was in sight, about a mile away. That was a fair swim, and the water looked choppy, with swelling waves.

She untied the laces in her boots, so she could slip them off if she had to go into the water, then loosened her sodden skirt, ready to step out of it. She looked around the deck, for anything to help her. In a nearby corner she saw washing hung out to dry and slipped over to take a look at the clothes pegged on the line. She grabbed a pair of sailor's trousers, pulled them up under her skirt, then moved back to the group of women. No-one had seen her, and she looked out to sea again, towards the coast of South Africa.

There was nothing else she could do but watch and wait. Thankfully, the day remained bright and clear. The sea moved with the breeze, and white lacy frills appeared on the tops of the dark green waves.

The ship's carpenter and his mate were lowered over the side to begin the repairs. Each man sat in a canvas sling that swayed while they hammered and patched the hole in the hull.

A long length of pipe was slung over the side of the ship and the flood water was pumped out of the bilges. The ship slowly began to right itself. After hours of pumping, it became clear they were no longer in danger of sinking.

Throughout the day, small boats came out from Cape Town harbour to investigate and offer help. By evening, all the women were exhausted, half-starved and chilled to the bone from sitting in damp clothes all day, but they were alive. The repair was successful and, as darkness fell, the ship got underway to Cape Town with just one sail hoisted.

Instead of joining the women to go back to their prison, Jane hid beside the line of laundry, forgotten in all the excitement of the day. She left her blouse on and slipped out of her skirt and boots, leaving just the sailor's trousers and her bare feet. Then she climbed onto the rail, sat and looked down at the water several feet below. 'Do it now!' But she hesitated. She had never swum at night before. The lights of Cape Town were just over the water, and were now less than half a mile away. She braced herself to jump. The water would be freezing. She held her breath, and flexed her arms to push off from the ship's rail.

A hand caught hold of her arm, and she heard a whispered word. 'Jack!' She turned and saw Owen Doran beside her in the dim light of the deck. 'What in God's name are you doing?' he asked.

'Don't stop me, please. I've got to get away.'

'There are sharks out there in the water. They'll eat you,' the sergeant said.

'You're lying. I can easily swim from here.'

'Get down off the rail now, or you'll be seen. I won't be able to help you then. You'll be flogged, first thing tomorrow morning.' He kept hold of her arm and pulled her back to the deck. 'Pick up your skirt and walk with me.'

Bitter tears ran down her face, but she did as she was told, and the two of them walked down the stairs back to the prison.

'You could have let me go,' she said.

'If the sharks hadn't eaten you, you'd have been found and caught in Cape Town. It's a British garrison town, for God's sake! No-one escapes from there.'

'I need to get back to Ireland, to Dublin. I had a job there. I was Jack Keating.'

'Well, I can guarantee you won't be taken for a boy or a man here,' Owen Doran said. 'Get some rest. We'll be docking in Cape Town soon.'

Only Lizzie noticed Jane's late arrival, but she didn't ask the reason. It was almost time for lights out.

Jane saw the hole in the hull was now covered with tarpaulin, a filthy bandage, held tight by lengths of timber nailed to the floor and ceiling. Some of the bunks were wet and the crew had hauled the soaked mattresses, including Jane's, up on deck to dry off. Lizzie's bunk had enough room for Jane to squeeze in beside her.

Jane wiped away her tears and scolded herself for being a foolish girl, allowing herself to be caught so easily. Jack wouldn't have been caught. Next time, she'd succeed, she promised herself.

* * *

The following morning, Jane's head ached from her failed attempt to escape. At least she hadn't swum all that way to Cape Town and been arrested, or worse, been eaten by sharks.

But the thought did nothing to ease her pain.

At breakfast, rumours swirled that the ship was too badly damaged to continue the journey to New South Wales. The convicts persuaded themselves they would soon be returned to Dublin. Jane's hopes lifted. Maybe she would serve her sentence in Ireland?

The women sat in their below-deck prison for another day and night until the captain found the time to come to speak to them. He had a smile for the women, who remained seated on their bunks as he spoke.

'Good morning. I'm sure you're all wondering what the position is. As you probably know by now, the ship's hull was damaged when we hit a submerged rock.' He pointed to the patched wall. 'You can see it's now watertight, but it needs a lot of work to be made seaworthy again. We won't be going anywhere in her for at least a month, if not more, so the ship and her crew will stay here for the duration.'

The captain held up his hand to calm the swell of questions from the women convicts, then he continued. 'Be quiet for a minute, while I explain. I've made arrangements for you to continue your journey. Her Majesty's ship, The Maitland, is due here next week from London. She's carrying over one hundred convicts from Pentonville Prison in London. You women will join the ship, in separate quarters from the men. Your army escort, and Mr Blake, the Superintendent, will travel with you to New South Wales.'

The captain didn't wait to answer any of the questions hurled at him by the women. He turned and left the crew members to lock up behind him.

Jane looked at Lizzie. 'Well! That's us told.'

They settled down to wait for The Maitland to arrive.

* * *

Sure enough, one week later, a great four-masted ship docked in Cape Town for revictualling. As soon as that job was finished, and it took the best part of three days, the women prisoners and their guards were gathered on deck ready to be transferred to the other ship.

Jane saw Owen Doran, and gave a small wave. He came over to her. 'Hello, Jane, or Jack. How are you today?'

'I'm fine, thank you. I'm sorry about last week. It was a stupid thing to do. I just wanted to get away and go back to being Jack in Dublin. I was happy there.'

'I don't understand any of this. What do you mean go back to being Jack?'

'When my father died, I travelled as a boy, it was safer for me. But then I found I could be accepted as a boy and when I got to Dublin, I got a job at The Nation newspaper. They trained me as a typesetter. I loved it. I think I'm meant to be Jack.'

Owen shook his head. 'Well, maybe it'll be different in Port Phillip. I have never been there, so I don't know. But be careful, won't you? You'll have to serve your sentence, whether Jack or Jane. No-one escapes.'

He put his hand out, and Jane shook it.

'The captain said you're coming with us to the other ship?' she asked him.

'Yes, we're your escort, all the way to Port Phillip.'

Jane pointed across to the dockyard and the dozens of ships lined up, each serviced by smaller boats loaded with barrels of provisions and water. 'I know it's Cape Town, but where are we exactly? It feels as if we're at the end of the world.'

'No, the end of the world is in New South Wales. That's where we're headed. Here, we're on the southern tip of Africa. See that flat-topped mountain across there? That's Table Mountain.'

'I see it. There's a mountain with a flat top like that, in Sligo. It's called Ben Bulben. I went there when I was a child. It's not as big as this one, mind.'

'I'd never been further than my home town of Wicklow until I joined the army,' Owen replied. 'South Africa is another British colony, much like Ireland.'

Jane shook her head. 'What are they doing here? The British?'

'I don't know, but I hear there's diamonds further north.' He nodded to Jane. 'I need to go. Listen, I'll keep an eye out for you on the next leg of the journey.'

'*Go raibh maith agat,* Owen. She thanked him in Irish and enjoyed feeling the sounds of the words on her tongue. She watched him go over to speak to the crew. He was of a narrow build, wiry, but when he had caught her arm the night before, she'd felt his strength. She liked his smile, but reminded herself that he worked for the British Government. She was fortunate he hadn't reported her to the captain.

Later, the gangplank was lowered and the women prisoners were chained together in a line. They were marched off the ship and along the dockside to The Maitland, their prison for the next part of their journey to New South Wales. As soon as they were on board, the ship raised anchor and sailed towards the Southern Ocean.

5

Annie Power: September 1846. The Sisters of Charity

Annie's next task was to get Finn and Katty enrolled in St Paul's school. They needed books and pencils if they were to start the following week. Bridie took them both shopping and found bargains at the street market where Annie had tried on the shawl.

'I'll repay you the cost of these, as soon as I earn some money,' she promised her aunt.

Katty and Finn were in bed early on the Sunday night before their first day at school. Annie and Bridie sat at the kitchen table and talked again about the job at the Sisters of Charity orphanage.

'I'd say you'll get work there,' Bridie said. 'If not, I'll ask at the Infirmary.' Bridie had been a nurse there for the last ten years.

At the mention of the Infirmary, Annie shook her head. 'I'd be no use in a hospital. After Da died, I just don't want to be around sick people. Do you remember Marie Duggan, our neighbour? She was great, and helped me with Da when he died. I couldn't have done it without her. But I won't do it again.'

Annie hadn't noticed Finn had come back in to get a drink of water. He sat down next to her, and put his head on her shoulder. 'I miss Da, too, sister,' he said. 'But you must take care of yourself, Annie. We need you. You're still not right after that fever on the ship, are you?'

Annie stroked her brother's face. 'Sure, I'm grand now. T'was only a little bit of fever.' They all knew well, that if it was the relapsing fever, the same fever that had killed Pat Power, then it could come back.

'Well then, you'll have to get work at the orphanage,' Bridie said. 'Lots of children and young people will keep you entertained. And if you don't, there's other work. You'll get a good job with those references. I guarantee it.'

* * *

Later that week, Annie's quest for a job brought her back along the Bowery to the orphanage school. Summer was changing into autumn, and she saw that the season in New York was different than in Ireland. In New York, stunted trees did their best to grow along the edges of the muddy roadways, and tried to display their autumn beauty. The leaves on many of the smaller trees had begun to turn from green to yellow to a pale crimson, whereas the foliage on the taller trees had deepened to a reddish brown. The colours here in autumn, or fall, as they called it in New York, were definitely more exaggerated than the changes she remembered from back home, where the weather and nature were softer, and always wetter.

She walked on, and thought of her friend, Jane Keating. She would be in the Southern Ocean by now, getting nearer every day to her prison for the next seven years. 'Blessed Mother, keep her safe. Bring her home, one day.' Annie prayed. She looked at the stunted trees on the sidewalk. 'And where's your home, Annie Power?' she asked herself. She smiled, of course she knew the answer to that question. 'Sure, it's where I can walk along the strand by the River Suir, hear the song of the blackbirds in the morning, sit and have a cup of warm, creamy milk straight from the cow, and talk to my father about the day to come. Where our neighbours call in to tell stories and sing songs of an evening.'

'Watch out there!' A hand grabbed her arm. 'Miss!'

'Oh! What?' She looked at the boy who had grabbed her arm.

'You nearly stepped under that cart,' he said.

'Thank you.' She shook her head and walked on. 'Wake up, Annie, don't be an *eejit*! Getting yourself killed. After all the trouble you took to get here.'

The orphanage was just up ahead.

* * *

'I've been wondering what you'd look like, Annie.' Sister Fidelma spoke with an American accent. 'When Sister Angela told me there was a teacher looking to work with the orphans, I imagined you must be older. What are you, seventeen, eighteen?'

They were in a small office just inside the main door of the orphanage and Sister Fidelma stood to greet Annie. The nun's face was shaded by a cowl-shaped hat, a few thin wisps of dark hair had escaped and lay at the side of her neck, but her smile lit up her pale, lined face and her eyes sparkled as she shook hands with Annie.

'I'm seventeen, Sister.' Annie replied. 'And I have my references here.' Annie offered the envelope to the nun.

'Thank you. I'll read them in a minute. Let's talk first. Sister Mary Angela tells me she showed you around last week.'

'Yes, she did.'

'Well now, it's my turn. Come with me and I'll explain our work here.' Sister Fidelma left the envelope on her desk and held the door for Annie to go out ahead of her.

They walked further into the building as the nun explained their mission. She was shorter than Annie, of square build, and despite her bulky uniform, a dark grey woollen top and pleated full-length skirt, she moved with a light, quick step along the hallway. Annie had to lengthen her stride to keep up with her.

'The Bishop Hughes, God bless him in his work, helped us to set up this orphanage. There've been so many poor children without a mother or father to look after them. We have over a hundred orphans, Annie, and they're from all parts of Ireland.'

They walked past the two classrooms Annie had seen on her last visit. Today, lessons were in progress and the classrooms were full. One held younger children, lots of them, and the other class had the older boys and girls. Annie saw no sign of Joanne Hayden.

The nun led the way up a wide staircase to the children's dormitories. As on the ground floor, there were two large rooms off the landing, here each room was filled with clean, single beds and not much else, apart from a crucifix on the

43

wall with a small statue of the Virgin Mary on a table below it. 'This floor is for the girls. The boys' dormitory is upstairs,' Sister Fidelma explained.

Back on the ground floor, they stopped at the chapel, went in and sat together facing the altar. Annie smoothed the skirt of her good dress, the one made specially for her in Dublin. She shook off thoughts of Dublin and home.

'Why do you want to work here, Annie?' the nun asked in a low, soft voice.

'I need a teaching job, Sister,' Annie said. 'I was trained by a good teacher, back home in Ireland. And I have a younger brother and sister to support.' She paused to gather her thoughts. 'We've been here just over three weeks now. We came in through Quebec, then down along the Hudson River to New York and my aunt Bridie's apartment on Princes Street.'

'What of your parents?'

'They're both gone to God,' Annie replied. 'My mother died when Katty was born. My father died earlier this year.'

'Ah, may the Lord have mercy on their souls.' The nun blessed herself. 'Well then, you've come to the right place. This is God's home on earth for orphans. Now, tell me about your teaching. Did you attend college in Ireland?'

Annie smiled and shook her head at the thought of college for a poor country girl like herself.

'No. Miss Nagel ran a school on the estate where I lived, just outside Waterford. She was my teacher and then she took me on as her assistant and trained me. I taught English, arithmetic and geography for nearly three years, mostly to the younger scholars. Miss Nagel taught the older children.'

Annie took a breath; her fingers kneaded the fine wool

of her skirt. 'Then on the ship coming over here, I set up a school for the children to learn English. I taught about twenty children and adults. They could all speak a little English by the time we reached Quebec. The ship's Captain, Joe Hennessey, gave me a letter of reference.'

'I see. Sister Mary Angela said you're an Irish speaker.'

'*Sea, tá Gaeilge ogam,*' Annie replied. 'Yes, I speak Irish,' she translated.

'That's good to hear,' the nun said. 'Most of our nuns are American, and many of our pupils only speak Irish. So we have a communication problem, and you may be able to help us, Annie.'

'Then you'll give me a job?' Annie asked. She tried to keep the tremble out of her voice and failed.

'Well, first I need to read your references. Let's go back to my office, and I'll do that now.'

They knelt in front of the altar and blessed themselves before leaving the chapel.

* * *

Bridie had a stew cooking for their evening meal and Katty and Finn were at the table doing homework when Annie arrived home. She hugged her aunt then her sister and brother.

'I got the job, I start next Monday. They're paying me as a trainee teacher, just three days a week at first. But I'll earn enough to pay for our food and board, Bridie.' Annie's eyes gleamed with tears of pride.

'You're a great girl, so you are. Well done. And don't worry about me,' her aunt said. 'Just pay me something towards the food and we'll manage nicely.' Bridie lived a quiet life, between work at St Vincent's Infirmary and her church attendance. She wasn't short of money, but the food bill had gone up considerably since the arrival of her nieces and nephew.

* * *

Later that evening, as they cleaned the kitchen before bed, Annie confided in her aunt. 'I didn't tell you, but three weeks ago, when I met Sister Mary Angela, I saw a girl at the orphanage. She told me that she came to New York on the same boat from Quebec. I don't recall seeing her, but she had spoken to Finn and Katty.' Annie paused.

'Bridie, do you know the legend of the Children of Lir? Well, she reminded me of one of the princesses.'

'What are you talking about?' Bridie asked, as she wrung out a cloth and wiped down the kitchen table.

'The Children of Lir, Bridie. Their stepmother put a spell on them, King Lir's children. They were changed into swans and exiled from their home.' Annie stopped sweeping and waited for her aunt's reply.

'Yes, I recall the legend. But what's it got to do with a girl in the orphanage?'

'That's what the legend is about. Exiled here in New York. Don't you see?' Annie sighed. It was obvious to Annie, the girl was the same as one of the King's children.

'Jesus, Mary and Joseph! What nonsense is this? You saved your life and that of your brother and sister. Aren't the three of you the children of Lir, too? Besides, what more could you do?' Bridie tutted and took the broom from Annie and continued to sweep the kitchen floor and answered her own question. 'You can make a life here for yourself, like I have.'

'I promised her I'd help her find a job, Bridie.'

'Why? How old is she? And what business is it of yours?' By now, Bridie had started to sound exasperated with her niece.

'She's fourteen, Bridie. Her family are back in Sligo, on a half-acre, like we were. And you know what that means. She came here to earn money and send it home. The nuns took her in, but she tells me she's stuck there and needs a job. Every day that she doesn't work, means she can't send money home.'

The kitchen was finished, the table cleared and wiped down. Bridie stood by the sink and looked at Annie. 'And how do you imagine you'll help her?'

Annie saw Bridie's face soften into a smile, as if she anticipated her niece's reply.

'I thought you might know, dear aunt.' Annie returned the smile. 'Is there any work in the hospital?'

'There's always work there, girl. It's hard work, mind. Mostly cleaning for women and it doesn't pay well. But if you think she could do it, I'll make enquiries tomorrow. If she's a good worker and can read and write, then with time, she may be taken on to train as a nurse.'

'She told me she can read and write, and I know she'll work hard. Thank you, darling. I knew you'd help.' Annie put her arm around her aunt for a hug, then leaned back against the sink. 'But Bridie, it made me wonder. What about the older girls like Joanne who come here on their own? Girls my age? Who helps them?' she asked. Since the day she had seen Joanne, the question had stuck in her mind, like a burr stuck in her hair.

'I don't know. Maybe they have jobs to come to? Anyway, there's not much you can do for them.' Bridie paused as she folded the cloths on the sink; she looked at Annie, then smiled again. 'You look so like your mother, may she rest in peace, and she could be a stubborn *divil*, too. Look, if you're intent on doing more, then you could get along to the cathedral one Saturday night. There's an Aid for Ireland group that meets every week. I'm not exactly sure what they get up to, but you could maybe go and find out?'

Annie kissed her aunt. 'I'll do that. Will you come with me?'

'We'll all go. But get your job sorted out first. Now then, let's get this place finished before bed.'

Annie put the clean cups, plates and cutlery in the cupboard, then took the bucket of dirty water downstairs to empty. In the morning, it was Finn and Katty's job to bring up fresh water for the day, while Annie emptied the night chamber pots into the shared privies at the back of the apartment block.

She checked on Katty, who was fast asleep in Bridie's bed. Then she went into the parlour where Finn slept on a narrow mattress. She kissed him goodnight and unrolled her mattress on the floor next to him, and made up the bed with a pillow and blanket. Annie lay down, blessed herself, thanking God for a safe place to lay her head. The pillow was soft, and in her dreams, the exiled princes and princesses were transformed into swans, singing their songs of desolation.

* * *

Two weeks later, as the month neared its end, Annie and Bridie arrived early at the orphanage to collect Joanne Hayden. Bridie had managed to find a vacancy as a nursing auxiliary at her hospital. It was a live-in position with food and board included in her wages.

Joanne was ready to go, her small bag was packed and she opened the front door when they knocked. She hugged Annie and shook hands with Bridie. *'Go raibh maith agat!'* Joanne thanked them both.

Annie was surprised to see how changed the girl was, her face glowed with pride. She was a young woman about to embark on her new life. Joanne turned and shook hands with Sister Fidelma who held the door open.

'Goodbye, Sister. Thank you for giving me a home.'

'You're welcome, Joanne. Say a prayer for me, won't you? And I'll pray for you and your family.' The nun smiled at Annie and Bridie. 'You've done a charitable act, ladies!' I'll see you later, Annie.'

'Yes, Sister,' Annie said. 'I'll be back here in time for lessons.'

The three women set off for the hospital. It was early morning, and promised to be a bright day. The streets were busy with people and horse-drawn traffic, all on the move around the city.

It took just twenty minutes to reach the hospital, then it was time to say goodbye. Annie hugged her new friend. 'I'm so happy for you. You'll do well here.'

'And I'll keep an eye on you,' Bridie added.

Joanne's smile filled her whole face. 'It's thanks to you both that I'll soon be able to send money home. I'll work hard, Bridie. I won't let you down.'

'We need to find the Matron and get you allocated to your room. Then you can start.'

'Slán, Annie!' Joanne said, and waved goodbye.

Annie watched her aunt and Joanne walk into the hospital. They were soon out of sight. She started the walk back to the orphanage to begin her own day's work. Joanne had helped her see that she could perhaps do something to help other girls and women make a life here. Now she just needed to find them.

6

Jane Keating: September 1846. In the Southern Ocean

Jane's whole world seemed to be made up of the yards of sailcloth that blew above her head like giant sheets hung out to dry. On days when the wind dropped, the sails hung from the yardarms and swayed loosely as the ship moved with the current. On days when the wind screeched through the rigging, the crew scampered around the masts to tie up the canvas.

Jane and the other women convicts would sit on deck in the shelter of the hull, and watch the live drama every day, up on the stage of the ship's masts. There was always the risk a crewman might slip and fall, what seemed to be a hundred or more feet, to the deck. Shouted orders from the mate below resounded through the rigging and added to the urgency of the work. When the weather closed in, and clouds were low, the crew could only be heard, not seen. The ship-board sounds echoed with the creak of rigging ropes as the crew moved around and their voices called to each other through the mist to be ready to haul the sails.

They had been at sea for weeks with no sign of land, after leaving Cape Town. There were very few seabirds, with just the odd sighting of a wandering albatross, its massive wingspan, white body and black wings, gliding across the sky. As it moved, the albatross dipped its head to glance at the ship below. At one time, Jane looked up to see the great bird perched on top of the main mast. It seemed to be studying her.

The Maitland sailed on towards the Southern Ocean, and Mr Blake, the surgeon-superintendent, continued his system of management of the female convicts for the remainder of the journey. Male and female convicts were segregated and mingling was strictly forbidden.

One evening after supper, Mr Blake, requested one of the crew to play some music for the women. Jane recognised the first tune played on the tin whistle and sang the words to the old song. She closed her eyes and imagined herself back at home in Galway. She sang and felt the presence of her mother and father, her brothers, Joe and Seamus, and smiled. When the music finished she saw Owen Doran standing close by. His eyes were fixed on her face. Behind him, the night sky blazed with wide swathes of glittering, silver, red and blue stars. Her gaze held his. He nodded to her, and joined in the applause, that she realised was for her singing.

The next few weeks passed without any further excitement as the Maitland moved closer each day to their destination of Port Phillip, and the town of Melbourne, where Jane would begin her new life.

7

Annie Power: September 1846. Annie meets McGonigle again

I t was Saturday morning, and Katty and Finn had a lie-in. Bridie had left the apartment early for first mass, then continued on, as usual, to her shift at the hospital.

Annie waited for the water in the kettle to boil, and made a pot of tea for herself, Katty and Finn, then called her brother and sister to get up for their breakfast.

She heard the steady low rumble from carts rolling along the street outside, shouts from impatient drivers, and the clatter of horses' hooves. Back at home there would be just the soft rustle of the breeze across the turf roof, perhaps their cow lowing in the field behind the cabin, and in spring and summer the songs of the blackbirds. And always, her beloved father's voice, the deep anchor to her days.

Here, the iron stove was kept on a low burn with coal and wood. Back home, the peaty smell of their fire permeated everything in their cabin, and the water tasted of the stones it had flowed across in the spring, whereas in New York city there was a sour metallic tang to both the air and the water.

'Annie, tell us about your job again,' Katty said, as she finished her porridge. 'I want to be a teacher when I grow up, just like you.'

'You know, it's near enough for me to walk there, on the Lower East side. I'm the assistant to one of the nuns, Sister Mary Rose, who teaches the younger children. Quite a few of them don't have any English, and I teach them. It's a lovely job.'

'So, are they all from Ireland, then?' Finn asked.

'Yes, there's over a hundred of them. All orphans.' She poured another cup of tea and sat with them. 'We're the lucky ones, to have this lovely home with Bridie. Now, *acushla,* it's your turn to tell me about your new school.'

'I love it there,' Katty said. 'The nuns are so kind, and my new books are beautiful.'

'What are the other children like?'

Well, most of them are Irish too, but some are from Germany and Italy. And I've got lots of new friends. My best friend, Orla, is from Kerry.'

'And you, Finn? How did you get on this week?' Annie noticed that Finn had that stubborn Power look on his face, for some reason.

He avoided her glance. 'I did everything back in Miss Nagel's class, in Ashling. Now I'm doing it all over again.'

'Well, I'm sure it'll get better when they see how clever my brother is.' Annie finished her tea. 'Now then, let's get our jobs done and we can go out and explore.'

* * *

Annie set to work in the parlour and rolled up the mattresses, folded them and the blankets, piled them on top of the pillows and tucked them all behind the oak armchairs. A basin and jug stood on a side table by the distempered white wall. She emptied the basin into the chamber pot and checked the room was tidy, then she joined Katty and Finn, who had made up the double bed in Bridie's room.

Annie covered one chamber pot with its lid, and made her way downstairs to the outside privies where she emptied it. At least these privies were only shared with the fifty or so people who lived in the apartment building, which was a great improvement to what they had on board the ship. Thankfully, the privies were emptied every week by the night-soil wagons. The tenants took turns to clean the outhouse, but it wasn't a place to linger.

A water pump stood in the corner of the yard, and on her second trip downstairs she passed Katty and Finn in the queue. They waited to fill their buckets for the day's cooking, washing and making tea.

Finally, the housework was done and the apartment was clean and tidy for their aunt Bridie to come home to.

'Katty, come and I'll do your hair, darling,' Annie said. She sat and brushed Katty's long, dark curls, and felt the weight of the silky hair in her hands. She used Katty's yellow ribbon to tie some of the dark strands into a topknot, then she hugged her sister. 'We'll need to buy you a new ribbon soon, *acushla*. This one is really frayed.'

'Don't throw it away, Annie. I need it,' Katty turned to her sister. 'It reminds me of Daddy. I have to keep it.' Katty's forehead creased into a frown and her eyes filled with tears.

'Darling, we'll put it somewhere safe, so you can keep it forever. But you need a new one for school.' She kissed her sister's cheek. and wiped away her tears. 'Now, are we ready to go out?'

Annie pulled her cloak around her. Katty put on a woollen jacket over her dress and boots. Finn wore a coat over his long trousers. Since coming to America, he had insisted on wearing American style trousers, no more knee breeches. He had grown up fast in the last few months, and was now as tall as Annie.

* * *

The three Powers left the apartment and walked along The Broadway, heading south. True to its name, this was a wide, rutted street and was already filled with hundreds of people on the move along the sidewalk and crossing over and back the road. The roadway itself was full of horses and their riders, carts and cabs all pulled by more horses; the larger carts were pulled by teams of oxen.

A ragged boy, about ten years old, and selling newspapers, held one out in front of Annie. 'Just one cent, Miss!' he yelled at her in a shrill voice, even though she stood right next to him.

A sharp breeze fluttered the newspaper in the boy's hand. Annie paid him for the paper and examined it. The name, The Sun, was printed across the top of the page, together with its motto, *'It shines for all'*. It was smaller than the broadsheets Annie had read in Ireland and had pictures on the front page, a thing she had never seen in The Nation. She tucked it under her arm to read later, then linked Katty's arm. She looked over her shoulder to find Finn, and saw him speaking to the boy who had sold them the paper. The newspaper boy held his bag up to show Finn something. Finn nodded, smiled and joined Annie. Then they continued on their walk.

'Mind out, Annie!' Katty shouted. Annie stopped and turned to see three huge pigs come trotting up behind them. They were large animals, up to Annie's waist; the lead pig was black with floppy ears that almost covered his eyes. The other two were a muddy, mottled pink; their bristly snouts and the insides of their ears were the only clean parts of them. The pigs trotted along the street, one after the other, and snuffled and snorted as they overtook the Powers. The animals seemed to know where they were going, and other people just ignored them, and went about their business.

'Sure, where did they come from?' Annie asked. The three of them laughed together. 'What kind of place is this?'

'Look!' Finn said. 'There's more over there, across the street.'

The siblings stood in a doorway and watched several even bigger pigs pass by. These were over three feet in height, and they muscled their way through the crowds, who still took no notice, and just stepped out of their way. The troop of pigs were followed by a gang of mangy, half-starved dogs.

'There's as many animals here as people, if not more.' Annie held tight to Finn and Katty's hands as they moved through the crowds of people.

She was used to animals, being a country girl, but was surprised by the sheer numbers of pigs, dogs and horses on the city's streets, not to mention rats and flies everywhere, and that was just the live animals. Then there were the dead animals, for sale as food.

Thankfully, there was no shortage of any meat. Hens and chickens with wrung necks, their feet hooked to the awnings of street stalls, swayed in the breeze and their russet feathers ruffled. Sides of beef and lamb hung with the white lattice of their rib cages on display in the windows of butchers' shops. Strips of unrecognisable offal swathed bowls of gleaming brown kidneys, wet red chunks of liver and creamy, petalled strips of tripe. Bloody back-bones of oxen and gristly pigs' trotters sat, side by side, on damp boards. And all at the mercy of black, buzzing flies.

'As long as you have the money to buy,' Annie murmured.

They needed to cross the street, but it was congested with horse-drawn traffic, all of them speeding to get somewhere else. The smell from the piles of horses' excrement gave the air a heavy, pungent odour. Somehow, they managed to get to the other side of the street.

'Watch your step, the ground is really filthy.' Annie spoke too late, as Katty slipped on a pile of dung, but she caught her sister before she fell into it.

'Annie, where are we going?' Katty asked, after they had walked on a little further.

'We're exploring our new home. It's time we got to know this place. Here's a test for you. Can you tell me which way we're heading, Katty?' Annie asked.

'I can tell you,' Finn said.

'I'm not asking you, Finn. I'm trying to see if Katty can work it out, too,' Annie said. 'Can you find north and south from the sun?'

'Yes, I think so,' Katty said. She looked up into the sky and saw the morning sun was to her left, turned and faced it. 'East is there, so south is on my right hand. Are we heading south to the docks?'

'Good girl. And north?'

'North is on my left hand.'

'Finn, a question for you now.' They walked on. 'We're facing south so where is auntie Bridie's apartment?'

'North-west.' Finn pointed back over his shoulder. 'That's easy!'

'Good, we're getting our bearings. So, if anyone gets lost they can find their way home from The Broadway.'

* * *

By this time, they had arrived at an intersection of four streets and saw a large open park across on the other side. They took a few minutes to cross the wide street and dodged more piles of horse dung, carts and carriages, mules and horses. Annie saw space on a bench near a fountain in the centre of the park, and they sat together and gazed at the water as it cascaded down into a stone basin. The park was a grassy area and people walked along the pathways, some at a brisk pace, on their way to places, while others, like Annie, Finn and Katty, strolled and explored their new home.

Oak and elm trees stood around the edges of the park. Their branches were visible on the skyline, as the chill breezes of autumn encouraged them to shed their leaves. Katty shuffled her boots through the crisp, faded orange leaves blown in beside the bench; the rustle and crackle was a familiar sound of other autumn days.

Annie pushed back the hood of her cloak and unfolded the newspaper she had bought to read some of the news items. The newspaper was definitely different. It was smaller, and easier to handle, and the news stories were about New York, and not just advertisements. This paper even had a letter of complaint about the pigs and dogs in it. She smiled, it seemed that even in this great city, nothing could be done to stop the pigs "lounging around Broadway". Finn sat next to her and read along with her.

'I spoke to the boy who sold it,' Finn said.

'Mm, I saw you.'

'I asked him how he got his job selling papers, so I can get a job, too.' Her brother looked at Katty, over by the fountain, then back to Annie. 'You still see me as your little brother, don't you?'

'That's because you are.' Annie laughed and looked at Finn. She saw he wasn't playing, he was speaking the truth.

'Annie, I had to grow up when you went to Dublin, and then at the docks, when that man took Katty. It was my fault for not watching her. I promised myself then, I'll take care of you and Katty from now on.'

'Finn, *a cushla*, it wasn't your fault. It was mine. Captain Joe warned me there would be criminals waiting for immigrants to step off the ships and they'd steal their money. I didn't think they'd take children! I was a fool, an *eejit*! And I'm really sorry.'

The brother and sister sat in silence for a few minutes and watched Katty throw pebbles into the water of the fountain. As well as the splash of water, there was music on the air. Annie could hear but not see the musician.

'If you need to get a part-time job, then do. But you must work hard at school, Finn. Promise me you will.'

Finn looked away, nodded, but didn't speak. She was puzzled by his silence, but decided not to question him just then. She'd ask him about it later. Everything will be fine, she promised herself.

'Right, so.' She folded the newspaper and tucked it back under her arm. 'Let's go on, and see what's over there. Katty, come on.'

They walked past a sign for Saint Paul's Chapel of Ease and the cemetery behind it. Annie had noticed two women standing beside the church wall and she wanted to get a closer look at them. One was young, with her hair uncovered and she definitely looked to be Irish. She was skinny with dark hair and she reminded Annie of Jane Keating. Annie greeted her in Gaelic. *'Dhia dhuit.'*

Annie was not surprised to see the girl, for she was not much more than a child, narrow her eyes at the words, then turn away. This girl, so young, did not acknowledge the Irish greeting here, but had recognised it. Annie was sure of that.

When she had spent the few weeks in Dublin, trying to meet their landlord, Annie had seen young women waiting to get a 'catch' to pay the rent. This girl was in the same situation, but she was only a girl. When had she come to New York? And where were her parents? The girl was scrawny, with sharp, hungry cheek and jawbones. Her dress, of purple velvet, was too large for her and was held up by a narrow belt at her waist, or it would have dragged on the ground. She had turned up the sleeves and wore a bright green woollen shawl around her shoulders. The other woman, older, had the girl linked by the arm, and was her mother, or grandmother, or something worse, perhaps, Annie decided. She was just about to speak to the girl again, when Finn called her.

'Annie, look! Over there.' He pointed to a huge five-storey building on a corner site facing the park. The facade of the building was covered with flags and banners that moved and fluttered in the breeze. A long queue of people snaked back around the corner from the entrance. Finn and Katty raced to the end of the park. 'Come on, Annie. Let's go and see!'

Annie turned back to see the girl walking away with her companion. 'I'll come back,' she whispered, then went to join her brother and sister.

* * *

The name above the building was Barnum's Museum of Curiosities. Signs on the wall near the entrance doors announced: "Entrance fee only 25 cents!" A ragged musician stood beside the main doorway and played a brass horn, while a girl next to him, about Finn's age, sang in a sweet voice. It might have been a folk song, but was sung in a language that Annie had not heard before. 'It's not just the Irish who come here to find a new home,' she thought.

They stood and listened until the singer finished her song, then held out a hat for coins. Annie found a few cents in her purse and threw them into the hat.

Finn pointed to a notice pasted on the wall of the building. 'What's a freak show, Annie? It says they have a zoo, and a freak show.'

'Well, there's a zoo in Dublin, but this place doesn't look big enough to have a zoo. A freak show? I don't know, I've not heard the word before,' Annie said.

A tidy-looking woman towards the front of the queue overheard Annie, and turned to speak to her. 'It's just fantastic! There's all sorts in it: a bearded lady, and a midget! The Siamese twins are the best; grown women with two heads and just the one body. I'll guarantee you've never seen the like of it. We've come back for another look.' The woman waved to Annie and caught her two young children by the hand, as the queue began to move towards the door.

Annie saw her siblings' excitement and frowned. 'Hm, I'll save up and we can go and look in a week or two. Maybe. Though, I'm not sure I like the thought of caged animals and freaks. Come on, I'll show you where I work.'

They walked along The Bowery and turned into East Street. Annie was annoyed that she had missed the chance to speak to the girl in the purple dress, but promised herself she'd find her the next time.

* * *

Later that day, Finn took himself off to find out about a job selling newspapers for The Sun. The street-seller had given him the address on Broadway.

He reported back to Annie and his aunt. 'I've got a job. I can sell the papers before I go to school in the week, on Saturdays and after mass on Sundays. Bridie, I'll earn some money.'

'Sure, aren't you the great man now. Just be careful out there on the streets, won't you?' Bridie said.

'I will, of course. Don't worry about me. I have to fetch the papers early tomorrow morning. Will you call me when you get up?'

Annie smiled to see that Finn was happy and looking forward to his new job.

It was agreed, Finn and Bridie would leave the house early for first mass. Then Finn would collect his newspapers to sell. Annie and Katty could have a lie-in and they would go to second mass.

* * *

The next day, when Finn arrived back from selling the Sunday papers, he brought one of the newspapers with him. Annie and Katty came back from mass and they had breakfast and read the newspaper together.

One article caught Annie's eye. She saw the words, 'County Louth,' and read the report.

The New York Sun. 25th September 1846

A house of ill repute, in Five Points, Manhattan, was raided yesterday after a charge of larceny was laid against Marie Smith. The young woman in question is just fifteen years old, and newly arrived from County Louth in Ireland. She was charged with stealing ten dollars from the pocket of James Walker. She has been locked up to await trial.

Annie stopped reading. 'How on earth did that girl end up in a house of ill repute?' Then she recalled the young girl she had seen at the park. Maybe Marie Smith had no choice.

Another article expressed concern about the numbers of Irish people pouring into New York, especially young, single women, travelling alone. She decided she would go and take a look for herself. She left Finn and Katty to get their dinner together. Bridie was working the early shift again, and would be home later that afternoon.

Annie wrapped her cloak around her, for the breeze had strengthened. She pulled the hood up around her face and walked fast. She headed south along The Broadway, past Barnum's and the Town Hall and kept moving until she got to the end of Manhattan.

The nearer to the docks she got, the more crowded and dirty the streets became. Annie recognised many Irish faces in the crowds. She gave an Irish greeting to some of the women and children she passed, '*Dia dhuit*,' and heard the response, '*Dia is Mhuire dhuit*,' back from a few. Others looked at her, as if to ask, 'and what business of mine is yours?'

* * *

At the docks, there were dozens of ships tied up beside the piers. Through the masts, out on the horizon, beyond the small islands in the bay, the pale sky melded into lilac and merged into the dark line of the sea. Out there, more ships queued to get into this great port, laden with their precious cargoes of people and goods.

Not all of the ships were emigrant ships. Many had cranes beside them, loading or off-loading barrels and crates of goods, but there were two ships with people crowded on deck, waiting to disembark. Annie guessed there must be hundreds of people arriving on just these two ships, on this one day. How was she supposed to find single women and girls in these crowds of people?

Shouted orders from the ships' captains to the crew on the quay echoed and bounced around the dockside. Each voice was louder than the next, trying to outdo the other and be heard.

She stopped near one of the gangways. Close to her, at the end of the gangway, she noticed small groups of men, who appeared to be waiting for the new arrivals to disembark. When they arrived in Quebec, Captain Joe had warned Annie not to speak to anyone on the quays; they were only out to get her money and baggage off her. And they were here too, the gangs. She had been caught unawares once, but never again.

She saw one of the men glance at her, then he moved away, and she lost sight of him. 'My God!' she whispered. He was the man, scrawny and dirty, with a bearded face and ragged hair. The man who had abducted Katty. She'd never forget that face. She guessed he didn't know her. He had taken Katty, and he might have seen Finn's face, as he chased him down the alley, but he can't have seen Annie, who was further behind. She'd know him anywhere; his head seemed to twitch and bounce as he moved.

She gripped the edges of her cloak to stop her hands from trembling. She looked around and spotted a group of nuns gathered at the side of the quay. She recognised one of them from the orphanage.

'Sister Fidelma!'

A small nun in the middle of the black clad women looked up and waved. 'Annie Power! What brings you here?'

'I came to have a look at the ships bringing the immigrants from Ireland. There was a man over there. He's the one who took Katty, last year when we got here.'

'Where is he?'

'He's gone. He didn't know me, I think.'

'That's good. This place is full of villains.'

'Is that why you're here, Sister?' Annie moved closer to hear above the shouted orders and the clatter of the gangways on the piers. Still anxious, Annie looked over her shoulder to check if the man had remembered her and followed her. He was nowhere to be seen.

'Yes, we try to get between the gangs and the immigrants,

before the poor souls get fleeced of what little they have. And they're pouring in, more every day. God help them. And many of them have come with nothing.'

They heard a commotion from one of the moored ships. Crowds of men, women and children piled onto the gangway and surged down to the dockside. Some of them knelt and kissed the ground. *America!* The noise was immense. Annie heard people shout and cry; saw them hug each other as they stood on the dockside. Some were barefoot and shivered in the autumn breeze, but their voices sounded a hubbub of relief. Gulls flew up into the air and their screeches added to the commotion.

'Can I help, Sister?' Annie had to raise her voice to be heard.

'Go with the nuns, and speak to anyone you can. Point them over here.'

Annie followed the small group of nuns and pushed through the moving crowds to the end of the gangway. The whole thing seemed to be a free-for-all, with no officials or even crewmen off the ship to help. The emigrants were just dumped on the quay, and left to get on with it.

She saw one of the waiting men reach out and catch hold of a young boy. Annie froze, it was Katty's abductor again. He seemed to be everywhere. 'There you are, young fella!' he said to the child. 'Where's your Daddy?' The child pointed to his father, who stood next to several small children and his wife. 'Right so, let's go and talk to him.'

Annie forced herself to go over to them and stood close enough to hear him speak to the newly arrived family. He held out tickets to the father of the family. As soon as the father reached for his wallet, Annie took a deep breath and stepped in between the two men. She put her hand out to stop the transaction. 'Wait!' she urged in Irish. The Irishman paused. He looked from Annie to the man.

The scrawny man caught Annie's hand and bent her wrist back. 'You're getting between me and my new friends here. I suggest you head off over to your nuns and mind your own business.'

He didn't recognise her, she was sure of it, and she leaned in towards him, despite the pain in her wrist. 'Those tickets will take them nowhere. They don't need your help, and you're not their friend. Shame on you!'

'Let go of her hand, then,' the father of the family said. He was a West of Ireland man; of small build, with dark hair and eyes, but unafraid, for all his low size.

The ruffian pushed Annie out of his way and turned to look for another victim. Annie kept her eyes on him. The nuns had spotted him too, and one followed him.

'*Go raibh maith agat.*' Annie and the father both thanked each other at the same time, then both laughed. His wife and their five small children joined in the laughter. It seemed the children hadn't understood or been frightened by the incident.

'He said his name was McGonigle, but he's not Irish. A chancer, I'd say.' The West of Ireland man said.

Annie nodded. 'My name is Annie Power. I'm from Waterford. What part of Ireland are you from?'

'Galway town. And I tell you, we're glad to be here with our feet on the ground. I'm James Conroy. Jean, here, is my wife, and these are our children.'

'And where are you heading for?' Annie asked. They were dressed in worn but warm clothes and they all wore shoes, unlike some of those disembarking.

'Upstate New York, I've a cousin there. We didn't have time to write and tell anyone we're coming, we just had to get out of Ireland. But my cousin will make us welcome.' James Conroy replied.

'That's good,' Annie said. She lowered her voice to a whisper so the children wouldn't hear. 'I left in June. Is it still the same, back home?'

Both husband and wife nodded. 'It's worse. Bad everywhere,' Jean said. 'And there's no end in sight. The blight is still in the ground. The main crop is rotten again. Sure, there's hunger, sickness and death everywhere you look.'

Annie put her hand to her heart. 'You did the right thing getting out now. I came with my brother and sister. We have an aunt here.'

'We surely did,' James Conroy agreed. 'There's nothing to go back to. Not for us, anyway.'

Annie pointed to the nuns. 'The nuns over there, they're the Sisters of Charity. They'll put you right about getting to your relatives. Just be careful who you pay money to. If those men see you have money, they'll have it off you.' She paused. 'Or they'll even take your children, and you'll have to buy them back!'

She looked at their shocked faces as they took in her words, and she nodded. She shook hands with the couple. 'May God go with you.' She watched as they made their way over to the small group of black clad nuns.

Katty's abductor, McGonigle, or whatever his real name was, had disappeared. He would know Annie the next time he saw her, of that she was certain. She shivered and looked at the purple bruise on her wrist. She would have to be careful, but she'd not be stopped.

* * *

Annie spent an hour speaking to more newly arrived emi-grants. She got between some gang members and felt their eyes on her, as she greeted families and couples. She was searching for single girls, but saw just two women, and they had travelled together from Sligo. She spoke to them and found both had jobs to go to. They were being met off the ship by their employer.

Maybe there aren't that many single women travelling alone then, she thought, but the newspaper report had said otherwise. Did they come in through Quebec like she had? It was cheaper to travel to British North America and then cross the border into America. Therefore, they would land on Pier Three, like Annie had, and not here. Annie promised herself she would pay a visit there soon.

Both ships were now empty, and the quays were clearing of people. She said goodbye to Sister Fidelma, and began to walk back to the apartment. On her way home, the voice of the newly arrived immigrant, James Conroy, echoed in her head. 'There's no going back now.'

The words echoed through her mind. She shook her head. Was there really no going back? Ever? Why should we all be thrown out of our country? Why don't people rise up and protest? She answered her own question. Sure, I tried, and got arrested for my trouble. But why must we live here? Away from our family, our friends and neighbours. She could almost hear the answer. 'You know why, Annie. They're all either dead, or they've left Ireland, like you. All your neighbours were evicted, gone from the village, to England or North America. You're one of the lucky ones. You're alive.'

'But there's plenty left. They could rise up!' It was no use, she knew that those left behind had their own struggles, if they were to survive this great harrowing.

She was soon at her aunt's apartment, and walked up the steps to the front door. She stopped to look back along the street. It was full of people like herself, strangers to almost everyone around them, in a strange, new country. And some were not friendly, some would cause harm to those she loved. She shook her head, blinked away bitter tears and went inside.

8

Jane Keating: October 1846. New South Wales

J ane Keating's journey from the Cape of Good Hope was finally at an end, and the Maitland docked in Port Phillip in early October. There, at the end of the world, it was spring-time, the seasons were opposite to the northern hemisphere, and the air was full of fresh breezes with lots of bright sunshine. Summer was on the way.

Their ship sailed into the wide blue waters of Port Philip Bay, and, for the first time in months, Jane saw land. She smiled at the sight of a long sandy beach towards the east. Beyond the beach, a forest of heavy-topped trees gathered on the skyline.

Up ahead lay the estuary and a wide river mouth and the port. She'd heard the crew call the river the Yarra as they reefed the sails, and left just one aloft to allow it to manoeuvre up to the dock.

Jane and Lizzie leaned on the railing. 'I'm happy to be getting off this ship,' she said to her friend, for she'd soon feel the earth beneath her feet again. 'But it's real, isn't it

Lizzie? We're here for seven years.'

'It'll pass, Jane. Seven years is not that long.' Lizzie said. From her expression, Jane was sure that her friend had the same worries. Would they survive and get back home?

On the banks of the river, people stopped to stare at the ship as it moved slowly towards the landing quay. She waved to a group of children playing on the quay, and they jumped up and down and waved back at her, calling out in high, piping voices. As they neared the docklands she saw long, low whitewashed buildings, and many more people, mostly men, working around the ships that were newly arrived from England. Beyond the town, dark mountains rose in the distance, shadowed against the brilliant blue sky.

* * *

On the crossing, Jane had heard rumours of a different out-come to the convicts' journey. They would not be prisoners, thanks to the objections of the many free emigrants now living in Melbourne. The citizens of Port Phillip and the town of Melbourne wanted nothing more to do with the convict past of their new town. Never mind that gangs of convict labour had built, and still worked on, the roads and government buildings. That was part of the past, not the present. It was eighteen-forty-six, and time to move forward. They conveniently forgot that there was still a demand for cheap labour, not only from sheep farmers, but the government, too.

Jane had heard that Lord Grey, a Government Minister in London, had come up with a scheme to rename convicts as 'Exiles' and give them a free pardon on arrival. The male convicts on the Maitland had already served part of their sentence back in Pentonville Prison in London. They would be the first of 'Grey's Exiles', and they would receive a pardon.

The women convicts, by a stroke of good fortune, were to be included in this scheme. In this way, Melbourne would avoid the stain of being a convict town. It seemed an incredible story, and Jane decided she would believe this when she heard it from the Captain himself. She didn't have to wait long.

Before they were allowed to disembark, the women prisoners were mustered below decks and the captain introduced the Superintendent of Melbourne himself, Mr Charles La Trobe. A tall man, he had to stoop to avoid the beams in the convict quarters. He confirmed the rumours. They were indeed to be given a certificate of Conditional Pardon. The prisoners had to promise not to return to England at the end of their sentence, but to remain in Australia. There were no questions from the women, who couldn't believe their good fortune and just wanted to get off the ship.

After La Trobe left, the women were given two choices; either sign up for work in the government factories where they would earn a wage and live in government accommodation; or they could meet with a woman, Mrs Chisholm, who was waiting on the quayside to speak to them.

'Mrs Chisholm runs a charity for women emigrants to Sydney and Melbourne,' the captain said. 'She has agreed to extend her service to you women, and help you find work and accommodation. Those of you who want to get work in the factories will go with Mr Blake. The rest will be directed to Mrs Chisholm.' The majority of the women left with Mr Blake, and Lizzie would go with them. She hugged Jane. 'Are you sure you won't come with us? By the sounds of it, the work is well-paid.'

But Jane had instantly decided against working in a government factory. If she was to be free, then she'd do it without the help of the British Government. 'No, Lizzie. I'll see what Mrs Chisholm has to offer.'

'Sure, Melbourne is only a small town, we'll meet again. Come and find me when you're settled.' Lizzie suggested. The two friends parted.

Jane and the remaining women prepared to disembark. She gathered her few bits of clothing; the shabby grey convict uniform, Annie's prayer book, and the precious journal she had been keeping for the last five months. Then they were led off the ship by their military escort, who left them to wait on the edge of the quay. Owen Doran had gone with the other women to the manufactories, and she'd not had a chance to say goodbye to him.

Jane stood with the other women prisoners, unsure of what to do next. Her legs felt strange, now that she was standing on firm ground. After months at sea, she had become used to the movement of the ship and her balance adjusted to the sway and rise of the sea. She still swayed slightly and, with each step she took, her feet hit the ground too hard, as if expecting the ground to give way beneath her.

The sun burned down from the wide azure sky and she squinted at her fellow convicts. Almost free. It was a strange feeling, to be free, yet at the same time, be trapped inside a great big prison. The only way out would be on one of those ships at anchor, and there were plenty of soldiers and crew to ensure no escaping convicts, or Exiles, made their way on board. Yet she felt no fear, just curiosity about this new place.

She looked along the quay and counted fifteen ships loading and unloading goods. Gangs of men hauled bales of wool onto some of the waiting ships.

Finally here. It was overwhelming and she couldn't imagine what would happen to her, here in Port Phillip. 'One thing is for sure and certain,' she promised herself. 'I'll be home in Ireland before seven years are up. Somehow.'

A warm breeze ruffled her hair. Yes, she could feel in the air, that summer was not far off. Having left Ireland last June, in summer, it felt as if time had almost stood still; as if the sea journey were only a dream and she was now awake. She moved out of the way of a dingy mule pulling a huge cart piled high with hemp sacks, bursting with creamy wool. The cart was about three times the size of the poor animal, and his head and long ears drooped as he clopped along towards the ship. The driver of the cart held a long whip and clipped the mule lightly to keep him going.

Anther ship had its gangway down to offload new emigrants. Young men and women, some families with young children, carried their belongings off the ship, ready and eager to start their new life in Melbourne. One young mother held an infant in her arms, while her husband carried their bags. They smiled at each other and both of them seemed to Jane to be filled with excitement at the start of their new adventure. She almost envied them.

Neither Jane, nor any of her fellow freed convicts, had any money. They each had their letter of conditional pardon, the clothes they stood up in and a spare prison uniform. Jane's hair had finally grown down past her shoulders, after keeping it short when she was 'Jack' in Dublin. She had been fed on board and had filled out a bit, yet, despite the attention to cleanliness on board, she was crawling with lice. She longed to strip off, scrub herself down, and set fire to her convict clothes.

Further along the quay, she saw a short, stocky woman standing on a stool at the side of one of the warehouses. Jane squinted to read the sign the woman held up: *Women's Work Here.* That must be Mrs Chisholm.

Jane and the other women walked over to stand in front of the woman and waited to hear what she had to offer.

When the fifteen, newly pardoned women had gathered, the woman spoke. 'Sisters, welcome to New South Wales.'

Jane almost smiled to hear this. Sisters? Was the woman mad? Maybe so, but she'd listen to what the woman had to say. There was only one other alternative.

'My name is Caroline Chisholm, and my home is in England, but I am here with my husband who works for the British Government.' Mrs Chisholm, spoke in a high, refined voice, but had a smiling, friendly face. 'I have made it my mission to help women emigrants to find work and clean lodgings so they can start to make a life here. Now, you know there is a government scheme which provides work and accommodation. However, I can help those of you who may want to take a different path. If you look at the building at the end of the dock just there.' She turned and pointed to a small shop front at the end of a run of warehouses. 'You'll see my office and the women's hostel. It's open now for you to go and have something to eat. There's a dormitory where you can sleep and eat until you get set up with work. And right next door, an employment agency, where we can put you in touch with decent employers. I invite you to come and see what we can offer.'

The woman stood on her stool and looked at the pardoned convicts in front of her. Jane put her hand up.

'Why are you doing this, Mrs Chisholm? We're Irish and you're English.' Jane frowned. Now she was puzzled.

'Because I'm a Catholic, and I expect you are too,' Mrs Chisholm replied. 'My faith tells the parable of the Good Samaritan. You must have heard it?'

Jane nodded.

'Then you understand why I came here today. Also, I know how hard it is for women on their own here. Why, some have even fallen into prostitution to earn money. I'm not suggesting that you will go down that road, but I'm here to offer some help. Will you walk with me to the office?'

She stepped down from the stool, picked it up, then waited for Jane and the other women to join her. With nowhere else to go, Jane followed. Mrs Chisholm led the way from the quay to the hostel. As they walked, she explained that the government had loaned her the building for her charitable work.

Jane and the other pardoned convicts looked around as they walked. It was getting on for late afternoon and Jane felt sweat break out on her face and neck. The sun hung low, like a great orange ball in a cloudless blue sky, but the heat was still intense.

'What will it be like here in summer?' Jane thought. The quay and the buildings alongside were built of pale grey stone that reflected back the heat and the sun's rays. There wasn't a breath of wind in the air from the river, a wide expanse of still water that, out beyond the anchored ships, mirrored the sky and the sun on its surface. Layered on top of the heat, she heard the shouts of the stevedores at work on the ships and the quay.

The Female Immigrants' Home was only a short walk,

and Mrs Chisholm introduced the women to Mrs Smith, the manager. They walked around the Home. 'It was an old immigrants' barracks, loaned to us by the British Government,' Mrs Chisholm said.

Constructed of yet more pale stone, the ground floor was divided into rooms for sitting and eating.

Mrs Smith pointed out the washroom and privies at the end of the hallway, then invited them into her office near the front door. It was a squeeze for them all to get in, but they saw she had laid out a stack of second-hand clothes on her desk. The women were able to choose two sets of clothes and underwear each. Mrs Smith accompanied Mrs Chisholm on the tour of the rest of the building. Upstairs in the dormitories, each room had twenty or so single beds and each of the women was allocated a bed and a small locker to store their new clothes and personal belongings.

After Jane had put her possessions on her bed, she opened one of the windows and leaned out to look up the river towards the jumble of low slate roofs a short distance away from the docks. A tower of red brick and dark stone rose in the distance above the other buildings. It looked to Jane like a church tower. This place was to be her new home. For a while at least. She corrected herself, for a short while, and followed her companions downstairs to the dining room.

Mrs Chisholm waited while they helped themselves to a plate of food, a stew of some sort, and sat down with them. 'You must be tired after your long journey. Mrs Smith, will look after you. Have your supper, rest, and get a good night's sleep.

'I'll come back first thing in the morning, then we'll get you into settled jobs. Most of the work is in domestic service, either here in the town, or further out on the sheep stations. So you'll have a choice of where you wish to begin your new life. God bless you all.' She raised her hand in farewell and nodded to Mrs Smith. 'I'll be back after breakfast.'

The dining room had whitewashed walls and more of the large windows. It was now evening, and the sun slanted in through the glass windows and glinted on the tin plates and cutlery. One thing Jane quickly realised was that there seemed to be very little shade in this part of the world. The women sat at a long refectory table, and ate their plate of stew with a thick slice of bread on the side.

After supper, most of the other, now-freed convicts, went out to enjoy their liberty and explore Port Phillip.

Jane was weary and didn't join them. She went to the washroom and scrubbed herself clean of the weeks of being at sea. She put on one of her new shifts and smoothed her hair. Then she went upstairs to her bed. She took her journal and a pencil out of her bag and carefully tore out a page and began to write.

Melbourne 19th October, 1846.

My dear Annie,

I'm writing to tell you that I am finally here in Melbourne, Port Phillip, New South Wales. The journey was long and arduous, but I met a young man from Wicklow, Owen Doran. He's a soldier in the British Army and he was our escort from Dublin and he was a friend to me on the journey here.

The seasons are topsy-turvey and it is spring here, but even so, it is very hot.

The good news I have to relate is that I am no longer a convict, for we were granted a Pardon on arrival here. I'm free, but not free to leave, yet.

I hope you got to New York and are now safe with your aunt. Give my love to Finn and Katty and tell them I hope to see them again. I'll send this letter to the address you gave me, and if by some miracle you receive it, then write to me at the Female Immigrants' Home in Port Phillip. Address your letter to Jane Power. I have kept my first name.

There is a Mrs Chisholm here and she helps young women and girls like myself to find work. I tore this page out of my journal and, as you can see, it is now full. I will ask Mrs Chisholm to advance me the cost of postage.

Please God and his Blessed Mother, we'll see each other again, if not in New York, then back home in Ireland. Your sincere friend.

Jane Keating

She lay down on her bed. It was still daylight outside and she listened to the sounds of birdsong in the trees near the dormitory window. She recognised the low, sweet call of blackbirds and the whistling chatter of finches. 'This time next year,' she promised herself, as she drifted off to sleep.

* * *

It was Jane's third interview. The first two didn't go so well. The jobs offered meant that she had to go and live out in the bush, miles away from Melbourne. She felt safer in town, perhaps because somehow Melbourne reminded her of Galway, both towns were built around rivers, although that was the only resemblance. Whatever the reason, she could write her letters and get them posted, something she'd never be able to do miles out in the bush. Mrs Chisholm, bless her, had loaned Jane the money to post her letter, and it was now on its way to America.

There had been almost no sign of anything amiss at the third interview in Caroline Chisholm's office. Just the one small thing. A glance she had caught from the man, the way his eyes flicked over her whole body. She'd seen something like it before, on the convict ship.

'I'm a retired Colonel in the British Army,' he said. 'I live in the town here with my wife and children. Our housemaid has gone off to get married, and we need to replace her.' The Colonel wore a lightweight linen suit, and had retained his short army haircut, greying moustache and sideburns. He was a handsome man, but no longer in the prime of his life. He had been polite, and anxious to offer good employment in his home.

He addressed his comments to Mrs Chisholm, as if to impress her and not Jane.

'Jane is one of the fortunate ones, Colonel.' Mrs Chisholm said. 'She had been given a free pardon. She is one of Grey's Exiles and will serve her sentence here as a free person.' Mrs Chisholm smiled at his look of surprise. 'Yes, times have changed. We'll not see many more convicts in this beautiful part of the world.'

The Colonel frowned and looked at Jane. 'What was your crime, then?'

'I'm innocent of any crime,' Jane said. 'I was wrongly convicted.' No use going back over old ground, she thought.

'Well, we should get on famously.' The Colonel's voice was dry and emotionless. It was then, that Jane caught the glance from him. It reminded her of the look from a cat before it pounced on a tiny mouse. At that moment, just for a single moment, she had second thoughts about taking the job.

'We have a housekeeper to look after the house and she

cooks for us, and a handyman to look after the grounds and the stables.' He looked at Jane and this time he smiled. 'You'll have your own bedroom in the cottage in the garden, there'll be just you and the housekeeper. All your meals and board are included and you'll be paid six pounds, twice yearly.'

'Colonel Johns,' Mrs Chisholm said. 'I require that all our employers provide clothes and shoes for their new workers. It will help Jane get off to a good start.'

'Very well. I have an account in the general store in Melbourne. Jane can get what she needs there.'

'That's good to hear. Now, there's just one more thing, Colonel. We insist that our young women have time off every Sunday to attend mass or a church service. Jane is a Catholic, like myself.'

It was agreed. Jane had a job and a roof over her head and her certificate of pardon in her hand. She would call into the general store later that day to collect her new clothes and report for work at the Colonel's residence. She put aside her doubts. This would be as good a start as any, to her new life in exile.

9

Annie Power: October 1846. Aid for Ireland Meeting

Annie's job as a teaching assistant was going well. The familiarity of a classroom full of Irish boys and girls helped her to almost feel at home. Although not situated in a barn, as back at Ashling, familiar Irish faces sat at wooden tables and benches. Even the nun who taught the class resembled Miss Nagel, the teacher who had taught and trained Annie. The difference being, that these children were all orphaned as a result of the famine following the potato blight. They had seen and experienced a lot in their lives, as Annie could attest to.

Back in her home village of Ashling, the children all had homes to go to, until everything suddenly fell apart. She daren't think where all her neighbours were now, only that they were gone, dispersed. All that land had been cleared by evictions. At least here, the orphans had the nuns, food and shelter. Annie's job was to help them learn to speak, read and write in English. She shook thoughts of home away and got back to her work.

* * *

Finn and Katty reported that they were doing great at their school. Finn's part-time job gave him the opportunity to move around a patch of The Broadway selling newspapers. And Bridie revelled in her instant family.

Only Annie felt no joy. Everywhere she looked she saw displaced Irish immigrants. Every night she dreamed about home and her father. 'Annie, don't dwell, girlie,' he would say, when she worried about not having enough oats left for their supper. Her father was a great one for finding a small bag of barley to thicken the broth, or exchanging some turf for oats with Marie, their neighbour. He could always find something to make their lives a little warmer. She determined that she would try to take on some of her father's optimism. Maybe she could find something to make her life a little warmer, more meaningful.

She remembered her aunt had told her about the Aid for Ireland group who met every week and decided it was time to go along to one of the meetings.

* * *

The following Saturday, after they had eaten their supper, the Powers set out with their aunt for the Cathedral hall.

Bridie led the way. Saint Pat's Cathedral had been built only recently and the separate meeting hall at the back was as wide as it was long. It had a raised stage at the top of the room and there must have been fifty or more people on benches facing the stage. Oil lamps on the stage cast a yellow glow along the seated committee members, while the rest of the room was in shadow. Annie and her family found an empty bench towards the rear of the hall and waited for the meeting to start.

The committee, there were ten of them, six men and four women, took their seats on the stage and faced out towards the people gathered in the church hall. Those on the stage were mixed in age; the men older, suited and most with grey sideburns. The women were younger, two wore the traditional Irish cloaks and the other two wore top-coats. From where she sat, Annie could see they were all well-shod in leather boots and shoes. A quick glance around her fellow audience told a different story. These people were shabbier and thinner, in general. However, she noticed, many were a lot younger, too. Recent arrivals, like herself, Annie thought.

The chairman cleared his throat and stood to speak. 'Welcome everyone. *Failte.* Now settle down there, will you?' He waited for the low chatter to stop then continued.

'Thank you all for coming out tonight. I see quite a few new faces here, so for those of you who haven't met me, I'm Pat Brady, the chairman of this Aid for Ireland committee. As you may be aware, we've worked hard these last months to raise money for the relief of the disaster back home. I want to tell you about a couple of special donations. I'll start with Jim Hanrahan. Where are you, Jim? Stand up there man! Jim and his wife, Cissy, have raised twenty dollars for the fund.' Jim and Cissy both stood and nodded to the crowd. Jim raised his hand to salute the chairman, who clapped and smiled, and the couple sat down to more clapping.

'Thank you, both. We'll be sure to put your money to good use. And the second large donation comes from Father Malachy, here at the cathedral. He had a special collection at mass last week and raised twenty-five dollars.' Father

Malachy, one of the committee members, stood, while Pat Brady clapped his large, square hands together. The audience joined him in the applause.

The chairman continued his address. 'The question we have to answer tonight, is what do we do with this money? There's now two hundred and fifty dollars in the pot. The committee here has looked into it and we have a couple of options. But it's turning out to be a tricky proposition.' The Chairman paused to look over his notes. 'The first option is to buy sacks of food, grain and oats and send them over to Ireland. There are plenty of charities over there and the Government Relief Committee will distribute the food for us.'

At the mention of the British government, the audience erupted into whistles and jeers. Annie's stomach turned at the mention of the Relief Committee. Her father had tried to get work on the roads last year. He'd been turned away several times, because he had a half acre of land and was not deemed to be homeless. They had gone hungry because of the British Relief Committee. And they weren't the only ones.

The glow from the oil lamps flickered and illuminated the top of the chairman's bald head and his bushy grey eyebrows.

He held his arms out to quieten the crowd. 'Yes, I understand.' He coughed and cleared his throat. 'Another option is for one of the committee members to take the money to Ireland, buy food and whatever is necessary and see to the distribution personally. But for this we need a person we can trust to spend the money wisely. First though, no-one need suggest I go. I'm far too old for that sort of thing.' He chuckled at the idea.

Over the next few minutes, various people in the audience made suggestions but no-one came forward to volunteer.

Annie frowned and looked at her aunt. Like probably everyone else in the room, they silently agreed it was too dangerous to go back right now. Everyone knew the whole island of Ireland was a disaster, with hunger and disease in almost every town.

The meeting dawdled on for half an hour, with no resolution, until eventually, the Chairman called a halt to the chat. 'If we can't agree on what to do with the money, then we'll either buy food and send it to the Government Relief Committee in Dublin, or we'll send over the money to them to use as they see fit. They'll distribute the money to local charities.'

Mr Brady looked around him, at the other committee members, and the people seated in the body of the hall. To Annie, no-one seemed to be satisfied with the outcome of the discussions.

The Chairman continued. 'We'll meet again next week, same time. If you have any ideas at all, then bring them along for consideration. Right so, the meeting is now at an end.' The Chairman pointed to Jim Hanrahan. 'Jim, will you and some of the men get these benches shifted so we can get on with the music?'

It took only a few minutes to clear a space in the centre of the room, and get the benches lined up around the wall. An older couple, a man and a woman, unpacked two fiddles and began to tune them. Then they started to play a reel.

'Bridie, you didn't tell me there was a *ceili* here.' Annie whispered.

'This must be a new thing, it wouldn't have been allowed before Bishop Hughes came,' her aunt replied.

'Well then, we'd better make the most of it before he changes his mind,' Finn said. He took his coat off and grabbed Annie and Katty and they joined the few brave dancers in a reel. For the first time since she had arrived in America, Annie felt her heavy load lighten as she danced with her brother and sister. Maybe these people could be her new neighbours? 'Dear Lord and Blessed Mother, grant this,' she prayed.

She danced on the hardwood floor of the church hall and recalled the evening, almost a year ago, when she had skipped a reel, barefoot with her friend, Eileen. It had been early evening and as the moon rose and dusk fell, the sky slowly lit up with a long sprinkle of stars that shone down on the leaving 'wake'. None of them were to know what was to befall Eileen and her entire family before the year was out.

* * *

On the walk home, Annie listened to Katty and Finn as they chatted to Bridie about the *ceili*. Katty was not the only child at the meeting; other boys and girls had joined in the dance and Katty was already friends with some of the children from school. Annie smiled to see her sister as she laughed and danced with her new friends. Finn, too, had met up with a few boys of his age and he spent time standing at the side of the wall talking to them. They all looked very serious. Finn didn't join in the dancing again, but he shook hands with the boys when he left. He looked happier than he had for a long time.

Annie recalled the discussion of sending money to the British Relief Committee. She remembered her father's description of the men with books of lists. Those who were on their list would eat that day, or get some money to feed their families. If not, they'd hear the dreaded words. 'Come back tomorrow, you're not in the book. Perhaps tomorrow.'

Heat rose through her body and she wanted to shout out her thoughts. 'Sure, can you not see he's walked miles in his bare feet? He left his wife and children at home to get a few shillings for bread? Do you not see death in his eyes for want of your help?' No, she decided, the money must not go to them sort. The ones with lists and books. 'I'd rather stand on a street corner in Waterford or Galway and give away the relief money.' She knew that going back wasn't an option, for she risked being arrested again and hauled back to Kilmainham Gaol. That was not a risk she could take, not after Jane had given up her freedom to save her.

Silently, she spoke to her father. 'Da, tell me what to do. I can't go back there. Jones, the agent, he'd recognise me for sure.' Annie heard his reply, as if he was right there beside her. 'Stay away from Ireland and look after yourself, your brother and sister, *acushla*. What about your friends in Ireland? Can they help?'

She stopped on the sidewalk, her eyes were full of tears, but she almost smiled and she reached out to touch Bridie's arm. 'I know what they can do with the money. I met a lot of people back home. They worked so hard to get food to the hungry.' Annie's voice broke and she swallowed hard. 'Teachers like Miss Nagel. The Dublin Quakers, those women who ran that soup kitchen on Saint Stephen's Green; and we met a priest, in Sligo, with dozens of orphaned children to feed.'

'Sure there's a lot of good people in the world, all the same, girl,' her aunt replied. They walked on and turned into Princes Street. Evening had drawn in, traffic on the road had eased, and lamps shone in some of the tenement windows, as people settled down after their supper.

She stood at the bottom of the steps and called Finn and Katty who were about to go into the apartment building. 'Wait a minute, and I'll tell you my idea for the money!'

She outlined her idea and they agreed it couldn't wait till the following week, so Annie took off back to the Cathedral to find the Chairman.

* * *

She prayed Mr Brady would still be there and ran all the way, her cloak flying behind her, her hair had pulled loose, the weight of it bounced on her shoulder. Five minutes later, she arrived, breathless, at the door of the cathedral hall, and there he was, Pat Brady, on his way out.

'Well now, Miss. And what brings you back here? You're Bridie's niece, aren't you.' He put the keys in his pocket and placed his hat on his head, for it was getting colder now night had drawn in.

'Yes, Annie Power. Mr Brady, I'm so glad you're still here. I have an idea, what you can do with the money.' Annie caught her breath, she felt her heart hammer in her chest.

'I supposed we'd better go back in then, so you can tell me. It's too cold to be standing out here.' He smiled and unlocked the door, opened it and stepped back to let Annie go ahead of him.

She started to speak as soon as they were through the door. 'Did my aunt Bridie tell you that I spent a couple of weeks in Dublin before we left to come here?'

He nodded. 'She did. We spoke after mass a few months ago. She told me you buried your poor father, too.'

They stood in the lobby of the hall; Pat Brady, tall in his

beaver hat, seemed to loom over Annie, who shivered in the cold air and pulled her cloak tightly around her. The only light came from the brilliant harvest moon that shone in through the small window beside the door.

'It was after my father died. And I travelled to Sligo with Speranza, a reporter from The Nation newspaper. She didn't speak Irish, so I was the interpreter for her. We met a lot of people on our travels. But also people who were trying to help; Quakers, priests and nuns, from all over, who were doing their best to help those poor starving families. And it was often their own money, or sometimes, the little they could get from the government. There are lots of them. If you send the money to them, it won't be wasted.'

'I'll stop you right there, Annie. That's exactly what we want to do, but how do we get it to them?' Pat Brady took his hat off and sighed. 'That's our problem, don't you see?'

It was dark in the hallway and he led the way through to a small office, where he struck a flint to light an oil lamp. 'Take a seat.' He sat opposite her and clasped his hands together and waited for her to reply.

She took a deep breath. 'At the meeting this evening, I thought, no-one dare go back there. Sure, it's far too dangerous. There's fever and sickness now, as well as the hunger, all over the country. But there's someone already there who'll help, I'm sure.' Annie paused. 'His name is Charles Gavan Duffy, he's the owner of The Nation newspaper, in Dublin, and he's a Catholic too. He'll help distribute the money. Speranza and I can give him the names of the people we met and he'll find them. He's a barrister. You can trust him with the money.'

'I must say I like your enthusiasm, young woman. Who is

this, Speranza?' Mr Brady asked.

'She's a poet, Jane Elgee. Speranza is her pen-name, and she has published articles in the newspaper. She helped me.' Annie replied.

'Well, I suppose it's worth taking at look at it. It might work. This Mr Gavan Duffy. He's a barrister you say?'

'I have a copy of the Nation newspaper at my aunt's. I can bring it to you and show you his name on it. He's a nationalist, he wants an independent Ireland. I think that's why he set up the newspaper.'

Mr Brady pursed his lips, and the wrinkles in his forehead creased as he appeared to worry about this information.

'I don't want to be getting involved in politics now, Annie. We're well out of it here. But I'll tell you what I'll do. I'll put it to the committee. We meet tomorrow after the eleven o'clock mass. Come along, and you can tell them about your proposal and we'll consider it.'

'Thank you, Mr Brady. I'll be there tomorrow.' Annie shook his hand hard, and left him to lock up again. Then she raced home to tell her news. They'd send the money to Mr Gavan Duffy, she was sure of it.

* * *

Annie got up early the next morning. Finn was off selling his newspapers and she had the parlour to herself. She took her time getting ready for mass and the meeting afterwards. She had two best dresses for Sunday wear. The pale blue dress her aunt had sent over to Waterford from New York last Easter. Its soft fabric and the white lace collar showed hardly any wear. The other dress, the Dublin dress, had been made by Speranza's dressmaker, Madame Celeste, and was in a different category altogether. She put it on and held up a tiny mirror to look at herself. Made of lightweight wool, the deep red colour contrasted with her copper hair. The wide neckline set off her pale shoulders and chest. She smiled at herself. 'Come on now, girl. Where do you think you're off to in that dress?' But she left it on. She felt different when she wore that dress. No longer a country girl, but an Irish woman. She wrapped herself in her cloak, pulled the hood up and set out for mass with Katty and Bridie.

* * *

After mass was over, she said goodbye to her aunt and her sister, and went round to the side door to the hall. The committee members had arrived at the same time, and took their seats. Annie joined them.

The chairman introduced Annie, and they waited to hear what she had to say.

'I visited Sligo and some villages on the west coast, just last May. There's terrible hunger and distress there. With the potato crop gone, there is just no food for the people who live on the land. Sure, you all know this. Forgive me.' A few of them nodded to acknowledge her comment.

'But I also met many people who are doing their best to help. They're priests, nuns and teachers, and Quakers. I heard some of the landowners are helping, too.'

One of the committee members, a young, red-haired woman in her twenties, slapped her hand down on the table as she interrupted. 'There'll be none of this money going to any of the landowners. I can assure you of that, Annie.' The man beside her put his hand on the young woman's hand. 'Julia, let Miss Power speak.'

Annie nodded to both of them. 'I know who they are, the Quakers, and priests, nuns and teachers. Some of them anyway. I can give you the names of the people who would spend the money and make a difference there. But I also know someone who can distribute the money you have raised, and see it gets into the right hands.'

'Well then, don't keep the committee in suspense. Tell them the name of this person,' Mr Brady said.

'He's the owner of The Nation newspaper, Mr Charles Gavan Duffy. He's a respectable man, a barrister and a Catholic. I have a copy of the newspaper he set up in Dublin.' She passed the newspaper to Mr Brady. He looked at it, saw the names of the proprietors and passed it around the table.

'If we ask him, I'm sure he'll agree to distribute your money. With your permission, I'll write and give him the names of the people I met and he'll vouch for them. And Miss Jane Elgee, she writes under the name of Speranza, she'll know who they are, too.'

Annie stopped speaking, took a deep breath and looked around the people at the table. No-one spoke, they just sat and stared at her. One or two nodded slowly, as if in agreement.

She broke the moment of silence. 'What do you say?'

'Well, thank you, Annie,' Mr Brady said. 'You've made a very interesting proposition. We'll need to consider your suggestion. And we'll do that now. You can make your own way out. I'll tell you next week about our decision.'

Annie stood, undecided whether to stay or go. This was her chance and she took it. 'There's another thing I must tell you. Something that happened to me recently. I walked down to the docks and saw a young woman, a girl really, younger than me.'

Mr Brady interrupted. 'I don't see what this has to do with our charitable work, Annie. We're here to talk about what to do with the money we have raised to help back home in Ireland. We need to get that money to them as soon as possible.'

'Yes,' Annie replied. 'But what about the people who struggle when they get here? What are you doing for the girls who have no-one to help them and no job? The girl I saw last week? She's working as a prostitute in Five Points, just a couple of miles from here.'

Julia, the young committee member, spoke up. 'Annie, we don't have a solution to all the problems. New York is full of immigrants. Sure, aren't all of us here on the committee Irish born? We all know what it's like to struggle.'

'Then hear me out, please. Just one more minute.' Annie's voice strained and broke. She cleared her throat. 'Those girls, the ones down by Five Points, need a friend who'll stand by them. I can do that. I can teach them, help them to find work.' She stopped to think for a moment of how best to get them to understand. 'There's no point sending money home, then forgetting about the ones who get here. They need our help, too.' Annie's voice rose and she felt her eyes sting with tears as she tried to make them see what was obvious to her.

The chairman reached over and caught hold of Annie's hand. 'Don't upset yourself, Annie. We're here to talk about getting the money we have raised back over to Ireland. What you're talking about is another thing entirely. Now take a minute and get your breath back.'

Annie sat down and closed her eyes. She should go. She

knew that she had made a fool of herself.

Mr Brady addressed the committee. 'Now my friends. I don't think we need to discuss this further. Our young friend here is right. We need to get the money over to Ireland as soon as we can. I say we contact Mr Gavan Duffy in Dublin. He looks to be a respectable businessman and a barrister. I'll send him a banker's draft and ask him to distribute it on our behalf. What say you?'

'Aye.' The decision was unanimous.

The chairman turned to Annie. 'I'd like to extend a vote of thanks to you.'

Annie tried to smile and looked at the men and women around the table. They had accepted her suggestion for the money. But she had also failed, and her heart ached.

'Now then. That's our decision. Annie, will you write up a list of names I can send to Mr Gavan Duffy?'

She bowed her head and tried to smile. 'Yes, I'll do it tonight. I want to thank you, all of you. I'll think of another way to help the young women who have no friends here. I won't give up.' She tilted her head back, and her aunt's words came to her. 'You're a stubborn *divil*, Annie Power. Like your mother before you.'

The meeting ended. The chairman arranged to collect the list of names from Annie at the orphanage the next day.

When she left, Annie stopped into the cathedral and knelt before the altar. Her mind was too addled to pray, and her breathing rattled in her chest. 'I'll help those girls. I know they're out there. Maybe I'm just not looking in the right place. Perhaps they're coming in through Quebec, like we did. I'll find them on my own, if no-one will help me. And I'll get money from somewhere to help them.'

She looked over to the right of the altar, to a statue of the Virgin Mary. The words of her favourite prayer came to her. 'Remember Oh most Blessed Virgin Mary, that never was it known, that anyone who implored thy help was left unaided. Despise not my petition but in thy mercy hear and answer my prayer.'

'Then they'll listen!' Annie heard herself say the words and looked around. There were a few women praying in front of the altar. They didn't turn round.

* * *

As soon as she got back to the apartment, Annie wrote up a list of names of the people and the organisations that she remembered from her travels with Speranza. Then she copied it out again. She now had one copy for the committee, and one to send with her letter to Charles Gavan Duffy at The Nation newspaper in Dublin. It would take a few weeks to get there, but she'd promised to write and tell him about her experiences.

Saturday 19th October 1846

13 Princes Street, Manhattan, New York.

Dear Mr Gavan Duffy

Greetings from New York. I hope you are well. We've been here almost two months now. Finn and Katty are in school already and I have a job as a teaching assistant with the Sisters of Charity orphanage.

I am writing to you about the Aid for Ireland Committee at Saint Patrick's Cathedral here. They have raised a lot of money to help people back at home.

I gave them your name, as they need someone in Ireland they can trust to distribute the money. As you can imagine, the committee members are unwilling to send the money to the British Government Relief Fund. The Chairman, Mr Brady, will be writing to you, to ask for your help with this. I have written up a list of the people that Speranza and I met in Sligo, Waterford and in Dublin. I'll give it Mr Brady, and I enclose a copy of the list for you, also. Please show it to Speranza, she will know more names. Please say you will help to get the money to these people. I send you my thanks.

As promised last June, I have written an article for The Nation. I'll put it in with this letter and I hope you will publish it. It tells about our journey from Quebec to New York. Please God, it will help others who plan to make the same journey. I will be forever grateful for the money you paid me for these reports. It saved our lives. I will send more news in the next few months.

I spoke to a family just arrived from Sligo earlier this week. They told me that the main potato crop has failed again. The news has filled me with dread about what is still happening to my fellow countrymen in Ireland. I will pray every day for an end to this terrible blight.

Please give my best regards to Speranza and Tom Meagher.

Yours with grateful thanks

Annie Power

Annie counted out some cents for the postage and put her letter on one side to post the next day.

Back home, almost a year ago now, she'd sent her first poem to Speranza at The Nation, from the General Post Office in Waterford. The counter clerk there had asked her what she wanted with "that Nationalist rag". She had told him to mind his own business, checked he put her letter in the postbag and left. That day, she had walked along the quay, then up to the market in the town, past the cathedral and said '*Dhia duit*' to familiar faces; people she had known all her life, who knew her father and her mother, her brother and sister. She refused to think about the Persephone, the transportation ship she'd observed at the quay in Waterford.

She remembered walking the road home in the company of Eileen, her best friend, both of them thankfully ignorant of what the future had in store. Eileen's future would end in her drowning in the Saint Lawrence River on her way to a new life in America. Annie's father would die of fever, just months later. Somehow, she, Finn and Katty had survived. To what end she didn't yet know. But she lived, still. In this land where she was a stranger, she had a life to live.

10

Finn Power: October 1846. Finn skips school

I t was a Monday morning in late October, and Finn walked with Katty to the school gate. The wind caught and blew her hair, and Katty's bright new ribbons, pink satin, fluttered at the ends of her plaits. The heat of late summer had ended and chill breezes blew in off the Bay and the Hudson River, and met in the middle of Manhattan, where brother and sister stood together outside Saint Paul's School.

'I'll meet you here later,' Finn said.

Katty nodded, said nothing, just turned away from her brother and went into the schoolyard.

Finn bit his lip. He didn't want to put Katty in this position of keeping his secret. It wasn't fair on her. By now, this was the third week Finn had skipped school. Well, not just skipped school, left school, finished. He hadn't told Annie or Bridie yet. He'd tell them when he was ready, as long as Katty kept quiet.

He turned back onto The Broadway and headed for the Sun newspaper, went into the yard at the back of the building and joined the line of boys who queued to collect their supply of the day's newspapers. He filled his rucksack with a stack of papers, and hitched the bag over his shoulder, then left for his pitch around Battery Park and the Piers on the Hudson. Most days he'd come back to collect another bag of newspapers. Last week he had made two dollars.

By noon, it had started to rain, but Finn's oiled coat and hood kept him dry. He bought a hot dog from a street vendor and found some shelter under a tree in Battery Park to eat. He had a bottle of milk in his bag and drank it while he ate the food and looked out over the grey Hudson river at the ships and barges coming and going. When he had finished, he put the cork back in the bottle and made his way back to the Sun to collect more newspapers.

By four o'clock, he had earned seventy-five cents for his day's work and waited across the road from the school to meet Katty. She walked out with a few friends, waved goodbye to them and joined Finn. One of the nuns on duty saw Finn and called to him, but he ignored her and caught Katty's hand in his. They walked off and turned the corner, where Finn stopped and hugged his sister. He had bought her a gift, a sweet pancake from a Russian street vendor, and her smile for him was his treat.

'Finn, have a taste. It's so sugary,' Katty held out a piece of the pancake.

'I've already eaten, Kat. That's for you. Here, I'll carry your bag.'

Katty handed over her bag and ate as they walked home. Katty coughed and covered her mouth with her hand.

'Finn, what's that smell? It stinks.'

'It's coming from behind those tenements. There's manufactories or butchers at work, I'd say. I'll take a look tomorrow. Might be able to sell some more papers over that way. Let's get on home.'

They walked on up The Broadway, and headed past the cathedral towards their aunt's apartment. Before they went up the steps to the door, Katty stopped and turned to face Finn.

'When will you tell them, Finn? Sister Rita asked about you today. I told her you're sick. But I don't like lying to the sisters, or to Bridie and Annie.'

He sighed. 'It'll not be for much longer, Kat. I'll tell them soon. I just need to decide what I'm going to do. I've got to have something to tell them. If not, they'll make me go back to school. You know what Annie's like.'

'But when?' Katty asked again.

'When what?' They both turned to see Annie on the top step. 'What are you talking about?'

Finn stared at Katty, then looked up to Annie on the top step. 'It's a secret, a surprise. What are you doing home from work?'

'Sister Mary Rose let me go early. I had a headache.'

'Ah, Annie. Are you better now?' Katty asked.

'Yes, I had a lie down and just came out to buy some milk.'

'I'll get it,' Finn said. 'Here, take the bags, I won't be long.' He ran up the steps, dropped the schoolbags on the threshold and grabbed the milk can from Annie. Then he raced off down the street.

* * *

The next day, Finn spent the morning selling newspapers. On

his round, as he came up from Pier 6, he came across the smell Katty had noticed, but it was stronger today. The stink made the air around him seem heavy, with a yellow taint. It was full of rot and blood and heat. He gagged and spat to get rid of the taste.

Out of curiosity, he followed the stink, off the main street and into a small alleyway behind a row of tenements. The ground was unfinished and muddy with channels of filthy water running along each side. Here the smell was pungent, thicker; the air was now a dirty brown that he could almost catch in his hand. He covered his nose and mouth with his scarf and continued along the lane towards a dilapidated building. Its roof and walls were made of badly planed planks of wood; a metal chimney poked through the roof and belched out a solid stream of pale grey smoke mixed with strips of dirty yellow haze. As he had guessed the day before, it looked like some sort of manufactory. The building seemed to lean against a large barracks place next door, home to several barefoot children who played in the road outside the lodgings, oblivious to the bilious air.

The door to the manufactory was open, he knocked and looked inside at an inferno. The air boiled around his face.

Four huge tanks stood on top of a glowing, molten furnace. A man, his nose and mouth covered by a rag, moved about on a raised platform, and stirred the tanks with a long wooden paddle. The man waved to him, climbed down a ladder and came over to the door. He stepped outside, pulled the rag down and took a deep breath before he spoke. 'Are you here about the job, young fella? If so, you're late.'

'The job?' Finn asked.

'This job. For the night-shift. Did you not come about that?'

The man went to turn away. His boilers were hopping on the furnace.

'Well, maybe. How much does it pay?'

'A dollar-fifty a shift. That's for the night shift, from six to six,' the man said.

'I'll take it.' Finn held out his hand. Six shifts would pay nine dollars a week. A fortune.

'Hold on there, young fella. What's your name? You Irish?' The man looked back over his shoulder at the boiling cauldrons.

'Finn Power. Yes, I'm Irish and I'm looking for work. I can turn my hand to anything. What is it you need doing here?'

'Come up here and I'll show you. That other fella hasn't turned up, so you might do.'

Finn followed him towards the inferno. He stood and watched as the man picked up a large metal scoop and climbed up the ladder to the platform at the side of one of the cauldrons. Finn watched as the man put the scoop into the bubbling yellow stink, and skimmed off a ladle of mottled grease, then turned and tapped the grease into a vat already half full of the jelly-like substance. When that was done, he climbed down to speak to Finn.

'We're bone-boiling.' The man pointed to the boiler above his head. 'We get carcasses from the slaughter-houses and boil them up. This stuff, the grease, makes soap and when the bones are clean, they're sold to char boilers, further along the lane.' He must have seen Finn's blank look. 'They make charcoal,' he explained. 'And I need a night-shift man. My last one got sick. Your job is to keep the furnace going and skim the grease off the cauldrons.'

Nearly forty dollars in one month, as well as the money

Finn earned selling newspapers. Finn stuck his hand out again. 'I'll do it,' he said. 'When do you want me to start?'

'Well, if you can start tonight, I'll give you a try, young Irish,' the man said, and shook Finn's hand. 'I'm Al, pleased to meet you, Finn. I'll show you the ropes later. If you can do it, the money's good, and you'll soon get used to the stink.'

'Thanks, Al. I'll see you at six.'

Finn stepped outside the ramshackle building and stopped outside the tenement accommodation next door. There was a basement, a ground floor and looking up, he saw windows built in into the bowed roof. The whole thing was made of timber, nailed together haphazardly, and looked as if it would fall down at any moment. He stepped around the children he had seen earlier. All were filthy, and clearly none of them in school. A few sorry-looking old men sat together on the steps. Finn wondered why they hadn't looked for work in the bone boilers. He shrugged, he'd soon find out.

He made his way back to the main street, and pulled his scarf away from his face to catch his breath. The stink had lessened here, but it stuck to him. It was in his clothes, his hair and in the back of his throat, no matter how many times he spat out.

Later, Finn went to the school and waited for Katty. They walked home together. It was time to tell Annie and Bridie.

* * *

Annie arrived home a little after her brother and sister.

'Did you have a good day at school?' Annie asked.

'It was all right, Annie.' Katty took off her coat and hung it beside her bag.

There was stew on the pot and Annie dished some out for the three of them.

Katty didn't speak. She began to eat, her head hung over the bowl.

'What is it, Katty? Is something wrong?'

Katty shook her head and put her spoon down. 'I'm not hungry.'

'Are you sick?' Annie asked. She looked closer at her sister. 'Why, you're crying, *acushla*. What's made you cry?'

'Ask Finn, he knows!' Katty shouted. She shoved her chair away from the table and ran into the bedroom. Annie followed her, but got no more out of her.

She went back into the kitchen and saw that Finn had just finished his bowl of stew.

'Well, tell me!' she said. She saw the look on her brother's face. As if he had been found out. But found out about what?

'I was going to tell you anyway,' he said, then got up from the table and shrugged his jacket back on.

'You're not going anywhere until I find out what's wrong with Katty. She said to ask you, so tell me now!'

Finn turned to face his sister. 'Here it is. I've stopped going to school. That's what.'

'You've stopped,' Annie frowned. 'Going to school? Since when?'

'Since last month. And I'm not going back.' Finn put his hand on the door handle. 'Will I tell you what I've been doing? I've been selling newspapers and I sell lots of them. And I make plenty of money.'

Annie struggled to make sense of his words. 'Finn, no, *acushla*. There's no need for you to do this. I have a job, we can pay our way.'

'Annie, I've had my education. I'm fourteen, for God's sake. There are no other fourteen-year olds in that school. It's time for me to work and earn some money. And I'll tell you something else, too. I've just got myself a full-time job. It starts tonight at six o'clock.'

Finn came back into the room. 'Look at me, Annie. You can see I'm not a child anymore. I took care of Katty when you were off in Dublin. I caught rabbits, and Marie cooked them. We didn't starve.' He went over to the door and opened it. 'I'm a man now,' he said, and slammed the door behind him.

Annie stood and looked at the door, then she went through into the front parlour, as if in a dream. Her's and Finn's single mattresses were unrolled for the night and filled the floor space in the middle of the room. She sat on the narrow horsehair sofa and put her head in her hands as her sight darkened and dizziness unbalanced her. She heard Katty crying in Bridie's bed, next door, but couldn't move to go and comfort her.

Of course Finn was old enough to get work. She knew that, but she just wanted to keep everything the same, the way it was before the blight had hit. She had tried to stop time passing and things from changing. Yet all she had done was alienate her brother.

It was done out of love, but also out of fear. After Katty's abduction, she lived in fear of anything happening to her brother or sister again.

She remembered their journey to New York, when the Grey nun in Quebec rolled the child's body into the pit, unrolled the blanket and let the small corpse fall on top of the others. The rain ran down over the grave and turned the earth to mud leaving just the child's blonde hair showing in the dirt.

And the black and white newspaper advertisement on the wall of the quarantine shed. What-was-his-name, searching for his missing brothers, who'd arrived three weeks earlier. A reward for information. Would the brothers by some Act of God be here in New York? She heard her father's voice. 'And who stood beside you on the ship and looked into the pit, and read the advertisement?'

She unpinned her hair and pressed her fingers into her scalp. 'Forgive me, brother,' she whispered,

But Finn stayed away. She tossed and turned; her mind swirled and ticked through the night.

* * *

Finn arrived at the boiler house, just as the Angelus bell rang out for six o'clock. He blessed himself and put his head around the door. 'Al?'

'Come on in, Irish!' Al called. He was skimming the tops of the cauldrons and Finn climbed the steps up to him.

'I didn't think you'd come back. I thought the stink'd put you off,' Al said. 'Here, put this rag over your mouth and nose, it'll cut down on the smells.'

Finn did as he was told and stood beside Al to learn the job.

'Now, watch me. You take this ladle and skim, like so.' Al hefted the long wooden scoop across the surface of the tank. 'Then tip the grease into the bin at the end of the platform. Keep going till all the grease is skimmed. It'll take you an hour to work your way across the four tanks. Follow me down and I'll show you how to keep the furnace going.

Finn followed Al and watched and learned, then took his

turn at shovelling coal into the furnace and skimming the grease off the boilers. Al observed Finn, announced he'd do, and promised to call back in an hour to check on him. Then he left.

Al was true to his word and came back to check on Finn. He showed Finn how to take out the cleaned bones and add more bloody bones to the tanks. Then he left Finn to get on with the work of tending the cauldrons. It was the start of a long night until the morning Angelus bell rang.

Al inspected the grease tubs and the cleaned bones for the char boilers. He pronounced himself satisfied with Finn's work. 'You'll do. I'll pay you at the end of the week, Irish.'

Finn walked slowly back to the apartment. Annie looked out of the apartment window and almost didn't recognise her brother, a skinny immigrant boy bent double on the street outside, as he coughed up and spat out yellow phlegm. He brought a smell into the small kitchen, of meaty boiled bones, thick, cloying marrow and underneath these, at the bottom, the scent of rotten carrion.

Finn went straight to the sink, stripped to his waist and washed and dried himself. He went into the parlour and put on clean clothes, then back into the kitchen to pick up a few oat biscuits and filled a bottle with milk.

He kissed Katty, who had just got up. 'Good morning, darling. I'm off to sell newspapers. I'll get some sleep this afternoon.' He kissed Bridie, but didn't speak to Annie. He left the apartment just half an hour after he had come home.

* * *

Annie shook her head. 'I don't understand. Why is he doing this?'

'He's not a child any longer, Annie,' her aunt said. 'It's time he made his own decisions. He's a Power, after all. And you're not the only stubborn one in the family.' Bridie smiled. 'Finn's clever, but you must let him grow up. If school is not for him, then don't drive him away because of something you want.'

Annie looked at her aunt. 'I'll make things right when I see him later.'

She cleared the table and started to get ready for work. Despite her promise, it would take her longer to fix things between herself and her brother.

11

Jane Keating: October 1846. Melbourne

The Colonel's house was on built on the side of a hill on the outskirts of Melbourne. It was a sprawling, white, timber-framed construction, with a pale green painted veranda on all four sides. Shade was provided by the extended grey, slate roof. The house was situated in the centre of large gardens overlooking Port Phillip Bay and the dockyards and army barracks beside the Yarra. On that morning in October, when Jane arrived to begin her new job, the sun beamed down from a pale, cloudless sky. Several trees shimmered with tiny white blossoms; two horses, a mare and her foal, cropped at the grass in their paddock.

Mrs Johns, the Colonel's wife, greeted Jane. A sallow-complexioned woman, she was bundled and corseted into an expensive cotton day dress, and appeared to be quite a few years younger than her husband. Mrs Johns didn't invite Jane into the house, instead she led the way through the garden to the small cottage at the rear of the main residence, and handed her over to the housekeeper, Mrs Carpenter.

'I do all the cooking and you'll help me with washing up and cleaning the kitchen,' the housekeeper informed Jane. It took just a couple of minutes to walk through the cottage and Jane quickly understood that she was not going to be on first-name terms with the housekeeper. There were two bedrooms; one for Jane and one for Mrs Carpenter; two more rooms completed the living quarters: the kitchen and a scullery for the laundry. A cast iron water pump stood just outside the back door and a dry privy shed took up a corner of the garden.

'You'll do the laundry and the ironing. You'll wait on table for the family's supper, set up and clear away. After that, your job will be to keep the house clean. The Colonel likes to have everything spotless and in its place. I'll go through it all with you, shortly.'

Mrs Carpenter was in her forties, English, and with no sign of a husband. She was comfortably settled in the tiny cottage on the Colonel's estate. Jane learned later that the housekeeper had been widowed shortly after travelling to join her convict husband, twenty years earlier. The Colonel and his family were now her family.

* * *

Jane met the other employee, Gerald, at supper the first evening. He was an ex-convict, an emancipist, freed after serving his sentence. He looked to be in his fifties, was short and wiry. His face was weathered by a lifetime spent out of doors, every inch of it deeply lined and wrinkled and topped by thinning, short-cut hair.

Gerald didn't say much, just nodded at Jane and ate his supper. He had worked for the Colonel after he had finished

113

his sentence, and looked after the horses, and tended the kitchen garden. He had a bunk in the stables and took his meals with Mrs Carpenter, and now Jane, in the cottage.

By the time she sat down to eat her supper on that first day, Jane had stripped and made all the beds in the main house and carried over the laundry to the cottage. She had stood with Mrs Carpenter to learn how to wait on table for the family's supper. Then cleared away and washed all the plates and cutlery from the meal and set up for breakfast the next day. Back in the cottage she stopped for a few minutes to eat her own supper. After eating, she mopped the stone-flagged kitchen floor.

Neither of the two employees had questioned her about her sentence, or had shown any interest in her, where she had come from, or how she had gotten to Melbourne. All the same, her new life had started, and she remembered her vow. 'Not this for seven years.' She shook her head. 'No,' she whispered, and emptied the bucket of dirty water out at the back of the cottage. By the time night had fallen she was exhausted. She dreamt about her dead mother, father and brothers. She was all alone in the world, and no-one here would care if she lived or died.

* * *

Soon after she had started the job, she woke early one morning. She'd heard a noise in the kitchen and walked through to investigate. It was Gerald. He had taken his shirt off and had bent over the sink to wash himself.

Jane stopped, and stared at his back for a moment, unsure of what she was seeing. Then she understood, and whispered.

114

'Ah, sorry, Gerald. I'm just going to the . . .'

She reached for the kitchen door, pulled it open and left before he could turn around. She raced to the outhouse and the privy and retched out dark green bile from her empty stomach.

She touched her own smooth shoulders through her shift. Dear God! Those scars on Gerald's back. Thick, gleaming, gristly, knotted strands of purple skin, as thick as her finger, ran from the tops of his shoulders across the width of his body, in all directions, right down to the small of his back.

The whips must have had metal tips to them, she thought, or knots, to so completely destroy his skin. How many lashes, how many floggings had that man endured in his years of detention? His poor back must have been full of blood and gore. What kind of people would do that to another, to abuse him and cause so much pain? And how had he survived all that torture?

Another thought followed. Would they flog her? If she broke one of their laws, tried to escape? She was certain she'd not survive a flogging like that. Sure, her mother and father would rise up from their graves to see their daughter punished so. She closed her eyes and saw again, the ruined flesh on Gerald's back, then shook her head and wiped her mouth. She'd not stay in this place here at the end of the world; she'd sooner be dead.

Her shudders eased as she remembered her vow to go back to Ireland. Now it was more that that. From now on she'd work to be free, or die trying.

12

Annie Power: December 1846, Annie starts her Commonplace Book

One dark December night, Finn was at work and Katty was in bed, Annie took out her block of writing paper, her pen and ink, and wrote the title for her narrative.

Annie Power's Commonplace Book or Eye-witness Account of a steerage passenger fleeing the Hunger in Ireland.

Then she began to write:

We had reached Dungarvan and were waiting for our ship to leave for Quebec, when there was a protest in the town.

As soon as the pen touched the paper, she wrote as if in a dream, and back there in Dungarvan. She covered page after page, and jumped when Bridie touched her shoulder.

'What are you writing, *acushla?*' Her aunt looked over Annie's shoulder at the tiny script on the page. 'My eyes are not so good lately. I can't read it.'

'It's about our journey here last June. I started with the protest in Dungarvan. I don't think I told you about it, Bridie. When we were waiting to leave on the ship, there must have been more than a hundred local people marching through the town. All of them angry about the grain, the butter, the beef and the pork, being exported to England, while their children went hungry.'

Annie dipped her pen in the inkwell and tapped off the excess. 'The army and the constabulary were everywhere and they had guns. I saw a man shot, Bridie. Right beside me. And I didn't go to help him. I just ran, with Finn and Katty, and all the rest of them. I don't know if he lived or died that day, but I can still see him fall. His legs seemed to go out from under him.'

'Dear Lord, that's an awful thing to witness, girl.'

'I'm writing it all down. It will help me if I tell these stories about what I saw. And someone might want to read them.'

'Well, I'll let you get on with it then. I'm off to bed. Don't stay up writing too late now, will you? God bless you, darling.'

'Good night, Bridie, and God bless you, too.'

Annie wrote up her testimony of the protest, then began to write an account of the journey from Dungarvan, away from Ireland and across to Quebec. She'd put off writing it because of Mary Sullivan, the lovely girl she'd met the first day on the ship.

Perhaps Mary is the reason why I'm so worried about these girls and young women travelling alone. Poor Mary got the ship fever from that old couple she had helped to nurse. The three of them died within a day of each other, and Mary was the last of her family.

Annie wrote it all down and only stopped when she got to the part where the ship arrived in Quebec. She didn't remember much of her own bout of the fever, only that the ship's captain had helped her to pass the medical inspection.

And what could she write about the burial pit outside the quarantine sheds? Leave it for another day. Time for bed.

But she didn't sleep well. It was as if just thinking about it had opened her mind's eye to see again that small child being rolled into the burial pit in Quebec. She tossed and turned but stayed caught in the dream. At times, she saw the girl's blond hair and the grey habit of the nun. At other times, the colour had faded, leached away and she saw only shadows, the movement, the fall of the child.

Then the man from Dungarvan fell, as if he was right beside her again. She heard his gasp of pain and jolted awake. She sat up in bed, her heart pounded in her chest, and her head felt dizzy. 'Dear God, let them rest in peace.'

* * *

Over the next few weeks, Annie went through her journals and wrote out her poems and some of her diary entries. She had an old copy of The Nation with one of Speranza's poems in it, and she added that, too. She thought hard about how she could raise enough money to set up a refuge, a place of safety for single women and girls. If no-one wanted to help her, then she'd do it herself. Every second day, she posted articles to the New York papers: the New York Daily Tribune, the New York Herald, and the Sun. When she heard nothing back from them, she wrote to the Boston Herald, and The Phoenix. Her friend on the ship, John, had told her there were lots of Irish in Boston. Maybe they'd want to read about home. Or maybe they didn't want to be reminded. No, they'd want to help, she was sure of that

* * *

Meanwhile, Finn worked long shifts at the bone boiler's. He slept at the apartment. His days were all the same. He started work at six o'clock every evening and finished at six the next morning. Then he called in home to get washed and changed and a bite to eat, and headed to the newspaper offices to pick up his bag of papers. He spent the morning selling papers. On his way home, around noon, he bought a hot dog from a street vendor. He went straight to bed and slept until five, got up, had his supper and left for work. He paid Bridie for his board and lodging and she sent his stinking trousers and shirts out to the laundry. He and Annie spoke only briefly, in passing.

13

Jane Keating: November 1846. The Colonel

The weeks passed quickly. Jane's days were full from early in the morning to late at night. Thanks to Mrs Chisholm, she had Sunday morning off work to attend mass. She had hoped to see Owen at mass but there was no sign of him. Jane was now clean and well fed, although her working days were long. She was up at dawn, and cleaned, scrubbed and helped the cook prepare meals for the household every day. She finished her work only when everyone was in bed for the night.

She hauled yet another bucket of water into the kitchen. It seemed that some days all she did was fill buckets with water and carry them into the cottage. Except here she was now, at the end of November, and it was getting on for summer, and two kangaroos hopped through the garden as she pumped the water. She stopped to admire their size and their long, grey tails and strong limbs. She kept well back, and let them go on their way.

Then there were the convicts, the poor *divils*. Gangs of them in chains, doing government work on the roads around the town. Every time she saw them, she was reminded of the work gangs she had passed on the road as she left Galway. Those men in Ireland hadn't broken any laws, yet she knew some would be working through the winter, barefoot in the snow and rain, without a coat to protect them from the weather.

* * *

One morning, the strangest thing happened. Jane knocked on the door of the master bedroom and waited a moment before she entered. As she did every morning, she brought the porcelain jug of warm water and a bowl over to the mahogany wash stand in the corner of the room.

She placed the jug and the bowl on the stand and glanced in the mirror on the wall. Her face and shoulders were still scrawny and her nose had that bend to it. Some of her black hair had escaped from the white cloth cap she wore, and curled around her cheeks. For one who had been a fairly ordinary looking girl, she almost didn't recognise the change in herself. She'd no longer pass for a boy or a young man, as she had in Dublin. That was for certain. Her face now had the look of a woman, not a sixteen-year old girl. Plain enough; the only saving graces were her grey eyes and black brows. She nodded at her reflection, and adjusted the towels on the wash stand. She caught a movement in the mirror.

It wasn't the Colonel's wife, for she was still asleep. No, it was the Colonel. He had sat up to watch Jane in the mirror; his small dark eyes focused on hers, then he let his gaze move lower. Jane froze for a moment, unsure whether to speak, and wake Mrs Johns. No, she forced herself to move. She turned and left the bedroom.

She had seen that look before, on board the ship, that crewman who had assaulted her had the same greedy look in his eyes.

She walked back over to the cottage and tried to persuade herself. 'It's your imagination, sure hasn't he got a lovely wife there in the bed beside him? Then why would he look at me like that?' Her eyes smarted with tears. She needed to talk to someone, to Owen, maybe? But he seemed to have disappeared. Maybe Lizzie could help, or Mrs Carpenter.

The rest of the day was devoted to the family's laundry. Gerald had filled the boiler in the scullery the previous night, and also the rinsing tubs. There was plenty of water for the job.

The wooden washboard was perched in the sink. She poured in a bucket of hot water and added lye soap. Then she filled the sink with the Colonel's shirts and let them soak for a few minutes. She rubbed the garments over the washboard, wrung them out and transferred them to the first rinsing tub, then to the second. She put the shirts through the mangle to remove the excess water and took them out to peg on the line at the back of the cottage. She did the same with Mrs John's cotton dresses and shifts, then the children's clothes and underwear. She hefted the boiler on to the range, refilled it and put the towels straight in to heat and soak.

By this time, Mrs Carpenter had arrived from the main house and the two women had their dinner, then worked together to rinse and wring the sheets and towels, and carried them out to the drying lines in the garden.

As they pegged out the laundry together, Jane asked the question that had been bothering her. 'Tell me, Mrs Carpenter, what was the name of the girl who worked here before me?'

The housekeeper glanced at Jane with narrowed eyes, then replied. 'Her name was Elsie Corcoran. Why do you ask?'

'No-one ever speaks about her. But the Colonel said she left to get married.'

Mrs Carpenter pursed her lips before she spoke. 'Well now, that's the story I heard, too. It was last September. She just up and left.'

'What do you mean? She didn't get married?'

Mrs Carpenter cocked her head as if she had heard a sound. A cry or an echo? 'Why do you want to know? Has something happened, Jane?'

Jane let the wet towel she was holding fall back into the basket. 'I need to find out if he is a good employer. Colonel Johns. Is he good to the people who work for him?'

'Well, between you and me, since you ask. I'd advise you to make sure you're not on your own with him. The Colonel had a soft spot for Sally. I don't know what they got up to, but she didn't leave to get married. She was here one day, and gone the next, and she was only a little bit of a thing.'

'Where did she go?' Jane continued to peg out the washing.

'I honestly can't say. She didn't get married, because she didn't have a beau, and she had no family here, that I know of. She was just a poor little orphan girl from somewhere called Skibbereen. Irish, like yourself, come to think of it.'

The look on Mrs Carpenter's face shut down any further questions, but Jane persisted. She recognised the name Skibbereen, a town in the south of Ireland.

'Does Gerald know?'

'Nobody knows. Now that's enough. Gossiping won't get this work done.' They finished pegging out the laundry in silence. A warm breeze lifted the sheets and towels, dresses and shirts. They flapped like the white sails on the ships in Port Phillip Bay. The brilliant blue sky and the fluttering sheets almost convinced Jane that she was worrying about nothing.

* * *

Over the next few days, Jane worked, as usual, from before dawn until late at night. After the family had eaten, and the two women cleared away, Jane had her supper with Mrs Carpenter and Gerald. They ate plainer food than the Colonel and his family. Generally something that Mrs Carpenter could leave to simmer on the stove all day.

Mrs Carpenter always ate a hearty supper, whatever it was. After all she had cooked it. Today's supper was boiled mutton with potatoes and carrots. Then, after a couple of large glasses of brandy, the housekeeper took herself off to bed, even though the evening sky was still bright.

Jane cleared away, cleaned the kitchen and walked over to the house to check the rooms and make sure all was tidy for the morning. It was getting on for night and the children were in bed. The Colonel and his wife were sitting together on a swinging seat on the veranda.

She came back to the cottage and spent an hour ironing the laundered clothes. She heated the irons up on the stove, sprinkled water on the Colonel's shirts and underwear, then swept the heavy iron over the garments until they were free of wrinkles, alternating the two irons, leaving one to heat, while she used the other to work with. She hung the shirts on hangers and folded the undergarments. She left the irons on the stove to continue the work in the morning.

* * *

The next day was Wednesday, the second of December. Gerald brought out bags from the house and loaded up the carriage. Mrs Johns and the children planned to spend a week visiting her mother in Geelong. Gerald would drive them over and he would return to Geelong the following week, to bring them home. The Colonel stood beside the carriage and waved them off.

Jane watched them leave from the scullery window in the cottage. Mrs Carpenter had walked into town earlier to buy fresh fish for the day's dinner and had left Jane to finish the ironing. As she folded away the remaining clothes and towels, she glanced out through the window again and saw the Colonel making his way across from the house. He walked straight towards the cottage. He'd never done that before. She'd never seen him in the cottage. There was no-one else around, and she froze for an instant.

Then she turned, rushed over to the range and picked up one of the smoothing irons. It was hot and heavy and she held it down, hidden in the folds of her skirt. As she did, she saw the Colonel pass by the scullery window and walk straight in.

'Ah, there you are Jane. I need you to come over to the house. I have a job for you.' He seemed excited, his face was lit with a hectic glow and his eyes glimmered in the dull light of the cottage kitchen.

Jane clenched the iron in her hand. What to say? 'I'm sorry, Colonel. I can't come just now. I don't feel well, my stomach is upset,' she said. 'I think I'm going to be sick.'

125

He moved across to her, came close and looked at her. 'Ah, you poor girl!' His eyes were dark brown, almost black, with tiny constricted pupils, and there was a light sheen of sweat on his forehead. He put his hand on her cheek and she felt it move back across her hair. Her skin crawled. He exhaled and she tasted his breath.

She pulled her head away. 'No! Don't touch me.' She reached up and pushed his hand away. With the other hand, her fingers squeezed around the iron, hidden in her skirt, and she flexed the muscle in her arm.

The Colonel blinked, as if surprised. 'There's no need for that, Jane. I mean you no harm.' He turned away. 'It'll keep,' he said, and left the door open behind him.

Jane's knees gave way and she knelt on the floor and leaned on the iron. 'Oh, my God.' Her breathing turned into ragged sobs.

There was no-one she could call on. Not one member of her family, all dead. Not one friend in this God-forsaken place. Owen and Lizzie were the only people she knew and she had not set eyes on them for months. It was as if they had vanished. A thought struck like a bell, and rang through her head. Like Sally, the last maid. She stood and closed the door. There was no lock on it, nor on her bedroom door.

* * *

Somehow she got through the week until Sunday, and her free time. The Colonel's wife was expected to return home on the following Wednesday. Until then, she put her mattress down on the floor in Mrs Carpenter's bedroom and gave no explanation.

126

Lately, when she dreamed, Jane saw the ghosts of her lost family. They were unchanged from her childhood days when they all sat together beside their fire on dark winter nights. Back home in Ireland, November and December saw the start of winter when the days shortened. The sun dipped early and rose late, and the family kept warm beside the turf fire in the cabin. For months in the summer, Jane and her father spent their days in the peat bogs where they cut and stacked piles of wet turf and left them to dry in the warm air, turning them over and over, until all the water had evaporated from the earthy lumps of fuel. They stacked the dry turf up against the outside of the cabin wall ready for winter. From November through to the end of March, the fire in the cabin was never let go out. A visitor who happened to pass by would see the warm glow and be sure of a welcome, and the best seat beside the fire. Then the whole family would settle down to listen to tales from the traveller. The long, dark winter nights passed in this way.

Here in Melbourne, December was the height of summer, and the days were warm and bright. The change of season disorientated Jane, as if a chick had wandered off from its nest and turned in circles, unable to find its way back home, with foxes on the prowl. Nevertheless, she persisted.

* * *

That Sunday, Jane attended mass in St Francis's church. An Irish priest recited the Latin mass and his voice and the words transported her mind all the way back to Galway. It was only a year ago that she had been at mass with her mother, father and two brothers. Now she was alone in the world and prayed for their souls. What would her mother say to her? She blinked away tears and tried to control her breathing, then stood as the priest prepared to give the final blessing and dismissal. *'In nomine Patris et Filii et Spiritus Sancti, Amen. Ite missa est.'*

Outside, it was a fresh summer day with a brilliant blue sky overhead. Jane made her way up the town. Melbourne itself, was barely ten years old, and crammed with timber-framed buildings; houses, shops, bars and hotels. Inhabited by immigrants and emancipists. Most of them came from England, Scotland or Ireland. By now, there were only a few government convicts left and they were used to build the roads and work in quarries.

Out on the fringes of the town, near the river, she saw a few small groups of tattered-looking black people, but they tended to slip away silently before anyone got near them. What was their life like with all these new people? And what had it been like before the new people came? She shook her head, and walked on towards the Yarra River and the dockyards, at the estuary.

She loved to be near water, to gaze on the limpid, glossy surface, barely moving at full tide. It was crammed with ships and smaller boats; some out fishing, others working to supply the ships at anchor. The salty air tingled on her tongue, and the tendons and muscles in her shoulders and neck eased a little. Her thoughts cleared. It would have been good to meet up with Owen again for a few minutes. She could have confided in him. She decided that she would go and seek him out, soon.

* * *

The Women's Employment office door was open and she walked in. Mrs Chisholm herself was there, seated at her desk, dressed in black from head to toe, with just a white lace collar at the neck of her linen dress. Her plump face lit up with a smile when she saw Jane.

'It's Jane Power, isn't it? You came over on the Maitland.' Mrs Chisholm gestured for Jane to have a seat by the desk. 'What can I do for you?'

'How are you, Mrs Chisholm? I'm hoping you can help me again.'

'I'm well, thank you. And of course, I'll help if I can. What is it?'

'I'm here to look for another job.' Jane saw the question on the other woman's face and continued. 'I need to get away from the Colonel's house. Do you remember Colonel Johns?'

'Yes, I remember him. Is it the work? Are they not kind to you?' Mrs Chisholm leaned forward until her corseted bosom rested on the desk. Whatever she saw in Jane's expression brought her to her feet and she came around the desk to kneel beside her. 'Dear girl, tell me.'

Jane hadn't planned on giving the reason, but when Mrs Chisholm knelt beside her and held her hand, Jane put her other hand over Mrs Chisholm's and held on tight.

Then she came out with it. 'It's the Colonel. At the interview, he said their last maid had left to get married. Do you remember?' Mrs Chisholm nodded.

'Well she didn't. The Colonel took a fancy to her, and then she vanished. I don't know what happened to her, but now he's been looking at me, and I don't feel safe.'

Horses' hooves clopped, wheels rattled past on the road outside, and disturbed the heavy silence in the office.

'God bless you, my dear,' Mrs Chisholm said, and made the sign of the cross. 'Are you sure about this, Jane? It's a very serious accusation to make. The Colonel is a well thought of man in Melbourne.'

'I'm sure. Mrs Carpenter, the housekeeper told me. I think she knows more, but she's not saying.' Jane's voice dropped to a whisper. 'And the Colonel came to find me, when his wife was away.' Jane forced out the next words. 'Mrs Chisholm, I'm afraid.'

'Well then, we must do something to make sure you are safe.' Mrs Chisholm leaned on the table to stand up. 'Dear Lord! There's no air in here. Come. Let's walk.' She put on her bonnet, tied it under her chin and pulled a black silk shawl around her shoulders.

They left the employment office together and headed towards the women's dormitories where Jane had spent her first few days in Melbourne. They walked in silence and Jane's fears calmed a bit, knowing that Mrs Chisholm would help her.

* * *

Further along the street, the two women passed by a large plate glass window in a business premises. An advertising poster caught Jane's attention, and she stopped to read it.

```
VACANCY!
Typesetter required
Must have experience
Immediate start
```

130

`Good pay. Apply inside.`

'Look, Mrs Chisholm.' Jane pointed to the window and laughed. 'I can do that. I can typeset!'

Mrs Chisholm leaned in and read the advertisement. 'Typeset? Is that for printing the newspaper?' Jane nodded. 'Where on earth did you learn that, Jane?'

'In Dublin. I worked at The Nation newspaper and I trained as a typesetter. Not for long, but I can do the job.' She read the name on the outside of the business, The Port Phillip Odyssey, and tried the door. 'Ah sure, they're closed!'

'They'll be open tomorrow. Come back then.' They walked on along the dusty sidewalk. It was now late morning and Jane's stomach rumbled, and she laughed again. 'Sorry, I fasted for mass,' she explained.

'Then we both need something to eat,' Mrs Chisholm said. 'Let's call into the hostel for some breakfast.'

* * *

Most of the residents had left for one or another church service, a condition of residency, but there was a kettle on the stove and porridge in a pot. Mrs Smith came in from the kitchen, greeted them, saw she wasn't needed, and left them to their breakfast.

Jane and Mrs Chisholm helped themselves to tea and porridge and sat down to eat.

'Now, Jane. Tell me, what will you do about the Colonel?'

'If I can, then I'll leave today. Might I stay here for a while?'

'I'll check, there usually a bed or two free. Wait here and I'll find out.' Mrs Chisholm was gone only a few moments. 'Yes, there's a bed here for you, and you can stay until you find another job. With luck, you'll get the job of typesetting, but there's plenty of manufactory or domestic work here, too.' Mrs Chisholm went back to eating her porridge. She clearly had a hearty appetite and finished her breakfast in no time, took a sip of tea, and waited for Jane's reply.

'Thank you, you're so kind.' Jane blew out a breath of relief. 'I'm half afraid to go back there at all, but my bag and my cloak are in the cottage. And I should say goodbye to Mrs Carpenter and Gerald.'

'Eat your breakfast, Jane. I'll come with you, make sure you're all right.'

'No, you've done enough. I'll only be there a few minutes. I won't stay.' Jane paused. 'Mrs Chisholm, you're a saint! Thank you.'

'Now then, don't exaggerate. I do what I can to help. You know Mrs Smith, she'll show you your bed.'

Mrs Chisholm left the housekeeper to show Jane to the dormitory and Jane lay down on her bed. The morning had somehow made her tired. What would she have done if Mrs Chisholm had not been able to help? The room was quiet, but it would soon be busy when the other residents came back from church. She closed her eyes and imagined herself working in the print room of the newspaper. She could smell the ink and the newsprint, hear the clatter and rumble of the press. Please God, it would happen.

She woke up when she heard footsteps coming along the corridor outside, but they continued on into the next bedroom.

She'd apply for the typesetting job first thing in the morning. She felt pulled to go back to say her goodbyes to the people she had worked with for the last two months. It would only take a few minutes. She'd be in and out in no time and she was not leaving behind her journal and Annie's prayer book.

* * *

Later that same afternoon, she went back to the house and found Gerald weeding the vegetable plot in the garden. He stopped work when she hailed him and pushed his hat back from his face.

'I'm leaving,' she said. 'I've come to say goodbye.'

He dug his spade into the ground, then nodded. 'You're right to go, I'd say, Jane. Mrs Carpenter told me you're not happy here.'

She didn't correct him. 'Is she up at the house?'

'No, she's in town visiting her sister-in-law. She'll be back in time to finish the Colonel's supper. With you gone, she'll have to dish it up, too!' Gerald's eyes crinkled as he smiled.

'Well, be sure and tell her I came to say goodbye, won't you? And we'll meet in the town. Sure, Melbourne's not that big a place!' Jane smiled at Gerald. 'I'm just off to pick up my bag, and then I'll go.' She waved to him and walked back to the cottage.

* * *

A few minutes later, the Colonel rode in on his horse and left it with Gerald to stable it.

Jane had her bag in her hand, and was at the door of the

133

cottage when she saw the Colonel walking towards her, just as Gerald led the horse into the stable. The Colonel looked at Jane, then glanced back over his shoulder. To check on Gerald?

He moved fast, and came right up to her at the door.

'Ah, there you are, Jane.' He pointed to her bag with his riding crop. 'Where are you off to?'

Jane couldn't breathe. Her fist tightened around the handle of her bag. 'I've come to get my things, Colonel. I'm leaving today.'

'What, and no notice?' he asked. 'That's not very friendly of you, now is it?' He moved closer, and she stepped back and tried to close the door and call out for Gerald all at the same time. He pushed the door open and walked in. She stumbled backwards.

'We need to talk about this,' he said. 'You can't just walk out on me. Who do you think you are? Just a cheap convict.' He raised the crop and lashed it across her shoulders and neck.

The shock and stinging pain of the whip made her gasp. No, no, no, were the only words she could think, but she was unable to utter them. She dropped her bag, and tried to get past him to the door. He slammed the door shut, then slapped her face hard, and pushed her to the floor. Her head banged on the wooden floorboards, and still, she could neither breathe nor shout for help. He knelt on her, his knee on her chest and forced her chin up with the end of the whip, leaned on it and half-choked her. Without breath in her lungs, her vision dimmed, as if night had fallen in an instant.

In almost total silence, just his harsh breaths, he tore at her blouse and skirt until she was nearly naked beneath him. She looked at his face and saw dead, dark eyes; the whites of his eyeballs gleamed and he bared his teeth and bit her on her breast.

Her vision seemed to black out. It could have been an hour, or just moments later, she opened her eyes and she was looking down at herself on the floor of the cottage. She lay there like a corpse, until he had finished with her. He buttoned his jodhpurs, straighten his shirt and jacket, then picked up the whip and flicked it across her belly and breasts in a stinging crack. 'You owe me for those clothes I paid for,' he said and turned to the door.

She stretched her arm out towards the range and wrapped her fingers around the warm handle of the smoothing iron, tucked away on the hearth. She had used it to iron the very shirt he was wearing. He spoke again, but she couldn't make out his words, they just echoed in her ears. She rolled over onto her front and bent her knees to stand. A kick landed at the side of her rib cage, and she groaned. She leaned her weight on the iron. His footsteps moved towards the door again, he was leaving her there. He was done with her.

The door creaked as it opened, and she stood, bloodied and trembling, half-naked. It took only a moment to cross the small kitchen and she let out a roar, and this time it didn't freeze in her throat. She hefted the iron to land a blow, when he turned. She caught him on his cheekbone. His look of surprise faded as his eyes rolled up in his head and he fell through the doorway onto the path outside.

Jane lifted the iron to hit him again, and stopped. She dropped the iron and bent over, her hands on her knees. Her heart almost jumped out through her chest and her whole body shook.

An arm went around her shoulders. 'Jane. What happened

here?' It was Gerald.

'I killed him. I think he's dead.'

Gerald knelt and checked the body. 'He's not dead. You knocked him out. Come back inside.'

She managed to get back into the kitchen and collapsed in a chair. All was in disarray.

'What the hell happened?'

'He raped me. I couldn't stop him. Then, when he was at the door, I hit him with the iron.' She shivered. 'He's not dead?'

'No. I'll look after him. You need to get away before he comes round.' Gerald shook his head. 'Jesus, Jane, what'll you do now?'

'If you weren't here, Gerald, I'd go back outside and finish him off. He should die for what he's done to me.' Her hand trembled as she held onto the edge of the table. Blood and semen ran in pink streams down her legs. She touched her neck where the riding crop had pressed and held her down and felt swollen ridges across her wind-pipe, she swallowed against the rawness in her throat.

Her clothes lay scattered and torn on the floor, the new blouse bought only a month ago was now ripped and bloody. He'd used her shift to wipe himself off and it lay in a tangled heap with her drawers.

'Will you be able to sort yourself out?' he asked. She nodded. 'Then I'll see to him. He's out for a while I'd guess. But be as quick as you can.' Gerald went outside and closed the door behind him.

Jane stumbled to the washing tub and emptied half a bucket of water into it, then stripped off the remainder of her torn clothes and washed herself down in the cold water. By the time she had finished the water in the tub had turned bloody and she could barely touch her female parts for the pain.

Then, naked, as if in a dream, she took a change of clothes out of her bag and got dressed. She smoothed her hair down and looked around the scullery; the overturned chair and her torn clothes strewn around. She picked up her bag and opened the door. Her attacker was still unconscious, and Gerald stood and walked a few steps with her.

'Don't worry yourself about him. I wouldn't say he'll report this.'

'No, but he will pay for what he's done to me. Somehow, Gerald.'

She left through the back garden. She still trembled and the darkness still ebbed into her mind.

She had walked half a mile back towards the docklands when her knees began to buckle. She sat on a low wall and rested for a few minutes. Some of the passersby looked at her face and her bruised neck. Her eyelids flickered and her body shook at the crack of a whip from a cart passing nearby. That evil man . . . .

She leaned forward on the wall, tried to breathe and stop her heart from pounding and hammering in her chest. Her head ached, her throat was on fire. Her sex was bruised and burned, and she felt the sting of his bite marks on her breast. She wrapped her arms around herself; shivered in the heat of the day and gritted her teeth to stop from crying out.

He would pay. He had left her alive, and somehow he would be held accountable. As long as she breathed, she would persevere and make him pay.

14

Jane Keating: December 1846. Gets a job and makes a friend

Soft, early sunlight streamed through the dormitory window and woke Jane. The room was quiet with just a low rumble of snores from the other women in their beds. She turned over and pain throbbed across her lower back and her legs. She had slept on her side and her arm was stiff and heavy; she massaged the sore muscle and the bruised bone where her attacker had caught her and dragged her.

Tears leaked from her eyes and ran across the sides of her face into her hairline. She put her hand between her legs and touched the swollen parts of her sex. She smelt the animal musk he'd left on her skin and her stomach turned. She felt like an injured bird. How must a chick feel, having just fallen from her nest and no way back to safety?

Yesterday, she'd recognised the danger, but not seen that she was in truly, mortal danger. Why had she let herself be overpowered by his strength? She lay on the bed and mourned for the girl she had been yesterday. Grief flowed through her body. What would her mother and father think to see their daughter abused like this?

She closed her eyes and her mind went blank for a few moments, until she heard birdsong outside. The sun still shone, the grass was still green, the blackbirds song was as sweet as ever. If the chick stayed on the ground, she'd be eaten alive by a bigger predator. She sat up and swung her feet out onto the bare boards of the floor.

That she had let this happen to her, rang through her brain like a gong. If she were still Jack, what would he have done? Just by disguising herself as a boy, Jane had got a job in Dublin and lived and worked freely. No-one bothered her as Jack. She shook her head. It wouldn't work here. For one thing, her certificate of pardon showed her as a woman. She must have her certificate to prove her identity. For another, she'd put weight on since leaving Ireland, enough so that she now had the shape of a woman, not the skinny boy she had passed for in Dublin.

Her neighbour in the next bed gave a light snore and pulled the blanket up over her face to get a few more minutes of sleep. Jane managed to get herself to the washroom at the end of the dormitory. She had a few minutes before the other women started to get up, so she picked up a jug and went downstairs and out into the yard at the back of the building where she used the privy. Then she filled the jug at the water pump. Coming back up the stairs to collect clean clothes, she felt some of the aches loosen. In the washroom, she soaped a flannel and scrubbed every inch of her skin; the bite marks on her breasts, her bruised neck, and more gently around her sex. She rinsed and soaped again, then rubbed the damp cloth through her hair until the smell of him was gone. She caught sight of her face in a small mirror on the wall. Her cheekbone under her right eye was swollen and red and would soon darken into a bruise. She could see the marks the whip had left on her neck when he had choked her into unconsciousness. She shuddered, closed her eyes and bent over to breathe and made that promise to herself again. He will pay.

After a few minutes, she went back to her bed and put on her skirt and blouse. The women around her stirred and rose to begin their day. A couple of them greeted Jane, but she just nodded and kept her head down, her hair loose around her face. She pulled stockings on and tied garters below her knees then fastened the laces in her boots. She picked up her bag, wrapped herself in her shawl and went downstairs, out into the yard. She filled a tin cup with cool water and drank it straight down, and felt the crystal liquid reach her stomach. She heard the song of a blackbird again, looked up at the bird, its golden beak and round, black body perched on a branch in a nearby tree, almost hidden by the glossy green leaves. The song was familiar to her from home, and she thought of her mother and father. She rubbed her eyes, then left by the back gate.

Outside the dormitories, the sun shone down on her as she made her way to Collins Street and the newspaper office. The fresh air, the drink of water and the song of the blackbird had helped to clear her mind.

She put aside the pains in her body and the vision of her attacker's face and his yellow teeth, the ferocious strength she'd had no defence against. She should have killed him as soon as she got the chance, and not just knocked him unconscious. Sure, it wasn't a bad attempt though, the iron was in just the right place. That brought a trembling smile to her face. She pressed her lips together and slung her bag over

140

her shoulder, adjusted the scarf she had wrapped around her neck, lengthened her stride and headed for the newspaper office.

* * *

The name of the newspaper, "The Odyssey and Advertiser", and the proprietor's name, Harold Stephenson, were painted in gold lettering on a sign over the window. The window itself was filled with notices and advertisements. One of them soon to be taken down, Jane decided.

The door was open and she walked in and went straight over to the clerk at a desk covered in what looked like the latest edition of the newspaper.

The young man's forehead was sweating, even though it was still early in the morning, probably from the heavy, buttoned-up suit he wore. He had flattened his light gold, curly hair back from his face in which, unfortunately, no two things matched. He had one brown eye and the other was green. His chin, what there was of it, receded under his protruding teeth and his skin tone ranged from a smattering of brown freckles across his nose and cheeks, to bleached white around his mouth and chin.

'Good morning.' He spoke an English accent. 'What can I do for you?'

'I'm here about the advertisement for a typesetter. I'd like to apply for the position, if it's still available.'

'Yes, we still need someone. Excuse me, but are you really applying to be a typesetter?' He seemed puzzled, then smiled, as if this were a joke.

'Yes, I am. I trained in Dublin at The Nation newspaper.'

Jane stood up straighter and tried to return his smile.

'I've seen that newspaper,' he replied. 'Yes, when we were in Sydney. I think I have an old copy somewhere here.'

'I'd love to see it.'

'Are you an emancipist then, or what?' he asked.

'I beg your pardon?' Jane feigned ignorance.

'What brought you to this part of the world?' he clarified.

'You've heard of Grey's Exiles?'

He nodded. 'Ah, you're one of those then? Pardoned.'

'Yes. And I need to find work. I'd be no use as a shepherd, and I've never worked as a builder either.' She waited for his reply. What was he not sure about? Did she look too young or more likely, too female? She pushed on. 'Have you had many applications?'

'None, so far. And I don't have time to train anyone up; we're too busy. But you look a bit young to be a trained typesetter.'

'I'm seventeen,' she lied. That was old enough for her to be trained for longer than the three months' worth she'd had in Dublin. 'And I'd say you won't find many typesetters here in Melbourne.' She waited.

Dust motes hung in the still, sunlit air of the room. Then he sighed and nodded. 'You're right about that. But I'll tell you something. The boss won't employ a woman. This is a job for a man.' He paused. 'Look, there's plenty of domestic work going in Melbourne. You'll get a job.'

Jane felt the opportunity slip away, stepped closer to his desk then paused, how much to tell him? Tell him nothing! 'Please, just give me a chance. You won't regret it. I'm really good at typesetting.'

He wiped the sweat off his forehead with a wrinkled

handkerchief. 'All right then. If you can tell me what happened to your face, then there's a task. Complete the task, I'll make sure the boss gets to look at it.'

'It was my last employer. He didn't want me to leave.' Her neck, her breasts and her sex were bruised and painful. The main damage was hidden from view.

He nodded and replaced his pen in the inkwell, getting more ink on his fingers in the process, then searched for, and found, a document in the drawer of his paper-strewn desk. 'Come, and I'll show you.'

Jane followed him through the front office into the printing room at the back of the building and nodded with relief when she recognised the printing press and the typeset. They were both similar to those she had trained on back in Dublin. The table for typesetting was angled to make it easier to work the type.

'What is the task?'

He handed her the document. It was scrawled in black ink, handwritten and almost illegible. 'This, in a three and a half inch column, with header. You've got fifteen minutes.' He looked at the clock on the wall above the table. 'I'll be back at half past nine. Good luck!'

The frame was already set up with space for the title. Jane smiled, as she read the words. VACANCY, then selected the metal header types and placed them in position. Next, she picked up the type holder and began to work, slotting pieces of type into the holder. She needed to do this fast and be accurate, to prove herself capable. The column was ready to print in ten minutes and she sat and waited for the clerk, or whatever he was, to come back.

He looked surprised to see the task finished and Jane relaxed in a chair, then he checked the typeset. He took the frame to a small hand printer by the window, inked the type and pressed a half sheet of paper. He read it, looked at her and chuckled. Jane had added just the one word, 'FILLED!' to the advertisement. She leaned over his shoulder and checked it. It was perfect.

'Well?' she asked.

'It's good. Very good, actually.' He kept hold of the printed page. 'Come and write up your application letter and I'll see the boss gets them both.'

She sat next to his desk in the front office and wrote about her job at The Nation and gave Mr Gavan Duffy's name as a reference. A reply would take months to come back, by then she'd be in this job, or God alone knew what else.

She handed her letter to the young man beside her.

'Come back later this afternoon. The boss will be in after dinner, so come around three. He'll have a decision for you. And bring your Pardon with you.'

'I will, and thank you for giving me a chance,' Jane said. 'What's your name?'

'Andrew Stephenson,' he said. The same name as the proprietor's name above the shop and she looked the question at him.

'My father owns the business,' he replied. 'I'm the reporter here. I do the printing and typesetting, but I can't do it all. And we're busier than ever lately, that's why I need some help.'

When he smiled, the oddities in his face came together somehow. His wide mouth and prominent white teeth balanced the lower part of his face and all was framed by those fair curls that threatened to fall over his forehead.

Jane put her hand out to shake his. 'I'm Jane Power. I'll

come back later. And thank you. If you give me this job, I'll work hard and I won't let you down.'

'There's just one more thing,' Andrew said. 'I found this. You might like to read it.' He handed her a copy of The Nation. She took the folded newspaper, wanted to kiss it, but didn't, just smiled her thanks and left the office.

On the walk up Collins Street, she decided she had done her best and was nearly sure that Andrew would give her the job if he could. But his father would make the decision. The newspaper felt cool and crisp in her hand. She turned it so she could see the banner and the date. It was an old paper and had been published earlier that year, in May, 1846. At that point, she had already changed places with Annie, and was in Kilmainham Gaol awaiting transportation.

She walked on, crossed the Yarra and headed to the beach. It was empty of people, just the fine yellow sand along the wide curving bay. She walked for about a half a mile, then sat down. The heat from the sand warmed her legs and bottom and she felt the rawness between her legs and the pain in her breast. Her fingers pressed into the fine sand and she pushed her palms through the soft grains. She lifted her hand and pressed it against her swollen cheekbone, to transfer some of the sun's warmth, then lay back and closed her eyes for a few moments.

* * *

After a few minutes, she sat up and opened the newspaper to scan the front page. The usual advertisements on pages one and two, then, there it was, a familiar name, at the top of page three.

"The Nation,Dublin.Tuesday,May 26th,1846.

Landlord and Tenant - Miss Anne Power
The case of Miss Anne Power from Ashling in County
Waterford is a rare occurrence in this country, for
it has not been, so far, the practice of our
resident landlords to oppress their tenantry.
Despite her apology to Lord Ashling's Land Agent, Mr
Jones, and despite Miss Power having an orphaned
brother and sister to take care of, she was,
nevertheless, sentenced to seven years
transportation to New South Wales."

* * *

The sound of the judge's voice flooded back to her, as she heard Annie sentenced to seven years' transportation. That had been the start of Jane's decision to change places with Annie and journey to Melbourne, as Annie Jane Power. She decided to read the rest later. She lay back and put the paper over her face to provide some shade and dozed.

When she opened her eyes, the sun had already passed over her head in the cloudless, azure sky and the wide blue-green sea that filled Port Phillip Bay. The surface of the water was still, with just a few lazy, white waves breaking on the sand close to her feet, for the tide was coming in. Small boats out on the water were busy fetching and carrying supplies to the tall ships at anchor in the bay, all with their sails furled. The skyline was a forest of masts, like dozens of trees with bare branches. Had they all come from England and Ireland? Were they going back there?

Dockyards and warehouses spread alongside the Yarra. Gerald had told her a few weeks ago, that he and other convicts had built the roads and completed the docks some ten years previously. The place was now attracting emigrants, for many of them had heard that wages were good and land was cheap here in New South Wales. Please God, she prayed, there'd be no typesetters arriving in the next day or two.

She caught the musical sounds of children's laughter further along the beach, where some young boys and girls played. Naked, they raced out into the water and splashed each other. She watched as they swam and chased each other through the water; their dark brown skin was glossed from the sun and the sea water on their bodies and limbs. Gradually, the children moved along the water in her direction. One of them looked her way; he was maybe eight years old. The same age as her brother, Seamus, would have been, had he been spared.

The boy raised his hand in greeting. Jane smiled and raised her hand in response.

'Hello, I'm Jane,' she said and she pointed to her chest.

He said his name. 'Jimmy!' He laughed and ran to join his friends at the water's edge. They worked their way back along the beach, chasing and calling to each other, then vanished into the woods above the dunes.

She looked at the space in trees where the children had gone. Where did they live, these people? She'd heard them called Aborigines. What must their mothers and fathers make of their new neighbours, the British? Were they neighbours?

Last year in Dublin, The Nation newspaper had reported on a Member of Parliament in London who had described the rural Irish as Aborigines. And here were more of them. Was this where the name came from? What is it about us, both peoples, that makes us Aborigines? Was it nothing more than both sets of people lived on land that was owned, or coveted, by the British?

The tide was now full in, almost to her feet. She kicked her boots off and tested the water. Then she stood and walked further along the beach, away from the ships at anchor, nearer to the dunes and the woods where the children had gone. She disturbed a bird she recognised, it was a cormorant, but smaller than those she had seen back at home, and white-breasted. The bird perched on a tree stump and spread its wings and fanned its tail feathers to dry in the sun. It looked at her with beady eyes and closed it hooked, yellow beak, then lifted off into the air and flew away, out over the blue-green waters of the bay.

Jane put her bag on the cormorant's tree stump, took her clothes off and folded them on top of the bag. Then, naked, she ran down to the water's edge and just kept on going, right out into the water. She lay back, closed her eyes and floated in the sun-warmed water of Port Phillip Bay. The salty water lapped against her bruised arm and neck and the bite marks on her breasts, as if to wash away the pain. She opened her legs to let the water bathe and heal her private parts, and began, finally, to feel clean.

Above her head, the azure sky faded to cornflower blue on the horizon. A large seagull glided overhead and, for a few moments, Jane allowed herself to join him in the sky. Together, they soared over the crystal water, just north of the Southern Ocean, thousands of miles away from her home, and the graves of every single one of her family.

After a while, she reached down an arm's length through

the warm upper layer of the sea, and touched the cold water beneath. The light pressure of the water supported her body as she drifted parallel to the beach. Small tugs of current tried to pull her out into deeper water. She corrected this pull with a few kicks, then turned over and swam back to the water's edge and sat on the sand to let the wavelets wash over her legs.

The water had helped ease the pain a bit, but in her mind's eye she saw her attacker's face and his flat, dark eyes just inches from hers. Was there to be any justice for her? If so, who would help her? She guessed most of the police would be ex-army, for they wouldn't employ emancipists. Somehow that man, she couldn't call him by his name, had to pay for his crime. At the same time she feared him. He could have killed her yesterday. Is that what happened to the other girl, the domestic servant who had supposedly left to get married? She made her mind up. She'd have to find Owen. He might advise her.

'Jane!' she turned towards the sound. It was the boy, Jimmy. He ran past her, still as naked as she, and into the water, where he was soon joined by his friends.

She sat for a while and watched them play, then rinsed the sand off herself and walked up the beach, to the edge of the woods, where she perched on the stump of the tree, like the cormorant had, to let the sun dry her off. Her skin felt soft and smelled of salt and the sea. She pulled on her navy twill skirt and white shirt. These were the clothes she had picked out in the hostel on her first day in Melbourne. The others, the new clothes she had bought on the Colonel's account were in a heap on the floor of the cottage. Would Gerald have cleared the place up, or left it to Mrs Carpenter?

149

The clothes she wore today were second hand, but they still had a lot of wear left in them. She wasn't the first or the last person to wear someone else's clothes; and smiled, for she felt an affinity with the previous owner, and silently thanked her. Then she tied her hair back, waved goodbye to her new friends and walked along the dunes towards the bridge. Her stomach rumbled to remind her she was hungry; she had no money to buy food, but she'd get a meal at the hostel.

* * *

Jane was back at the newspaper offices promptly at three o'clock. The editor and owner, Andrew's father, was a different type to his son. He looked to be in his fifties, his dark hair had receded to a peak at the centre of his forehead, with a shiny, bald crescent on each side of it. At least his eyes were both the same colour, a faded blue, and he wore gold-rimmed spectacles. The only thing father and son shared was the receding chin, but this man had a sharp nose that only pointed the observer down towards his chin.

Jane shook his hand. 'Thank you for seeing me, sir.'

'Come in, Jane. My son told me you were in an accident lately.'

'Ah sure, it looks worse than it feels,' she said. 'Mr Stephenson, sir, Did you get a look at the typesetting I did this morning?'

'I did. Come and we'll talk.' He opened a door and led the way into his office and sat behind a wide oak desk. 'Have a seat. I've read your application letter and I've a few questions. First of all, tell me what brought you to Melbourne, and what brings you here to the Odyssey?'

Jane explained about her conviction. 'It was mistaken identity, sir. I've never committed a crime in my life. Thank God, I got a Pardon from Lord Grey.' She handed over the paper.

Mr Stephenson's spectacles glinted as he read the pardon. 'Yes, I've heard of this. You're very fortunate, I'd say.' Then his eyes rested on her bruised face. 'It says here you arrived in October. What did you do then? You're a bit young to manage on your own.'

'I got lodgings in Mrs Chisholm's hostel, do you know it?' He nodded, and she continued. 'I found work as a domestic here in Melbourne. It didn't work out well.' Her lips had begun to tremble and she pressed them together, and looked at him. He nodded slowly, and spent a moment examining the test piece again. Then he cleared his throat.

'Well, you certainly know how to typeset. The only problem I have is this. How do I employ a woman?'

Jane shrugged and tried a tentative smile. 'It's your newspaper, Mr Stephenson. Surely you'll employ who you want. And you've looked at my work. You can see it's good.' She held her breath.

'Mm, you have a point. And you'll be in the back, working in the press room. Given that we've had no other applications for this job, I'm prepared to give you a chance. Just for a trial period, though,' he added, and took another glance at her face. 'I'd say your last employer won't be giving you a reference, so I'll write to your previous employer in Dublin, but that will take a while to come back. If your work is of a high standard, then we'll look at making the job more permanent. What do you say?'

Jane's smile broadened. 'That sounds fair, Mr Stephenson.

Thank you. I have just one question for you, sir. What will you pay me?'

'I'll pay half the going rate for the first month. If it works out, then you'll get the full rate. What do you say to that?'

Jane stood and stretched out her hand. 'We have a deal and thank you. Thank you so much!'

She was to report to Andrew for the afternoon shift the next day to prepare for the following morning's edition.

Andrew was at his desk in the front office and stood up when Jane came out.

'I got the job,' she said. 'Thank you, Andrew.'

'I told Pa that you'll do a good job. When do you start?'

'Tomorrow, for the afternoon shift. I'm on trial for a month, at half pay.'

He laughed. 'Good news, and not so good news. Well done, and I'll see you tomorrow at three.'

That night she added to her journal entry.

Monday, 7th December, 1846

Thank God, I got the job at The Odyssey. Mr Stephenson didn't want to employ a woman, but I think he had no choice, Andrew just has to have some help. I went for a swim in the bay. I feel a little better. I must write to Annie.

15

Annie Power: January 1847. Annie and Finn

It was the new year, and Manhattan was almost knee-deep in snow and battered by icy blizzards.

That evening Bridie sat down beside the stove and motioned to Katty to come over for a hug. 'How's my darling?' she asked.

Katty perched on Bridie's knee and put her head on her shoulder. 'I like this, Bridie.' The two sat for a while without speaking. Katty seemed to doze in the quiet room, while Annie sat on the chair next to them.

Outside fresh overnight falls kept the snow pristine in the early morning. In the day, it turned from white to muddy brown, as the horse traffic left their droppings and churned the snow into filthy frozen lumps. The dark days of winter dragged on, as if it were a slow funeral procession trailing round and round a graveyard.

Annie wore a long, dark green, knitted jacket over her woollen vest. A heavy black skirt and knee socks covered her lower half. For all this, she was just about warm enough if she stayed near the stove, which seemed to eat coal.

While the kettle heated on the hob, she began to prepare for bed. She collected a small shovel of hot coals from the stove and brought the fire into the parlour where she and Finn slept. She shivered after moving away from the fire; she could see her breath as the warm air from her lungs met the frigid air in the unheated room. She lay the burning coals on the few bits of kindling in the grate and went back for another shovel of fire and did the same in Bridie's and Katty's bedroom. After unrolling her mattress, she filled two porcelain bottles with boiling water, corked them, and placed one in Bridie's bed and the other on her own mattress.

Katty was asleep on Bridie's knee by the time Annie had finished. Finn would be back in the morning after his night shift. The two women sat and relaxed in each other's company. The room was lit by the yellow glow from the oil lamp, and shadows in the corners of the room deepened and surrounded the three of them, hunkered down for the night. Distant, muffled street sounds reached them at the top of their building.

'Did you ever want to go back home to Ireland, Bridie?' Annie asked.

Her aunt nodded and spoke in a low voice. 'I did, girl. It was all I wanted for the first few years. But, sure, what was the point? I had a job here and I could send some money home to my mother and father when they were both alive. Then, when your mother died, they were broken-hearted. Sure, they didn't last long after that. May God have mercy on their souls.' Bridie sat for a while, and seemed to think. 'Besides, I would have been just another mouth to feed and no work for any of us. You saw that with your father, trying to find work.'

Annie leaned across to open the stove door and looked into the heart of the fire. Her face warmed from the heat, and she waited to hear if there was more.

'Then I met Kevin. He was such a lovely man, although we were never blessed with children of our own. I've had a good life here, Annie. I have my own home, never in Ireland. I'd like to see Waterford again, but not now. I can't bear to read the reports in the newspapers. It's just so sad.' Bridie closed her eyes.

Annie reached over and put her hand on her aunt's knee. 'I'm sorry if I upset you with my questions. But I promised myself I'd go back. When I was on the ship, I looked back at Dungarvan, and made a vow I'd get Katty and Finn to safety. Then I'd go back.' She shook her head. 'I want to help here, but I want to go back and help, too. Ah, Bridie, what'll I do?'

Bridie brushed her tears away and caught Annie's hand in hers. 'Don't be so hasty, *acushla*. At least stay here until Katty is grown, and do what you can to help these poor girls you've seen. Sure, if things still haven't improved in Ireland by then, well, maybe you can think about going back.'

Bridie let Annie's hand go and stroked Katty's hair. 'Look at her. She's almost settled here and I'll take care of her. But give her a bit more time, then think about going back, if you still feel the same way. And don't forget, you can't go home with your hands hanging, now can you?' For a moment, Birdie's face appeared older and worn. 'There's enough starving people over there without you adding to the problem. Hm?'

Katty stirred, her eyes were closed, as if still asleep, but both women heard her whispered words. 'You can't leave me again, Annie.'

* * *

That night, Annie dreamt she was on the ship back to Waterford. She leaned over the rail as they sailed up the river past the village of Passage East. Beside her, a bag of money and sacks of oats and vegetables in the hold. Then she saw herself, as if from above. She wore a black dress with a shawl, woven from green and purple wool, around her shoulders. The sun glinted on the gold streaks in her hair and sparkled on the river water. She looked like the princess in the fable, *Sorcha Eireann*. Her heart was light and she turned and saw her friend, Jane, beside her. They both smiled.

* * *

Early the next morning, Annie threw some kindling into the stove to wake up the fire then added a few pieces of coal, filled the kettle and put it on the hob to boil. She'd get washed and dressed as soon as the water was warm enough to melt the ice in the washing bucket. After that, she'd wake the others for their breakfast. But first, she made tea for herself and her aunt.

Bridie had left for work, and by the time Finn came home, Annie was dressed and having her second cup of tea. She filled a basin of water for Finn to get washed, and went down to the yard to fetch another bucket of water to heat. He poured out a cup of tea and sat with her at the table.

'Annie, I want us to be friends again. I can't live like this, not speaking. I need you on my side, sister.'

'Ah sure, Finn, will you forgive me? I don't want to fight with you.' Annie's tears came. She knew that she should have said those words, and not left it to him. She leaned over and held his hand in hers, felt the rough skin and callouses, bent down and kissed the burn marks on the palm of his hand.

'There's nothing to forgive, Annie. As long as we have each other, and we have Katty and Bridie, we'll be fine.' Finn stretched. 'I'm tired. But I have good news. Last night was my final night at the bone boilers. I have a plan. Do you want to hear it?'

Annie reached up to hug her brother. 'Yes, tell me. Then I'll tell you mine.' For the first time in weeks, she felt a smile light up her face.

The two sat and talked until it was time for Katty to get up for school. They were reconciled.

* * *

As for Finn, he had saved every cent of his money, apart from the few dollars for board he paid Bridie. He had almost fifty dollars put aside. In December, when he was out selling newspapers, he had enquired about renting a stall on a street market he discovered on Pier Three.

It was a simple idea. He would set himself up as a street vendor, selling sandwiches from early morning until the afternoon. Around the Piers, there were lots of workers and travellers who needed a handy breakfast or dinner. He made an agreement with a local baker to buy fresh bread every day. The dairy next door to the baker provided milk, butter and cheese. Finn charged ten cents for a cheese sandwich and a mug of milk. Even though the winter of 1847 was a hard one, his sales increased each week. Katty joined him at the weekends to help. It was below freezing, some days even the milk froze, but they wrapped up well and put sacking around the milk churn.

He experimented with a portable brazier to make a pot of tea. Then he tried to toast a cheese sandwich on the brazier and burnt more than he actually toasted. Bridie came along one morning and helped him figure out how to toast the sandwiches. He charged fifteen cents for a toasted sandwich and a mug of tea.

* * *

Now that they were friends again, Annie asked Finn to come with her to meet some of the barges that brought Irish emigrants along the Hudson River from Quebec. She was searching for single girls and young women. Her plan was still more of a vague idea of what she could do to help them. Annie remembered the girl in the purple dress, she had seen several months before, and hoped to see her again.

They went in the evening when Finn had finished his work. The sun had already set and a freezing wind blew along the streets of Manhattan. Annie shivered and pulled her shawl around her head. 'We won't stay out long. It's too cold.' Finn's breath turned white as he exhaled. He glanced at his sister and smiled, his teeth gleamed in the winter half-light.

On their way, they walked through the park and saw young women and girls, lined up to get customers. She saw two girls, both were about fourteen or so, and they looked like china dolls, dressed up, and with rouged lips and cheeks. They leaned against each other, arms linked to keep in a bit of warmth. It took only Annie a moment to cross over to them.

'An Gaeilge tú? Are you Irish?' she asked.

One of them, the youngest, whispered. '*Is ea.* Yes.' Then glanced at the girl beside her.

A rough voice behind Annie startled her. 'What are you after here, ma'am?'

'I'm just saying hello to these girls,' Annie said, and turned towards the ragged man who stopped right next to her. It was McGonigle. His head twitched and she saw a look of recognition in his eyes.

'You!' He said. He looked over at Finn, and squinted his eyes as if to try to recall where he had seen Finn before, then back to Annie.

Annie saw that he had remembered the failed abduction of Katty the previous September.

'They haven't got time to talk to the likes of you. Now be on your way.' He spoke in a low voice that only she could hear.

'I'll only take a minute,' Annie said. Now that she stood so close to him, she felt no fear. He wasn't much taller then her, and his agitated, twitching head almost made her smile.

She switched to Irish to speak to the girl in the purple dress.

'What's your name?' Annie felt the man's hand grip her arm and squeeze hard.

At the same time, the girl whispered. 'Sinead.'

'Did you hear me?' The man hissed. 'My girls are working.'

'Let her be,' Finn said. He was right next to Annie.

Annie shook her arm free. 'I'm going.' She forced herself to stare into his bearded face. Shaggy, greying eyebrows hung over his mottled eyes. She smelt tainted meat and tobacco off his stubs of black teeth. By now a few people on the park had turned to look at them.

He pointed his finger in her face. 'You heard me. Get away from here!'

'And you heard me,' Finn said. He put his arm around his sister's waist.

'You, and your young lady, are sticking your noses into my business. Again.' The man said.

'I remember you,' Finn said. 'You tried to take my sister, last year.'

'I don't know what you're talking about. And who'll believe you, anyway?'

Annie interrupted their argument. 'Finn, this girl is from Ireland. I just asked her name, that's all,' Annie turned back to the girl and continued to speak in Irish. 'Where do you live?'

'Fuck off out of here, with your foreign language,' the man shouted. He pushed Annie and Finn, grabbed his two girls by the hand, and hurried them away from the park.

The girl called back in Irish. 'Five Points, the Barracks. Can you help me?'

'I'll come and get you,' Annie replied. 'Look out for me. I'll come as soon as I can.'

Finn and Annie looked at each other and nodded. They both knew they had got away lightly. But now, Annie had found a girl that she could help, and nothing was going to stop her. They half-ran home together. It was getting late.

* * *

She wrote about the girl in a letter to The Sun.

Her name is Sinead, and she's from Mayo, by her accent. She's a small girl, in a woman's purple, velvet dress, and it's too big for her. Her hair is pinned up and her cheeks and lips rouged to make her appear older than her years. In truth, she must be only around thirteen or fourteen years old.

160

I spoke to her for a minute or two, before her minder took her and another girl away. By the look of her she is an orphan, like me and my brother and sister. We are fortunate. We had our aunt Bridie to take us in. Who will offer a Cead Mile Failte to Sinead?

I've written this article to serve as a warning to single girls coming to America. Beware of those who would trick you with promises of a safe haven.

Sorcha Eireann.

Annie used her pen-name for the first time. It felt good. Then she made a copy of the letter. She posted one to The Nation, in Dublin, and hand delivered the second to The Sun.

She planned to keep writing under her pen name. With luck, her work might be published more often throughout the winter.

16

Jane Keating: January 1847. The army barracks

I t was now mid-summer and Jane had found out where the army barracks were situated on Flinders Street. It had taken a while for her to physically recover from the rape, but now she was ready to speak about it. She went to the barracks determined to report the Colonel to the people in charge of the army.

The barracks was built on a large site with two storey, wooden-framed buildings constructed around three sides, leaving the front open to the road. A low wall enclosed the parade ground in the centre. To the left, a row of stables with grooms and stable lads out working on their horses in the sunlit paddocks.

Directly ahead of her, what looked like the main offices stood at the top of a run of stone steps. She passed groups of soldiers in their black and red uniforms. Some of them whistled as she passed. She ignored them and began to climb the steps but stopped when she heard her name. 'Jane, Keating or Power!' She turned and knew him straight away, Owen, the young soldier from the ship who had helped her. He ran up the steps to join her and touched his shako in a salute.

'Sergeant Owen Doran, at your service,' he said, and did a mock bow. She remembered his open, smiling face, framed by dark sideburns, and now a wispy moustache grew over his wide mouth. His uniform was the same, but the bright red jacket with epaulets and white trousers looked cleaner and smarter, and his black leather boots gleamed in the morning sun.

'I never got to thank you for helping me on the ship,' Jane said.

'Well, here I am. You can thank me now,' he replied. 'Where are you off to?'

'I'm looking for someone in charge. I need to report a crime.'

'The one on the ship?' he asked.

'No. This is different.'

'Walk with me, while you tell me,' he suggested.

They climbed the steps together. Jane glanced sideways at Owen. 'It's about my last employer - he attacked me. I have to to report him. He's a Colonel, or a retired Colonel, so he says.'

'Jesus, Jane, that's a terrible thing to happen. When did this happen?'

'At the beginning of December.' Jane glanced around to make sure no-one was near. 'I thought he was going to kill me, but he beat me, and left me there.' She couldn't say the word, rape.

She heard Owen draw in a quick breath, looked at him and nodded. 'I hit him with the smoothing iron. The groundsman, helped me get away. I've not seen Colonel Johns since.'

* * *

Later, they walked together along Flinders Street towards the hostel. Neither spoke until finally, Owen said. 'I'm sorry we couldn't get any further with this.'

They were at the corner for Spencer Street and stopped to wait on several carts laden with fleeces to pass by on their way to the docks. They held their breath to avoid the stink and the clouds of tiny flies, then continued on their way. There was no shade from the sun, now almost directly overhead. Sweat beaded on Jane's forehead and ran down her neck.

'He didn't believe me. And I told him about the last housemaid, how she disappeared.' Jane shook her head and swallowed back tears.

Owen caught her hand and held it. 'What else did that man do to you, Jane?'

'I told them, he hurt me.' She closed her eyes and whispered. 'I couldn't say it, but he raped me.'

They stood together on the corner of the street, Owen still held her hand. His touch was warm and gentle. Time stood still for a moment.

'*A Dhia.* Dear God. And how are you now?' Owen asked.

'I'm better. And I've been fortunate to get another job, at the Odyssey newspaper. I've been there for more than six weeks, now.'

'That's good to hear. Where are you living?'

'At the hostel. Mrs Chisholm said I can stay there for as along as a I like. I feel safe there.'

'I'm not sure what to tell you to do about the Colonel, Jane. You could see a solicitor but that'll cost. What do you say if I ask my commander? He might have some advice for us.'

'Do that, Owen, and thank you.' They walked along in silence and turned onto the road leading to the docks.

'What about you, Owen? Jane asked him. 'I know you came on the ship from Dublin, but how did you end up in the army?'

'I have two older brothers in the British army, and I joined when I was eighteen. I send money home to my family. They'd be in right trouble with the blight if it weren't for me and my brothers.

'Do you have a wife?' She was curious about him and tilted her head to watch his face as he laughed.

'Ha! No, thank you! I'm only twenty-two. I have a mother and father and five younger brothers and sisters still at home. Paddy and Michael are stationed in Dublin, and I'm here. The one thing we Dorans can do is fight. Oh, and have big families!' He laughed.

'Well, you're not that great at the counting. That makes two things,' Jane said, and smiled, secretly relieved.

By now, they were back at the women's hostel. Owen held out his hand and she took it in hers and held it. 'All men are not ruffians, Jane. I'm not!'

'*Go raith Maith agut,* Owen.'

'It's been a while since I heard an Irish thank you. If I get any news I'll come here and let you know.' He saluted Jane and walked away a few steps, then he turned back. 'I've told you my story. Next time we meet, I want to hear about your family, and what brought you here, Jane Keating or Power.' He smiled, as if he knew there was a good story there.

Jane stood at the door and watched until he was out of sight. He was a good man, a kind man, and he warmed her heart.

The place was quiet, with most of the women out at work at this time of the day, and Jane helped herself to some bread and soup in the kitchen. She sat and ate the soup and pondered what part of her story she could tell Owen. The part about the orphaned girl, Jane Keating, from Galway, or her Dublin life as Jack Keating working at The Nation, or taking her friend, Annie Power's, place on the transportation ship to Melbourne? Perhaps one day she would tell him all of it. But not yet.

She finished her soup and rinsed out the bowl and spoon. For now, she needed to get ready for her shift at the newspaper. Despite the rape, she felt that her life here might be bearable with a friend. She felt a small hope, as if she might begin to heal. It was only a tiny hope, but it was a first step. Until she could go home to Ireland.

Before she left the hostel, she wrote in her diary.

January 1847.

I met Owen Doran again. I think we can be friends. He says he'll help me bring a case against Mr J. It's high summer here and the whole place is sweltering. Thank God there is a breeze from the river and the bay. My cheek still feels sore. I think I might have a broken bone. The job at the Odyssey is going well.

* * *

Jane arrived promptly at 1 p.m. for her shift at the Odyssey and Advertiser.

Andrew was already there. 'Come and see the news for the day and we'll get started,' he said.

Jane focused completely on her job of typesetting. Most of the work was for advertising job vacancies for shepherds and domestic servants, and Melbourne was a young town, in need of carpenters and builders. The advertisements provided the main income for the newspaper and filled the front page. While she worked at the typesetting table, Andrew wrote up a news article. Jane smiled when she read about the Lord Grey scheme for 'Exiles'. She was one of them.

By late evening, the paper was ready to print.

17

Annie Power: February 1847. The Bishop's palace

Dear Annie
   I'm sending this letter to you in the hope that you, Finn and Katty are in good health.

I am well although there were some difficulties after I arrived here in Melbourne last October. I wrote to you then. Did you get my letter?

My first job as a domestic worker didn't go well. Now I have a job as a typesetter at the Melbourne Odyssey newspaper and earn good money.

Have you heard any further news from Ireland? There is very little news here at the far end of the world.

One day, please God, we will sit and talk together. It is lonely here, but Mrs Chisholm has been very good to me. I stay at her Female Immigrants' Home in Port Phillip. She's a Catholic and helps single women find work when they first arrive. I don't know what I would have done without her help.

I still long for the quiet rivers, the soft rain and to speak the Irish language with friends and neighbours. And you, Annie? Have you *friends in New York? Write and tell me.*

God be with you and your family.

Your dear friend, Jane Keating. Melbourne, Port Phillip, December 1847.

* * *

Annie read the letter from Jane. She had written back to her friend, but knew that it could take months for a letter to get to Australia.

She read again the part about Mrs Chisholm's Female Immigrants' Home. Yes, that's exactly what she wanted to do, or something similar, here in New York. Set up a home for female immigrants. Then she'd be able to have a safe place for the young girls and women she'd seen. 'Thank you, Jane,' Annie whispered. She could try.

Now, Annie just needed to decide how to go about it. She'd talk to Bridie and Finn. They'd help, for sure.

* * *

Soon after the letter from Jane arrived in the middle of February, Annie received a letter from Bishop Hughes at the cathedral, inviting her to come and talk to him. He had read her letters and articles in the newspapers and wanted to meet Sorcha Eireann.

On her way to the Bishop's Palace, next door to St Patrick's Cathedral, Annie walked through the cathedral cemetery and stopped to look at the monuments. Most were simple white stone crosses, a few graves had larger headstones made of more expensive marble or granite. She stopped by one and read the name on the weathered stone:

Pat Kelly, beloved husband and father.

A long way from home.

Annie walked on and read more of the stones. Almost all were Irish names and on some of them the words were carved in Gaelic. She ran her fingers around the sharply-etched designs and letters on a particularly fine Celtic Cross. 'A long way from home, indeed.' She blessed herself. 'Eternal rest grant unto them, Oh Lord.' Her voice was the only sound in the graveyard filled with granite headstones and crosses. The trees around were bare of leaves, and a chill breeze ruffled her hair. She shivered and remembered the ghost stories of her childhood. She hurried towards the gate, then, still inside the cemetery grounds, she noticed a small path that led away towards the back of the cemetery.

Out of curiosity, she followed the path. It led to a cottage, built in the shelter of the high wall. The dwelling was timber-framed and clad with dark oak wood. There was a front door and two windows on the ground floor and a couple more windows in the shingled roof. The place had a deserted look about it; leaves and twigs had blown in and lay in a tangled heap right up against the door. She peered through the narrow window nearest to her and looked into a dimly lit kitchen that ran from front to back. Through the room she saw another small window on the back wall, above a stone sink. On the side wall she saw a dusty cast-iron stove with a long metal chimney to the outside. The only furniture in the room was a table and four chairs with a glass-domed oil lamp in the middle of the table.

Annie went past the front door and peeped into the other window to look in on a parlour, the same size as the kitchen, with a fireplace next to the outside wall. The walls and floors were all timber; planed planks were laid for the floor and were full of dust balls; rougher planks formed the walls. The two glazed windows were fogged and cobwebbed on the inside. No-one had looked out of them for a good while.

She turned and walked away from the cemetery and the church grounds, along the main street towards the Bishop's palace. An abandoned house was a sad place. It called to her mind, their own cabin back home. That had no doubt been levelled to the ground long ago. The eviction notice had been served the day before Annie had got back from Dublin. They got out before it was pulled down around them. This cottage still stood. But it had a cheerless and neglected air about it. Then she had an idea.

* * *

The leader of the Catholic church in New York, Bishop Hughes, was a bear of a man. His black soutane gave him the appearance of a solid block over which he wore a gold crucifix on a chain fastened to a wide belt. To Annie, he seemed to be a man past his prime, maybe fifty, but his dark hair and blue eyes gave the appearance of a younger man brimming with energy. Annie saw the curious gleam in his eyes as he greeted her.

'Come in and sit down there, Annie,' he said.

The Bishop's Palace was a huge place, and underlined the authority and power of the Catholic Church. Annie sat opposite Bishop Hughes's gleaming desk, polished to within an inch of its life. He sat with his back to a window that overlooked the garden adjacent to the cemetery. Annie caught

171

a glimpse of the roof of the cottage behind the wall.

She'd never seen or spoken to such a high-ranking priest before and had no notion of how to address one. 'Thank you for inviting me here, Bishop.'

'Well! It's Sorcha Eireann. I hear you're Bridie Foley's niece, from Waterford?'

'Yes, we came over last September.'

'I read your letters in The Sun. Tell me all about yourself.'

'I work at the orphanage with the Sisters of Charity. I help young Irish immigrants learn English.' Annie told him how she had found a job for Joanne, a girl she had met at the orphanage. 'And I've seen other young women, down around the Piers and Battery Park. In my opinion, they need someone to help them. Most of them are very young, Bishop, younger than me, and they seem trapped in that life. One of the girls I spoke to, Sinead, is a tiny little thing, from Mayo. I promised I'd find her and help her. So I wrote about what I'd seen.'

The Bishop nodded. 'It's most unfortunate, I agree. But what do you think your letters will accomplish, Annie? And what can you do?'

The Bishop's question seemed to be a challenge and he looked at her and waited for her reply. She smiled at him, for she had the answer.

'Bishop, instead, can I show you something? It will help me explain.' She paused to gauge his response. He still looked curious, and she had nothing to lose, so she continued. 'It's not far, but it might be a way you can help me.'

'A mystery! But I have a few minutes to spare. Where are you taking me?' He pushed his chair back, went to the door and held it for her.

'Just as far as the cemetery,' she replied.

'Let's go then.'

* * *

They walked back through the cathedral grounds towards the cemetery. It was colder now, and she felt the winter breeze burrow into her chest. She coughed to clear her throat and explained how she came to be at the committee meeting and her suggestions for the Aid to Ireland money. 'They didn't want to hear me. They were only interested in sending money back home to Ireland.'

'The Sisters of Charity do a lot of work with immigrants here. Have you spoken to Sister Mary Angela?' The Bishop asked.

Annie was aware that Sister Mary Angela was Bishop Hughes's sister, as well as head of the Sisters of Mercy. 'Yes, she helped me get work at the orphanage as an assistant teacher. But I can't see how these girls would let nuns help them. There's such shame in what they do. I can help them because I'm like them.' Annie caught the look, and corrected herself. 'I mean, I could be their neighbour. I've been fortunate to have my aunt to take in me, and my brother and sister. And they won't all be fallen if I can catch them first. That's my plan.'

By now, they had arrived at the empty cottage at the back of the cemetery.

'I found this on my way to see you,' Annie said. 'Does this belong to the church, Bishop?' She saw him nod, and continued. 'It can be a home for some of those girls and not just sit here empty.'

'It's the gardener's cottage, it's been empty for a while. Joe

173

lives with his mother and has no need of it. But I'm not too sure about bringing fallen women to live here. I'm not sure about that idea at all.' He touched the crucifix. Annie saw the gesture and thought of Mary Magdalene. The Lord had forgiven her.

After a pause, the Bishop sighed and said. 'Let's take a look at it while we're here.' Then he took a set of keys out of his pocket, tried a few of them, and finally opened the front door. They stepped over the debris on the threshold and into a long, narrow hallway. A steep stairwell at the far end led up to the roof-space.

The kitchen to the right was much as Annie had seen from outside, but there was an indoor pump next to the sink. She had never seen a water pump indoors, and ran her hand over the cold iron handle. She tried it, pumped the handle, and saw fresh water run into the stone sink. She shook her head in amazement.

The floorboards were in need of a clean, but felt sound under foot. They walked into the empty parlour across the hall, then came back out to climb the stairs to the roof space. The whole of the attic space was divided into two rooms and must have been used as bedrooms at one point. The eaves angled down at the front and back, but there was still room to walk around. The wooden floor and shingled roof gave the feel of warmth, even though it was freezing outside.

'This would make a home for someone,' Annie said. Then she changed the subject. 'Bishop how long is it since you left Ireland?'

'It must be thirty years, Annie. I was a young man when I left. Why do you ask?'

'Things have changed a lot, since you left. These girls will have been forced out of their homes, like I was. Since the potatoes failed last year, they will have gone hungry, and now they have nothing. Many of them can neither read nor write, and a lot of them don't speak English. I don't know how they got here, but many of them have been picked up by gangs who make them sell their bodies for rent.'

'Annie, I, and the Church, is doing all it can to help the immigrants. There have been thousands of Irish coming in over the last year. '

'Yes, Bishop. But, these girls in particular, have nowhere to go. Lend me this house for one year and I'll help some of them get out of this trap they have fallen into.'

She followed him back down the stairs and out into the back garden of the house. 'We'll grow our own food here and keep chickens. We can feed ourselves.'

Her aunt had told her that Bishop Hughes had worked as a gardener before he trained as a priest. He glanced at her, and nodded.

'I'm not keen on this idea, Annie, but I'll talk to Sister Mary Angela. If I do agree to lend you the cottage, it'll be on the condition that she oversees the work you do. And never forget, this is consecrated ground. It is part of the Cathedral grounds, the cemetery and the Bishop's Palace.'

They had reached the roadway. 'One more thing, how would you feed and clothe yourselves? It'll take a while for food to grow in the garden.'

Annie smiled. 'I have a plan, Bishop. I've saved the money I earned from my articles in the newspapers. But I want your permission to speak at masses around the city. And to have a collection made to pay for the upkeep of the Refuge. I think when people hear about these young women and girls, then they will want to help.'

The Bishop shook his head. 'So, you want me to give you a house and let you ask for money from the diocese.'

'Yes.' There, it was said. She pressed her lips together, for she wanted to throw her hands up and shout. 'Do it, Bishop!' But she had done all she could. Her heart hammered in her chest. If she failed in this, she would keep trying. She knew that, on her own, the task would be almost impossible.

'I tell you what you can do. Come and speak at a few masses for the next month. Where are we? The middle of February.' The Bishop said. By now they had reached the Bishop's Palace.

'There are ten Catholic churches in Manhattan, I'll ask my secretary to write the names down for you. He can book you in to speak at the end of the Sunday masses for the next few weeks. If you can raise fifty dollars, then I'll know you're serious about this project. What do you say?'

'I'm very serious, Bishop. I'll raise the fifty dollars. And you will lend me the cottage for a year?'

The Bishop put his hand out to shake Annie's hand. 'We have a deal.' He opened the front door and called for his secretary. 'Father Sean, come and meet our new speaker.'

* * *

Annie was exhausted by the time she arrived back at the apartment, and lay down on Bridie's bed. She slept for an hour and woke when she heard heard her aunt come in from work.

'I met with the Bishop. I told him about Sinead. And on the way there, I saw a lovely cottage at the back of the cemetery, just lying empty. I told him about my idea, and asked him to lend the cottage to me.'

'My God, Annie! And what did he say to that?' Bridie asked.

'He said if I can raise fifty dollars through speaking at masses in the next month, then he'll lend me the house. Father Sean is writing to the churches about me.'

'Sure, that's great news.' Bridie leaned over and hugged Annie. 'You've set your heart on this, haven't you, girl? I believe you'll do it. But keep up with your writing, too. That way people will read about you in the newspapers.'

'Thank you, Bridie. After supper I'll think about what I'm going to say at the masses.'

'Well, let's get the supper started, shall we?' They set to work in the kitchen. Later that night, Annie sat down to plan her talks.

18

Annie Power: February and March 1847. Fund-raising

Annie was at the six o'clock early mass at Our Lady of Padua's Church for the first of her fund-raising talks. She had met the priest before mass and joined the congregation with Bridie, Finn and Katty.

At the end of mass, the priest instructed the congregation to sit down, and he introduced Annie. 'One of our own, a recent arrival from Ireland, is here to speak to you about her experiences back home. Annie won't keep you long, but we will be taking up a collection at the end of her talk. She has the Bishop's blessing to ask you to support her fund-raising to open a refuge for young Irish women who have no family here in New York. I hope you will be generous.'

Annie stood at the oak pulpit, and looked out at the congregation. She knew that the majority of the parishioners here were Irish; some were immigrants and some were second generation, born in America. She thought that there were German and Italian immigrants in the congregation, too. They looked more prosperous than their Irish neighbours.

To Annie, that was a good sign. They'd open their purses and wallets.

She had brought along her Commonplace Book, and opened it at the chapter where she had recounted her visit to Sligo, in May 1846, almost a year ago.

'Good morning. First of all, thank you for your kind attention, and thank you, Father Pat, for letting me speak at this mass. I want to open a refuge for young, single women who come to New York, so that I can help them find work and a safe place to live.' She had decided not to mention that some of them were working as prostitutes.

'Some of you will know what is happening back home, in our dear Mother Ireland, but some of you have lived in America for a while, or even been born here. I want to tell you what I have seen with my own eyes.' Annie held up her book to show them. 'I'll read you a chapter about my visit to Sligo on the west coast last year.

'Some of the details are upsetting and this is why I have come to this early mass. I can see a few younger children, so you may want to take them home before I begin.' Annie waited for a few families to leave, then she began to read from her Commonplace Book.

"The start of our investigation into the plight of poor cottiers around Sligo. May 1846.

It wasn't long before we found a cabin that was inhabited. Dear reader, you must know, at the outset, that the human inhabitants of this small home were no longer in the land of the living, but had crossed the border into the realm of death.

The only living creatures were rats. Black and sleek. Indeed they

179

had a sheen upon them and their eyes glittered in the dark corners of the cabin. The only sound was their excited squeaks, undimmed when I pushed open the door to let daylight flood in. There must have been above one hundred of these vermin piled one on top of each other on the straw mattress in the corner. They writhed and fought with each other to get at what remained of the occupants of the mattress.

My companion, Speranza, and I, both stepped back, and pulled the door closed against the stink of death. I found a long-handled rake, my companion picked up a shovel, and we went back inside to put the run under the rats. They scattered around the room, some raced outside, others hid in the turf walls of the cabin, their red eyes watched us in the gloomy interior.

No words can describe the sorrowful sight on the rotten mattress. What had been a woman and her two small children, were now long departed from this life.

Speranza and I stood together and said a prayer over their ravaged corpses. We dared not stay, for the charnel smell of death invaded our own bodies. The rats waited for us to leave.

I ran to a cottage back along the lane, and begged a shovel of fire from the wretched woman there. When I got back to the cabin and opened the door, the rats had resumed their feasting. I threw the shovel of fire across their squirming bodies, then stepped back outside and pulled the door shut.

After a few minutes, orange and crimson flames caught the shutter on the window, flared then flashed, as the night air crept into the cabin.

We sat on the low stone wall across the lane and watched the place burn. The cabin door cracked and split as fire engulfed it. I kept the shovel at the ready if any rats tried to escape the inferno. Leaping flames burned through the turf roof, and lit up the black *sky. Soon after the entire roof collapsed down into the cabin and finished the job.*

Speranza and I knelt and prayed to God to have mercy on the souls of the dear departed family, first starved to death, then feasted on by great, sleek rats. May God forgive us all for this disaster."

Annie closed her book. 'Last month, I met a young homeless girl, Sinead. She was only about fourteen or fifteen.' Annie held her book up. 'This is where she came from, Sligo. Please, if you can spare a few cents or dollars, then your money will help me to make a home for Sinead, and others like her.'

A few sniffles sounded from the congregation, and the altar boys handed round the collection plates.

At the end of the mass, she helped the priest count up the collection money. She had raised eight dollars. Father Pat offered the money to her.

'No, please send it to Bishop Hughes. I want it all to go him, so he can see when I have raised fifty dollars.' Annie smiled. 'The Bishop has set me a target.'

* * *

By now it was the end of February. There was still two feet of snow in Manhattan and freezing blizzards blew around every corner. Annie walked home with Finn, after speaking at another mass. 'I can raise fifty dollars. I just hope I can do it in time.'

'Don't do too much, now Annie,' Finn said. 'You're out in the cold every morning, either at work or these masses, and it's not doing your cough any good.'

'Ah sure, I'll have to do it. I have to raise the money. At

least until they get sick of listening to me.' She smiled. 'I'll get barred from them soon. Come on, let's get home for some breakfast.'

They arrived back to a warm kitchen and a bowl of hot porridge each. Annie took off her wet stockings and put a pair of hand-knitted socks on. 'Thanks for these, Bridie. I've thawed out now.'

Katty and Bridie were ready to leave for second mass, and they left Annie and Finn to relax by the fire. Annie would go with them to second mass next week and speak there.

* * *

Annie sipped her tea and warmth flowed through her body. She glanced at a newspaper on the sideboard. Although Finn had stopped selling the New York Sun, he generally brought a copy home on Saturday to read Annie's letters and articles. By now, she was getting regular payments from the newspaper for her tales of emigration. She had a flick through the paper to see if any of her work had been published.

A word caught her eye in an article on page ten. She began to read aloud.

Tragic drowning: Report from the Coroner's Office.

The body of a young girl was discovered on the banks of the River Hudson on Wednesday night. It appears she had drowned. The deceased was about fourteen years old, of small build. She wore a purple velveteen dress. No injuries consistent with foul play were ascertained at the inquest. The Coroner concluded that the deceased either fell into the river or committed suicide. The body, unclaimed, has since been buried in a paupers' grave.

Annie stopped reading and looked at Finn. She crumpled up the newspaper and threw it across the kitchen floor. 'No! Tell me it's not her.' Tears flooded her eyes and poured down her cheeks.

Finn picked up the newspaper and smoothed it out to read the article for himself. 'Not who, Annie?'

'Sinead. Do you remember we saw her? Just after Christmas. She told me her name and where she lived. And she was only a girl for God's sake! I told them about her at mass, last week.' Annie said. 'I promised I'd find her. But I left it too late, didn't I?' She laid her head on her hands and cried bitter tears.

* * *

Later that day, Annie wrote a poem for Sinead. She sent it to The Nation in Dublin and The Sun in New York. It wasn't published in the Sun, for suicide by drowning was a common enough occurrence. She was confident The Nation would publish the poem.

To my Young Friend from Auld Erin
I saw you with another girl
at Battery Park. You wore a dress, too long and too large.
I knew you, from your Irish face, and we spoke together in Gaelic.
You left this hard world before I could help you.
Sleep in the arms of the Lord, dear Child.
Sorcha Eireann.

19

Jane Keating: February 1847. The beach at Port Phillip

'I've been sick the last few days. I must have eaten some tainted meat. And there's been a lot of sickness in the town from the dirty water, so it may be that. Work at the newspaper is really busy. We have increased our advertisers and the number of newspapers we sell. Andrew is a good person to work with, but we don't agree about the Aborigines. He doesn't see them as people. I do, they remind me of Brendan and Aoife and their children. Brendan was murdered because he wouldn't leave his land. Aoife and the little ones were put out on the road.'

That morning, after she had washed and dressed, she drank a cup of strong tea to settle her stomach. She wasn't due to start work until one o'clock and she'd work through the afternoon and evening until the paper was ready for the next day.

She headed out for a walk. On the way she called in, as usual, to the Post Office to see if Annie had written. A letter was there waiting for her. She stopped on the bridge to read it. From the post mark it had taken three months to get to

Melbourne.

My dear friend, I received your letter from Melbourne and I read it over and over. My prayers have been answered to find you arrived safely and have comfortable lodgings. Mrs Chisholm is a wonderful woman to look after you.

Our mother's sister, Aunt Bridie, has made us welcome. Katty is in school and getting an American accent already. Finn has a job.

Shortly after we arrived here, I found that there is an Aid for Ireland Committee at St Patrick's Cathedral. They have arranged to send money to help back home. I gave them Mr Gavan Duffy's name at The Nation and have written to ask him if he will help give out the money. Finn and Katty send their love.

Write to me and tell me your news. I think of you, and will always be thankful for your sacrifice.

Annie

Jane folded the letter and put it in her pocket and began to continue her walk. She felt a hand on her arm and turned to see the man she thought she had killed. Her attacker, Colonel Johns. She hadn't seen him come up behind her, and she froze at his touch.

He tipped his hat to her. 'Jane Power. Now where have you been hiding, these last few months?'

'You,' she said.

'I've been keeping an eye out for you,' he said. She stood there and felt his gaze on her. 'Are you working?'

'Did the army get in touch with you?' She ignored his question and asked one of her own. 'I reported you for the rape. Did they tell you?'

His face hardened. 'Now why would they do that? You know that I'm a decorated officer of Her Majesty's army.'

'I'm saving up to pay for a solicitor. I'll bring a case against you. I'm not finished yet,' she said. All the time she was speaking she felt light-headed. He could just reach out and strike her again. Would he care if there were people crossing the bridge, witnesses?

He took a step back and looked her up and down. 'Your new life must agree with you. You're getting fat, Jane. Now why would that be, I wonder? I think there's two of us who are not finished yet.' He tapped his riding crop against his boot, walked off and left her standing there.

Jane leaned against the stone wall of the bridge and looked down into the river. What does he mean, I'm fat? What business is it of his? He can't sue me for rape and he doesn't know where I'm working.

Her fingers grabbed onto the rough surface of the top of the wall, and she watched the river water flow out towards the bay. He can find me any time he wants to, she thought. She could still feel his touch on her arm, where he had squeezed her. She felt the sting of his whip again, and the weight of his body on hers almost stopped her breath. She stayed there for a while, just watching the river and the boats and ships, until her breathing calmed and the sweat cooled on her forehead.

* * *

Over the next few days, Jane took care when going and coming from work. But she saw no sign of the Colonel, and began to lower her guard a little.

One Sunday towards the end of February, she left the church after mass for her usual walk across the beach. It was almost midday, and the heat weighed down on her. Thankfully, a light sea breeze got up and blew in from the bay.

She walked along the beach and looked out towards the estuary, where the Yarra joined the sea and at the horizon beyond, where the sky and sea melded into a lilac heat haze.

Jane's feet sank into the fine, pale sand and she sat for a minute to take off her boots and hitch up her skirt. Then she continued to walk to the far end of the beach almost to the woods. The same group of children she had seen before, were playing in the water. The boy, Jimmy, waved to her and gestured for her to join them. Jane smiled and waved back and undressed down to her shift and drawers. Then she ran straight down to the water's edge to feel the cool saltwater between her toes, cover her feet and then on to her legs. The sun had taken the night-time chill off the water, but she still gasped as her warm skin touched the sea. She ran straight out and swam to join the children.

Jimmy and his friends splashed each other and raced to see who was the fastest swimmer. Their arms and bodies gleamed from the water and the sunlight and Jane was enthralled by the beauty of their skin.

She joined in their games for a while, then waved goodbye and swam parallel to the shore. When she started to get cold, she swam back in to the shore and walked across the sand to pick up her clothes and towel. Her feet were heavy with damp sand by the time she reached the trees to find some shelter to dry and dress herself. She had brought along dry underwear and she wrapped her wet shift and drawers in the towel and carried her boots.

The children were still playing in the water and she waved goodbye again. As she walked away, she heard Jimmy call, 'Jane!' She saw him run up the beach towards her. He had a small girl by the hand, who struggled to keep up with the older boy. Jane smiled at her new friend. 'Hello, Jimmy.'

He held up the little girl's hand. 'My sister, Rose.'

Jane crouched down to say hello. The child had a shy smile; her small white teeth gleamed in her heart-shaped face.

'Hello. What a beautiful girl you are.' The child was about six or seven years old, Jane guessed, for she was missing a few milk teeth. She was of narrow build with long, slim arms and legs. Drops of water sparkled in her dark hair, and she held out her hand to Jane, who laughed and shook it.

'Where do you live?' Jane asked.

Jimmy pointed towards the woods.

'Goodbye, Jimmy and Rose,' she said and waved, then went on her way. She turned to see brother and sister run back into the sea to continue their game.

* * *

She enjoyed exploring the land to the south of the Yarra River, and stayed by the coast to walk around the bay. She was alone, no other humans, just herself and the most beautiful birds, of a type that didn't exist in Ireland, with bright scarlet and iridescent green feathers. She stopped suddenly, as a group of kangaroos hopped out of the woods, and came bounding towards her. The tiny head of a baby kangaroo stuck out of its mother's pouch and looked her way, a small passenger travelling in comfort.

Jane smiled at the sight of the kangaroo and her baby. 'What a way to carry a baby,' she whispered. The troop of animals took no notice of her and continued on their way along the beach. She stood still for a moment, then blinked and looked at the kangaroos, as they disappeared into the woods.

'It can't be!' She put her hand on her belly. When did she have her last monthly? Not since Christmas? No, before Christmas, before . . .

She fell to her knees. 'Oh, dear God, no!' Her mind went blank and she let herself fall down on the sand. She curled up, one hand still on her belly.

He knew. The Colonel had known, just by looking at her, that she was pregnant.

* * *

After a while, she rolled over and looked at the sky. The sun was almost directly overhead and the day was hot. Time hadn't stopped, and she had to be at work soon.

Jane picked up the damp towel with her underclothes and boots and brushed sand off herself. Then she hurried back along the beach. The waves danced and glinted in the sunlight, the children had gone and the beach was deserted. There, in her mind's-eye, she saw again the alert face of the mother kangaroo with her baby in the pouch as she lolloped across the beach.

Jane knew it was true, she'd been through so many hardships and hunger but her monthly menstruation had always been on time. How had she not noticed its absence? She hadn't prayed much since her family had died, but she murmured a prayer to the Blessed Mother. 'Help me.'

* * *

She arrived a few minutes early for her shift, used the privy, then washed her hands and smoothed her skirt and blouse. She smelt the salt water on her skin and the scent calmed her a little. The taste of salt on her lips helped her to focus on her work.

* * *

Two weeks later and it was the first week in March. Jane could now typeset almost automatically and focused on the cold edges of the metal type, sometimes clutching them so hard the edges cut into her fingertips. By now, she had learned to read Andrew's crabbed handwriting on the advertisements and editorials. Once he had Jane to work in the office, he spent more of his time out chasing up stories and advertising. The newspaper was definitely in demand.

* * *

Owen Doran came back to the hostel to tell Jane about his enquiries to his commander. His advice was the same. Bring a civil complaint against the Colonel. The army weren't interested.

'Thank you for asking. If I go to a solicitor will you come with me?'

'I will, of course, Jane.' Owen paused. 'I tell you what, I've got a couple of hours off this morning. Shall we go for a walk? I've got a few names for you of solicitors we can speak to.'

It was a fine autumn morning in March and sea breezes blew along the Yarra River and over the town of Melbourne. The air was fresh that day, yet for a moment, Jane was sure she could smell the ice at the bottom of the world. A frigid draft from the Southern Ocean filled her nostrils with briny fumes and stung her tongue. She couldn't say the word, pregnant, to Owen. She pushed it out of her mind with a sweep of her hand through her hair.

'Let's go to the beach. I love it there,' she said.

They crossed the river and began to stroll along the tree-lined beach. Jane pointed out her favourite spot to swim.

'You can swim?' Owen asked.

'I swam in Galway Bay, ever since I was a child. It's the most beautiful part of Ireland. Did you never learn to swim, Owen?'

'Why do you ask?' Owen smiled and his eyes crinkled at the edges.

'I can teach you, if you'd like,' she said.

'There's not much chance for swimming up in the Wicklow hills, Jane. The only water there is in rocky rivers. Sure, it'd sweep you away!' Owen paused for a moment. 'But sure, I'll have a go. If you promise not to drown me!'

They made an arrangement for the next week and finished their walk with a stop at a food stall on Collins Street. Owen treated them both to a chicken pasty. She still didn't tell him. This friendship was a precious thing, and she daren't risk it.

20

Annie Power: March 1847. Annie buys some books

Annie had just seen the last of her class off at the end of the day. They didn't have to go far, only to the end of the hall to get their supper before starting on homework. The nuns did their best to create a homely environment, but an institution could never replace the homes they had lost. However, the orphans were generally well-behaved in lessons. For those who were not, a quiet word often helped to settle them back to their work.

That day, Annie had kept a boy back to speak to him when the other children left. He had been distracted in the lesson and refused to finish his assignment.

'I hate it here, Miss,' he said. 'Not just the orphanage, this city, this country. I want to go home.' His slate grey eyes filled with tears, and he blinked them away.

'Sure Pat, I know it's hard. Even harder for you children all on your own.' Annie said.

'I'm tired of people calling me names and telling me to go back to Ireland. I wouldn't be here if I had a choice!' He was thirteen, almost the same age as Finn, and feeling himself a man nearly.

'Some Americans worry about us Irish taking over New York,' Annie said with a wry smile. 'They don't need to worry just yet, do they?'

'As soon as I earn the ticket money, I'm going back. I'll join the Young Irelanders and we'll kick the British out of Ireland.'

'That sounds like a good plan to me, Pat,' Annie said. 'Get your education first, then work and save. Before you know it, you'll be on the ship back home.'

They left the classroom together. The conversation seemed to echo the argument she'd had with herself for the last months. Had Pat articulated her own dream of going back home? And would she take her own advice? Work and save? And see Katty grow up, first?

* * *

She had reached the front door of the orphanage, when she heard Sister Fidelma call her. 'Annie, wait! There's someone here to see you.'

Two nuns hurried along the hallway to catch up with her. One was Sister Fidelma, the other, Sister Mary Angela.

'I'll walk with you, Annie,' Sister Mary Angela said. 'That way I won't delay you.'

'Thank you, Sister,' Annie replied. They left the building and walked along the busy street. They had to dodge crowds of fast-moving people, some of whom overflowed onto the roadway and tried to skip between clattering cabs, carriages and horse-drawn carts, as the vehicles hurtled along, and churned the ground into thick, freezing mud. Most of the buildings they passed had shop fronts on the ground floor with apartments above. All were at least three storeys tall. Annie felt that familiar sense of being shut in a chicken coop. Yes, she could see the sky above, and today it was filled with low clouds, more grey than white, which sat like a lid on the roofs of the buildings.

The one thing she longed for was a distant view. Back home on the beach, she could look down the River Suir to the sea and the horizon, miles off. There, it felt as if her soul ranged across those miles through the air like a sea-bird. Here, her wings were clipped and her eyes blinkered, her world had become bounded by tenements and strangers.

* * *

She felt a hand touch her arm and jumped, startled. 'I'm sorry Sister. I just got to thinking. What did you say?'

'I said, Bishop Hughes is very impressed by your determination, Annie. He asked me to talk to you about this refuge you want to start.'

'I haven't heard any more from him. I've raised the money he asked for. Fifty dollars.'

'That's why I'm here. I have a message from the Bishop. He says to go ahead.'

Annie stopped walking. She covered her face with her hands. 'Dear Lord, thank you,' she prayed. Then she turned to the nun. 'It will be wonderful! Thank you.'

'I have something for you.' The nun opened her purse and took out an iron key ring with two long keys attached. 'These are for the cottage in the cathedral grounds. You know the Bishop is my brother? He has asked me to oversee your work.

I'm sure you'll agree that's a wise thing to do?' The nun didn't wait for a reply. 'The fifty dollars you raised should pay for the furniture you'll need, and for the upkeep of the Refuge for a while. Bishop Hughes has asked the Aid for Ireland Committee if they will consider a donation to the Refuge. You'll be pleased to hear that they have agreed.'

Annie took the keys, she clutched the cold iron in her fingers. 'I'll make a success of this, I promise.'

'You've got three months to prove it. After that, we'll review it together, and see if it is worth continuing. Tell me, have you thought about how you'll manage?'

'Yes, Sister. I've almost finished my Commonplace book about the Famine. I'm going to try to get it published. If it sells, then I'll have money to keep the place going.'

They turned the corner onto the Broadway. 'If not, then I'll keep giving talks at masses and begging for money. People have been so generous.'

Annie felt her face stretch into a relieved smile. 'Thank you, Sister. I'm sure, with your guidance, this will be a success.'

'I think it's a very good idea. There's definitely a need for your shelter or refuge. But have you thought about the consequences of doing this? You could be putting yourself in danger. These young women and girls are usually controlled by men, sure, they're criminals, and they'll not stand by and let you take away their living.'

Annie nodded. 'I've seen the men, and some women, too. But I have to try. I feel these girls are like my sisters in a way. Sure, I could have been one of them, if not for Bridie.'

* * *

195

By now, they had reached a street market, and one long stall caught Annie's eyes. It was filled, almost overfilled, with books that were piled, one on top of the other, and threatened to topple into the frozen mud of the street. She paused to steady a leather-bound tome and picked it up to show to her companion. 'We're going to need some of these, Sister. My boarders will need to improve their English.'

'Well, there's no better way than through reading.' The nun laughed and corrected herself. 'And speaking, of course! Right, let's see what they have here.'

The two women rummaged through the piles of books. Sister Mary Angela picked up a bible, opened it then put it back. It was a Church of England version and definitely not for Catholics. Annie found a pile of damp, tattered school texts and readers; on one of them she read the name, *McGuffey's Eclectic Primers for Beginners.* She picked out three of the best copies and held them, while she kept on looking until she ended up with a stack of books and showed them to the nun.

'What do you think of these, Sister?'

Sister Mary Angela looked at the authors. 'Mmm,' she said. 'Mary Shelley's *Frankenstein*. I've heard of this, but I think it is called a horror story. Ah, I know this one, *The Poems of Currer, Ellis and Acton Bell.* They're sisters, their name is Bronte, an Irish connection, I think, but they used men's names to get their poems published. And, yes, you have an American author here, Edgar Allan Poe, *Tales of the Grotesque and Arabesque.* It's a collection of short stories. I remember reading *'The Fall of the House of Usher'*. It's in here somewhere.' The nun opened the book and pointed to the contents list. 'There it is. Do you think your young women will like horror stories, Annie?'

'I don't know. I've never read a horror story. But I like the sound of the words, Grotesque and Arabesque.'

'Well, it's a new form of writing, I understand. Read the stories, and tell me what you think. What else did you find?' Sister Mary Angela peered at a yellow covered book. 'Mm, this looks interesting, *Narrative of the Life of Frederick Douglass*. Look! It was published in Boston. I've heard of this, and I heard him speak, at a meeting on emancipation, only last year. It's a new book, too. Douglass is a freed slave and this is his story. How did it get here, I wonder? May I borrow the book, Annie? I have a particular interest in the emancipation of slaves.' Annie smiled her assent. The two women stood shoulder to shoulder at the book stall. Their heads almost touched as they examined the stack of books Annie had chosen.

'I'll read it this week and I'll be sure to let you have it back for your library.' Annie's companion lowered her voice. 'Right, time to get ourselves a bargain.' Then she began. 'Good man, come and tell me how much you want for these books here. I don't know, but they are really overpriced, in my opinion.'

Annie watched, and was soon mesmerised, as the nun began to haggle over the chosen books. From being a small, anonymous woman in black, Sister Mary Angela was transformed into a hawk ready to pounce on the stall-holder.

Both she and the stall-holder argued over each book. She pointed out damage to the leather bindings, and he pointed to the illustrious author. She returned the *Life of Frederick Douglass* to him and the trader tried to get her to take it back; she accepted, but only after much debate. As the two haggled, a crowd of onlookers gathered to listen and comment on the proceedings. There was much amusement when the trader threw his hands up in the air and turned away in exasperation. The nun stood there and waited for him to come back to her. Then they had at it again. It took a while, but they finally agreed on a price for the pile of books.

Sister Mary Angela pulled out a purse from the pocket of her cloak and began to count out four dollars and seventy-five, in cents, dimes and quarters. The trader checked the money, and tied the books together with twine. As they shook hands on the deal, Sister Mary Angela picked up the Catholic bible she had found. 'Look at this. Sure, I forgot all about it!' She laid the bible on top of the parcel then blessed herself. The crowd of onlookers applauded and the stall-holder laughed at her audacity and waved her away when she offered to pay. The show had gathered a crowd of potential customers and he seemed eager to get on and make some more sales.

The nun handed the parcel of books to Annie and they walked on. 'Now, my child, you have the start of a library for your refuge. I pray the good Lord will bless your work.'

'Sister, you are so generous. Thank you, we'll look after them. Tell me, where did you learn to strike such a hard bargain? You must have got these books for half price.'

The nun laughed. 'I've had years of practice, Annie. I was brought up on a farm back in Ireland. Every single thing that we bought and sold at the market was bargained for.' The nun stopped. 'It's time I was getting back. So, Bishop Hughes said you are to call after mass on Sunday and collect the money you've raised. You can spend it on furnishing the cottage. Will you need help with that?'

'No, thank you, Sister. I think I know how to bargain, now that I've watched you, and Bridie will help me.'

They arranged to meet at the cottage the following week. Annie wanted to get started. She hurried home to tell the good news to her family. There would soon be a home for lost girls like Sinead.

* * *

Later that evening, Annie and Bridie were chatting about the refuge. Annie decided it was time to tell Bridie about her plans to move out.

'What do you think, Bridie? I need to go and live at the cottage as soon as I get some tenants. They can't stay there on their own. But I'm worried about Katty. What'll I do?'

'Why not ask her? Finn's gone to meet her out of school and they'll be home any minute.'

'I don't want to upset her.'

Bridie jumped up and started to make a pot of tea. There was an hour until supper, so they'd have tea to keep them going.

As soon as Katty and Finn came in, Bridie said, 'Katty, love, come and sit down. You too, Finn. Annie wants to talk to you both.'

Annie wasn't sure how to say it. Katty had a bag of books she had borrowed from the library and put the bag on the table. Katty turned to Annie and smiled her lovely smile. 'I know what you're going to say, don't I, Bridie?'

Bridie laughed. 'And what'll your answer be, Katty, my girl?'

'Annie, I know you've got to live at the cottage, but it's only around the corner. I've got to stay here with Bridie. She says she wants to be my mother. And I'd like that.' Katty put her arm around her aunt's waist. 'I think mammy would have wanted that.'

Annie looked from her sister, Katty, to her aunt and then to her brother, who seemed unsurprised.

She smiled. 'You sorted this out between you, didn't you? Come and give me a hug, all of you.'

They embraced. Bridie, not a one for too much emotion, poured the hot water over the tea leaves in the pot. 'Now, let's have a cup of tea and celebrate. Annie Power is opening her refuge. Well done, Annie!'

21

Jane Keating: March 1847. Melbourne's Botanic Gardens

One afternoon in March, the heat of the summer still hung over the town, despite it being the start of autumn. Andrew decided they needed a break from the office. The typesetting was completed and the office was quiet. 'We'll get some air, and something to eat, then we'll start the press.' He took his hat from the coat stand and held the door for Jane. She pulled her summer shawl around her shoulders and tucked it in at the waist. It was good to stop and rest her eyes.

They left the newspaper office, locked the door behind them and strolled along Collins Street towards the river and the food shops. They paused on the bridge, to look out at the river.

'What's that?' Jane pointed to a huge, fenced off area of land on the other side of the Yarra.

'It's planned to be a new park,' Andrew explained. 'Come on, we'll take a quick look and see how it's coming along.'

The sign on the fence said it was soon to be the Melbourne

Botanic Gardens. The large tract of land seemed to be just wetlands and swamps with a few gnarled, ancient trees.

'It doesn't look much like a garden. How will they do all that?' Jane enquired.

'I expect they'll drain the swamps, so that people can walk around and look at the trees,' Andrew said. 'I don't know much more about it, apart from the name of that big tree, over there, which is a eucalyptus tree. I hear that Mr La Trobe, the Superintendent of Melbourne, has great plans for the town.'

'I met him. Well, he came to speak to us on the ship, when we got here, last October.' Jane pointed to a small group of Aboriginal people sheltering in the shade of the great eucalyptus tree. Parrots flew in and out in the canopy; their brilliant green plumage illuminated by the creamy white bark of the tree. 'What are they doing in there?'

'Where? What, those Aborigines?'

'Yes. I think I know that boy. Yes.' Jane raised her hand and waved at the boy. 'Jimmy?'

It was him. He waved back at Jane, and said something to the woman beside him. They both came over to the fence. The woman looked to be Jimmy's mother, both were handsome, with matching smiles for Jane.

'My English name is Sally. My boy says you are his friend.' The woman spoke in English, too.

'We met on the beach. Jimmy's a very good swimmer,' Jane replied. 'Do you live here?'

'Yes, just there, under the sacred tree.'

Jane frowned and looked at Andrew, who fidgeted, as if the mention of the sacred tree had set off an itch. 'We need to get back to the paper,' he said.

Jane smiled at Jimmy and his mother. 'I must go back to work. We'll meet again.'

They walked back to the office and stopped at a bakery to buy a mutton pie to share for their dinner. Jane made the tea and when they had eaten they started the print run.

* * *

The owner of the Odyssey, Harold Stephenson, left the editing and printing to his son and only appeared at the office for an hour or so each day. Jane enjoyed Andrew's company at work and she relished the challenge of typesetting to a deadline.

One morning, shortly after they had met Jimmy and his mother, Jane spoke to Andrew. 'I've written an article about the Botanic Gardens. Will you read it and tell me what you think?'

'I'll look at it now,' he said and held his hand out.

She handed him the sheet of paper.

New Botanic Gardens for Melbourne, March 1847

Work is due to start soon on Mr La Trobe's latest project, a grand Botanic Gardens for the people of Melbourne to enjoy.

There is just one problem. The land is already taken. It is home to Aboriginal people and at least one of the trees is sacred to them.

Andrew laughed. 'Is this a joke?'

'No, not at all. I think we need to write about new things. What if we add a picture of the eucalyptus tree we saw the other day?' Jane added. 'Is that possible?'

'We print pictures on some of our leaflets. They're wood-cuts and more expensive, so we don't use them in the newspaper. But that's not what I mean, Jane. I think it's a good thing to write about the new Gardens, we can develop the idea. But you can't write about the Aborigines who live there. That will have to come out.'

'Why?'

'Because no-one's interested to read about them.' He dipped his pen in the inkwell and struck through the lines.

Jane stayed silent. Andrew seemed confused, unsure what to say next. She decide to try another tack.

'And there's another thing,' she said. 'The front page of the newspaper. It's all advertisements.'

'Jane, it's the Odyssey and Advertiser. That's why people buy it!' Andrew shook his head. 'I don't know!' She saw him relax a little, as if on safer ground, maybe.

'Yes, they buy it for the advertisements, but they want news about Melbourne as well, don't they? Perhaps if this article were on the front page, then people would buy the paper to read about the Botanic Gardens. Then they'd read the advertisements, too.'

'I don't think that would work. Anyway, what would Mr La Trobe say? It's his project.'

Jane rubbed her hands together. 'Exactly! We need to interview him and find out his plans. Then we can print this as a report.'

The two looked at each other. 'Don't tell Pa! We'll surprise him.' Andrew said. He said no more about her struck out lines in the article.

* * *

Jane's diary entry for 25th March, 1847.

Andrew liked my idea for an article about the new Botanic

Gardens. He's got us an interview with Sir Charles La Trobe. The Botanic Garden is his idea. Sir Charles will like people here to read about his ideas for Melbourne. I'm going to ask him what will happen to Jimmy and his family. They live on that land. Does he plan to evict them?

* * *

They were to meet Superintendent La Trobe at his home in Jolimont, only a short walk from the newspaper offices. They arrived at a simple cottage, it certainly wasn't the grand house Jane expected to see, and completely different to the mansions under construction nearby. Nevertheless, the cottage was easily many times the size of Jane's home back in Galway. This was clad with timber, had plenty of glazed windows and a chimney at either end of the long, low building.

Mr La Trobe's housekeeper showed them into his office. The sound of children playing in the back garden carried along the hall as they came face-to-face with Charles La Trobe. He was a handsome man in his forties, and his friendly smile dominated a narrow, lively face.

They knew from his title as Superintendent of New South Wales that he was a busy man, yet he seemed pleased to sit and talk with them about his projects.

'I've got great plans for Melbourne,' he said. 'It will be a beautiful city in a few years' time.'

'We want to tell our readers about your plans, in more detail,' Andrew said.

La Trobe outlined his ideas for Melbourne. 'I've set aside land for five parks around the town. You've seen the site for the Botanical Gardens, and there's more land for more parks and gardens around the town. In the next ten years, I plan to open libraries and set up a university. This town will be a great city for you young people, and the next generations.'

Jane was puzzled. The money to pay for all this work seemed to be of no concern to him. 'How will all this be paid for, sir?'

'That's a good question, Jane.' La Trobe smiled, as if he had the perfect answer. 'There is a lot of very good land around Melbourne. And it's Crown land, so the government of Melbourne gets to keep some of it when it is sold. The rest goes back to the Government in London, of course. The money we keep will be spent on developing this beautiful part of Australia.'

'Thank you, Mr La Trobe, it's a privilege to hear your plans for Melbourne,' Andrew replied, before Jane could ask another question. 'I'll write up this interview. I'm sure our readers will be delighted to hear your plans.'

'You're welcome, both of you.' Mr La Trobe stood and held his hand out to Andrew.

Jane saw the interview was over and she spoke quickly. 'May I ask a last question, sir?'

The Superintendent smiled at Jane. 'You may, of course.'

'It's to do with the Aboriginal people who live on that land. There are families who live near that big eucalyptus tree.'

'What about them?' La Trobe asked.

'What will become of them, when the gardens are finished?'

'They have no business there, they're trespassing. As soon as work starts in that area, they'll be moved on.'

'Moved where, Mr La Trobe?'

'There'll be somewhere for them further away from the town. There's a Protection Society to deal with the natives.'

La Trobe's tone had hardened, he finished abruptly. The meeting was over.

'Now then, you should have enough information to write a good report about the new Botanic Gardens and the rest of my plans for Melbourne.' He looked at Andrew, and ignored Jane. 'What do you say?'

'Thank you again, sir,' Andrew replied. 'It'll go on the front page of the newspaper.'

They left in silence. Andrew said nothing until they were outside the Superintendent's residence. 'Why on earth did you ask about the Aborigines? He really wasn't pleased. And what have they got to do with the Botanic Gardens?'

'Sure, they live there, Andrew. And because I've seen this before, back home in Ireland. My cousin, Brendan, was evicted from his home, just last year.' Jane paused for a moment. 'His cottage was burned down, and his family put out on the road.' She couldn't say the words to describe his murder. But the sight of Brendan's bloodied face came back to her. She almost tasted again his blood in her mouth and swallowed hard.

'Jane, I'm sorry to hear about your family. But it is different here.'

'Tell me, Andrew, what is different?'

'Well, for one thing these people are natives and they don't understand what we are doing. You can't stop progress.'

'Andrew, wasn't this their land before the English came?'

'I suppose that's true. But it's time for them to make way for us. All that beautiful land around Melbourne is perfect for sheep. It's not been used and it's really valuable land. There's money to be made here. No-one can get in the way of progress, no-one.'

They walked on. In Jane's mind's eye, she saw Brendan's murdered body on the frozen ground; his wife, Aoife's, face livid with fury and grief; their small children stunned, as if under a spell. Make way for 'Progress'. Is that what they all had to do?

* * *

Back at the newspaper, Andrew handed his notes on the La Trobe interview to Jane and left her to add more information to the article while he went to arrange a woodcut of the ancient eucalyptus tree. They agreed to print the article in the Saturday morning edition. The whole front page would be given over to Charles La Trobe's great vision for Melbourne. The usual front page advertisements for jobs, wool auctions, rooms in boarding houses, and the rest, were shifted on to page two. There would be no mention of the fate of Jimmy's family.

* * *

Jane's diary entry for Saturday, March 27th, 1847.

The meeting went well. Sir Charles told us all about his plans for parks and gardens around the town. He said in the next ten years there will be libraries and a university. He is really keen to leave his mark on the town. Andrew and I wrote up an article about the gardens. Sir Charles wasn't pleased when I asked him about the Aborigines who live there. He said they were trespassing and told me to talk to the Protection Society.

Later that same day, Andrew's father, arrived earlier than usual. He slammed the main door shut behind him and locked it. 'Get in here, Andrew and Jane. Right now!' Mr Stephenson shouted.

Jane was in the print room and came through to see what the commotion was about. Stephen was at his desk and she went over to stand next to him, while Mr Stephenson shook the newspaper at them.

'What the hell is all this? What have you done to my paper?' He held up a copy of the first edition. He must have bought it on the way to the office, and he threw it on the table in front of Andrew.

'Pa, we decided to try something different,' Andrew said. He picked up the newspaper and smoothed out the pages on the desk.

'And whose idea is this?' Andrew's father turned to face Jane. 'It's you, isn't it? My son would never do a thing like this, behind my back!'

'Yes, sir. It was my idea. We wanted to surprise you. Have you read the article?' Jane clenched her hands by her sides. She hadn't thought the owner would be enraged by a small change in layout. Maybe she had misjudged.

'Of course I haven't read it yet! I don't need to! I saw this picture on the front page and came straight here. You don't come in here and change my paper behind my back.' His face turned an even brighter puce colour than when he first arrived. He caught his breath and started again. 'I'll lose my advertisers, they're always on page one and two. And I'll have you two to thank for bankrupting the business!'

The owner's rant was interrupted by a rapid knocking on the front door. Jane breathed a sigh of relief, and went to open the door. It was urgent, whatever it was.

Two paper-boys stood at the doorway with big smiles on

their faces. The older one spoke. 'We've been sent from Smith's. We need more newspapers. They've sold out.'

Jane looked at the boys, then, as she realised what this meant, she clenched her fist. 'Yes!' She looked at Andrew, who had understood, and smiled at her.

'Come with me,' he said to the paper-boys. 'I'll get you some more.' He glanced at his father. 'I've done a second print run.'

He took the boys off into the print room, and left Jane alone with the owner.

Mr Stephenson picked up the paper from Andrew's desk and headed for his office. 'I'm going to read this now. If I don't like it, you're sacked, Jane Power !'

* * *

Jane's diary entry for Sunday, March 28th, 1847.

Mr Stephenson was very angry we printed the article on the front page of The Odyssey. I was sure he would sack me, because he can't sack his son. He said we had upset his advertisers, but the paper sold out in all the shops yesterday.

Mr Stephenson gave Andrew the job of explaining the new editorial policy to the advertisers. News about Melbourne will go on the front page from now on. Now we have to find stories to print every day. I got a pay rise. I'll write and tell Annie.

It was her day off, so after mass, she went to find the man in charge of the Port Phillip Protectorate Society. She found the Assistant Protector, Mr William Thomas. He was a stout man in his fifties, and he finished harnessing his horse to the small cart while she explained her reason for coming to find him.

'I read the article about the Botanic Gardens, Miss Power.

Most informative. But why do you want to investigate the Aborigines?' he asked.

'I met a family of Aborigines who live in the Botanic gardens and they will be moved off soon. Mr La Trobe said you would know where they'll be resettled.'

Mr Thomas took his hat off and scratched his head. 'Mr La Trobe, you say? Hm! There's a new settlement further inland right enough.' He looked at Jane. 'And you'll write an article about this?'

'Yes, I'll write what I see. And if you tell me about your job, I'll write about that too.'

'I'm off on a visit now. You're welcome to come along, Miss Power.' He loaded a few blankets onto the back of the cart and hauled himself up and took the reins. 'Will Mr Stephenson print your article would you say?'

Jane threw her bag onto the cart and climbed up to sit beside Mr Thomas. He looked across at her as he flicked the reins. Neither spoke.

* * *

They drove up towards the west of the town and out to the grasslands. The Aboriginal settlement they headed to was just a few miles further inland. Before they got there, Jane saw a plume of smoke on the horizon, and smelled the sharp tang of burning on the breeze.

The Assistant Protector glanced at Jane. 'Dear Lord,' he murmured. He gave the horse an extra tap with the whip, and the cart jolted across the grassland, towards the smoke, then it stopped at the burnt-out site.

There was not a soul to be seen, just flattened grass

211

surrounded by smouldering poles and bark, the covering used for the Aborigine's huts. They both jumped down from the cart.

'Where is everyone?' Jane asked.

'They have been dispersed, I fear,' her companion replied.

'Where to?' she asked again.

'They will have gone into the hills,' he pointed further to the north. 'There's another reservation over that way.'

'Then shall we go and find them?' Jane looked at the blackened poles of the Aborigines' shelters. She saw shattered pots, and picked up a broken spear.

Mr Thomas nodded and held his hand out to help her back up on the cart.

They set off again across the open meadowland. In the distance she saw a dark forested area, but there must have been miles of undulating grasslands, with small stands of trees dotted along the horizon.

After a while they slowed down to make way for a great flock of sheep, led by one shepherd, on foot. The sheep had dense, creamy white fleece. The animals were fat and clearly fed well on the rich grassland.

'There must be hundreds in this one flock,' Jane said.

'Yes,' Mr Thomas replied. 'This is perfect land for sheep rearing. The whole place is given over to sheep runs.'

He called out to the shepherd. 'We're looking for *abos*. They've just been moved on from further down.'

'Keep going, they're on the new reservation,' the old fellow said.

Just half an hour later, they saw the reservation up ahead. It was near a stream, and there were a few eucalyptus trees for shelter.

Then Jane understood why the Mr Thomas had brought blankets with him. One family group consisted of three generations, and most of them, young and old, were nearly naked. The father of the group came over to speak to Mr Thomas. Jane caught her breath to see such thinness in a man, every bone in his body on display, just under the surface of his skin. Only in Ireland had she seen its match. 'It's here, too,' she murmured.

She stood back and watched as her companion spoke to the man. Mr Thomas shook his head, then handed over a small parcel of blankets and came back to the cart.

'Is that it?' she asked.

'Their elder told me they were sent here last night. They were cleared off the site by an armed gang. They said they were police, but that can't be true.' The Assistant Protector sighed. 'It's happening more and more. If the Aborigines refuse to move, they threaten to shoot them and drive them off the land.'

'Tell me, sir, how is this a reservation? Sure, there's nothing here.'

'It's my job to arrange food and clothing for them. But in times like this, I don't get any warning. I'll arrange for food supplies to be sent out in the next day or two. If I can get some money. '

'Do you have anyone to report this to?'

'You mean the clearances?'

Jane's stomach turned at the familiar word, but she nodded. Mr Thomas explained. 'The Superintendent, Mr La Trobe, is in charge. I have a duty to these poor people, but I don't have any money to spend on food and blankets.'

'And what will become of them in winter? That's not far

off.'

'They tend to move away before then, Jane.'

'Where to?'

'I think they head into the forests and the hilly land out west,' he replied.

They both got back onto the cart and Mr Thomas clicked for the horse to move off across the wide green meadow. The autumn sun was lower in the sky, and the breeze had an edge to it.

* * *

On the way back to Melbourne, the cart trundled past the burnt out village. The flock of sheep they had seen earlier in the day had already colonised the grassland, hungry for more grass. It was as if the Aboriginal families had never lived there.

22

Annie Power: March 1847. The Refuge

Annie was nearly ready to open the cottage. She would call it the Refuge. She knew that she'd have to give up her job when she got her first residents and had put Sister Fidelma on notice about her plans.

That morning in March, she made her way along the Broadway, towards the orphanage. She tried to push through a crowd of people, but stopped when she saw that they were waiting to cross the street. A similar crowd of dark-clad people stood on the opposite side of the road. As soon as a gap appeared between the speeding traffic, the two groups of people stepped onto the road and rushed across. The first few had a free run, the ones who followed had to dodge the oncoming pedestrians, as if all were running in fear for their lives.

Annie was jostled and stumbled. She caught hold of the arm of a man next to her. She turned to thank the man, but he shook her arm off and rushed onwards.

Annie reached the pavement and stepped into a doorway.

Her head felt light and dizzy, so she stood for a moment to catch her breath. A dark cloud floated across her eyes, and she bent her knees and crouched down, leaning her back against the side of the doorway. She felt a tear run down her cheek, then closed her eyes, unable to keep them open. After a moment or two she heard a groan, and knew it was her own voice. She felt a hand touch her shoulder.

'Miss, miss, are you all right?' She heard the voice but couldn't open her eyes. She breathed out, then in, and forced herself to speak. 'I feel a bit dizzy. I'll be fine in a minute. Thank you.' The person moved away.

Annie brushed her hair away from her face and finally managed to open her eyes. She pushed her arms out and pressed her hands against the gritty red bricks of the alcove and forced herself to stand up. The blackness receded. Her legs trembled for the first few steps, so she took her time and let the crowds flow past her. 'Don't fall, take your time,' she urged herself.

She was a few minutes late for the start of lessons, and by then the dizziness had passed, but it had left her puzzled and unsure of herself.

By the end of the day, Annie felt better, but it had taken most of that time to shake off the weakness in her limbs.

She got back to the apartment and started the dinner. An ox-tail had been simmering in a big pot on the range since the night before. Annie scrubbed, peeled and chopped some carrots, onions and swedes and threw them into the pot on top of the meat. She added more coal to the range and the pot started to bubble, the lid puffed lightly off the rim of the pot, then down again, as the stew cooked.

She sat and helped Katty with her homework and waited

for Finn to come home. At every meal they said Grace, and thanked God, and their aunt Bridie, for the food on the table. They remembered those who had nothing to eat and prayed for an end to the Famine in Ireland.

* * *

After supper, the three siblings walked round to the Refuge to continue the work of getting it habitable. Annie and Finn had scrubbed the floorboards and washed down all the windows. 'Glass in the windows. I just can't get over it. Sure, you'd rarely see glass in windows in Ireland, apart from in Dublin, of course.' Annie smoothed her polishing cloth across the inside of the sash window, as if burnishing a precious jewel. 'It'll be my job to keep these clean.'

Katty was making a pot of tea in the kitchen and poured out three cups for them.

Finn had made a start on building some bookshelves in the parlour of the house. He had found a few planks of wood at the end of the garden. Then he borrowed a plane, a saw, a hammer and nails from the Bishop's gardener. After he had planed the timber, he measured it and and had already installed two of four shelves he planned for the space next to the chimney breast. Annie huffed impatiently. 'How much longer will you be? I want to put these books on there.'

'Annie, look, you can see I'll be done in another few minutes.'

Annie took herself off to the kitchen to wait for the shelves to be finished.

* * *

217

On the following Monday evening, Annie helped Bridie to tidy up the kitchen after they had eaten their supper.

She got ready to go out again, and saw that Finn had put his coat and boots on and waited for her at the door.

'Where do you think you're you going?'

'I'm going with you, sister.' Finn replied. Annie saw a look pass between Finn and Bridie.

'You've hatched this between you, haven't you?' Annie smiled. 'I don't need any help.'

'You always need help, Annie. Admit it!' Finn replied. He passed it off as a joke, but she could see that he was serious.

'Well, it is getting a bit dark out there. Let's go now.'

The two siblings went off arm-in-arm and walked down Broadway towards the park where Annie had seen the girl, all those months ago. Night was drawing in and Annie began to have second thoughts about her decision to venture out so late.

'I'm not sure if coming out now is such a good idea, Finn,' she said. 'There's not much light.'

'That cloud will move away from the moon and we'll see better in a few minutes.' Finn was as tall as Annie, at almost fifteen, and still had more growing to do. He had a huge appetite for food ever since they had arrived in New York. Maybe it was because he had gone hungry in that hard year before they left Ireland.

Lately, they had stopped talking about back home, but to Annie, he looked more and more like her father, not just in his looks, but in his mannerisms, his dry sense of humour, and his care for his sisters.

They arrived at the park, and with arms linked, strolled around the outskirts. The fountain had been switched off over the winter, and remained silent and empty. A full moon overhead illuminated the stone construction and the seats around it. Although it wasn't late, around eight o'clock, there was business going on in the dark corners. Annie saw transactions arranged and couples walk off together to find an alley for their trade.

'Where is she?' she whispered.

'Why does it have to be her, Annie?' Finn asked.

Annie sighed. '*Acushla*, I saw her with Sinead in February. I think she could have been Sinead's sister.'

Finn pointed out a girl beside an older woman. 'Her?'

'No, they're just out for a walk, would you say?'

The older woman stopped a passerby and they spoke for a minute. The man shook his head and moved off. Annie and Finn glanced at each other both nodded and approached the two females.

'*An Gaeilge tú?* Are you Irish?' Finn asked the younger woman. She glanced at him and replied in the affirmative. '*Is ea.* Yes.' She was Irish, then. The two words betrayed her northern Irish roots.

The older woman gave her companion a light punch on the arm. The girl looked to be about fourteen or fifteen, just a slip of a thing.

'*Dhia dhuit,* God be with you.' Annie greeted the girl who responded in Gaelic, '*Dhia is Mhuire dhuit.* God and Mary be with you.' The girl's eyes glittered with tears. Annie knew the feeling of hearing her own language, in this English-speaking world, and she nodded to the girl.

'What are you saying?' The woman was old enough to be the girl's grandmother, but she spoke with an American accent. The punch had let Annie see that this was not a caring adult, and possibly not a relation.

'We want your girl,' Annie said.

'Oh, I see!' the woman replied with a smirk. 'For the young man, is it?'

'No, we're taking her with us,' Annie clarified, and saw understanding in the woman's eyes.

'Don't you come down here do-gooding. Clear off!' The woman caught the girl's arm. 'She's mine. I look after her, don't I?'

The girl's eyes darted from Annie to the woman and back to Annie, who smiled at her. In truth, Annie could barely breathe, but she spoke with a strong voice, not to the older woman, but to her Irish compatriot and in Gaelic.

'My name is Annie Power, and this is my brother, Finn. We've come to help you. What's your name?'

'We're going.' The older woman hadn't understood what they saying but she pulled at the girl's arm and began to walk off with her. The girl looked back at Annie. 'Colleen O'Brien.'

Annie followed them and spoke again in Irish. 'Will you come with us? We'll help you.'

The girl said again. '*Is ea!* Yes!'

At that moment Annie heard an owl hoot in the nearby tree. She glanced up and saw the creature, wings outspread as he flew past them, his white face swivelled to look at her.

She laughed, then stepped forward and held out her hand. 'Come on, then!'

Colleen freed herself from the woman's grip and caught Annie's hand. Annie embraced the girl. She was small, she only came up to Annie's shoulder. Annie felt her tremble.

'We're going. Don't try to stop us' Annie shook off the older woman's hand and she and Finn and Colleen raced away and out of the park.

The screams and the shouts of the woman followed them across the road and could still be heard when they turned on to Broadway. They walked fast and soon the sounds were lost in the distance.

* * *

They went straight to the Cathedral, then to the cemetery behind the great church. Annie led the way to the Refuge, unlocked the door and held it open. Colleen walked through to the hall and looked around her.

'Come into the parlour,' Annie said

They sat together on the sofa beside the embers of the fire Annie had lit earlier that day.

'Do you live here?' Colleen asked.

'I do now,' Annie replied. 'I've set this up to help single women, and I've been waiting for my first resident, and here you are.'

Annie pressed her hands against the seat of the horsehair-stuffed sofa. The seat was firm, all the springs worked; she'd tested it when she saw it at a second-hand furniture market. In Ireland, they'd never had a sofa back in their cabin. Just the chair for Da, a couple of stools, and the bed in the corner. This was luxury.

She'd spent half her money on furniture, for the parlour and the beds and bedding; there were three doubles and a single bed upstairs, all second-hand, but in good condition. She'd scrubbed the mattress covers and bedsteads then made them up with warm blankets and a bolster for each bed. The beds would sleep a total of six, sharing, and a single bed for herself in the small bedroom. And there was room for more beds if the refuge filled up. Annie had bargained hard for the sofa and stools for the parlour. She planned to use the money she had left to buy clothes for the new occupants. The kitchen was stocked up with vegetables, oats and barley. She'd buy fresh milk and Bridie had promised to show her how to bake soda bread. But now, they were ready to open. Just the one job left to do. Ask Bishop Hughes to bless the Refuge. She'd do that soon.

* * *

After she had related the story of the Refuge to Colleen, they went through to the kitchen where Annie cut some bread and cheese for a supper for her new resident. There was hot water on the stove for tea and the three young people sat around the table while Colleen ate.

'Thank you,' Colleen said, after she had eaten her fill. She had a low voice and Annie tried to place her accent. It was somewhere from the north of Ireland.

Annie put her hand out to her first resident. 'Tell us how you got here.'

'I left Ireland after my mother and father died from the hunger. My brothers were put into an orphanage, in Letterkenny, but I was too old, I'm fifteen. I looked for work in the town. I just wanted to get my brothers back.' She stopped speaking. Annie saw the heartbreak in Colleen's eyes.

'There was no work, was there?' Annie asked.

'No. One of our neighbours was emigrating to America and they brought me with them. I thought I'd earn some money here and send for my brothers.

222

'Then my neighbours heard about the free land further west, and they set out last November. Mrs Stapleton, who ran the boarding house, said she'd look after me and help me find work. But I've worked as a prostitute for months now. She told me she'd kill me, if I left.' Colleen's tears, like hot beads, fell down her narrow, haunted face. 'But I had to take a chance with you. Please don't let them take me back.'

Annie put her arm around Colleen's shoulders. 'They won't take you back. You're here now and you're safe. We'll talk again, tomorrow. You look worn out. I'd say you'd like a good wash before you go to bed. Finn, there's hot water on the stove, will you . . ?'

Finn, who had sat and listened to Colleen's story, jumped up. 'I'll do it now, ladies.' He filled the sink with warm water from the kettle on the hob and fetched a towel, flannel and soap.

'Annie, I'm away home. I'll tell Bridie and Katty.' Finn kissed his sister. 'Good night, Colleen. You'll be safe here. Annie will take care of you.' Then he left.

Annie locked the door and came back into the parlour and saw Colleen's head drooping from exhaustion. 'Come on. I'll help you to get ready for bed, then show you where you're sleeping.'

In the kitchen, Colleen began to undress. She wore a dirty white blouse and frilled, green patterned skirt, not much cleaner than the blouse. Annie didn't comment on the bruises and marks on Colleen's small body, but saw that she had been hard-done-by in recent weeks and months.

'I have a clean shift upstairs, I'll go and fetch it. You can wear it in bed and you can borrow one of my dresses till we get you some new clothes. They'll be only second-hand from the market, but you can choose. We'll go tomorrow.'

She left Colleen to get washed and dressed in the clean shift and came back a few minutes later, then they went upstairs together to the larger of the bedrooms.

'You're my first resident,' Annie said. 'And you are welcome to stay here until you find your own job and place to live. I can help you do that. Now, here's your bed, have a good rest. You'll have to share when the place fills up, but it'll be only girls and women.'

Colleen sat on the bed and looked up at Annie. 'Thank you, Annie. Do you pray?'

'Every day, Colleen.'

'I pray for my brothers. I have to earn money. Then I'll send for them to come and join me.'

'We'll talk tomorrow.' Annie promised. She went to get ready for bed herself. This would be her first night in the Refuge. She knelt beside her bed and blessed herself. 'Thank you, dear Lord, and your Blessed Mother, for helping me to start this Refuge. Keep us safe here, under your protection.'

She slept well that night, for knew she could help Colleen, and was determined to find others like her. That was her mission, to fill the Refuge with women and girls; yes, some like Sinead, the girl she had failed to save, and others who had travelled alone from Ireland in search of a better life.

* * *

The next few weeks were busy ones, and Annie forgot to speak to her aunt about her dizzy spells, until she suffered another spell of fainting. This time she was with Bridie in the kitchen of the Refuge.

'How long has this been going on for?' Bridie asked.

'I get dizzy that's all, Bridie. I think it's a bit of the fever I had on the ship.'

'Sure, that nearly nine months or more ago. It can't be that.'

'Then, I don't know what it is.'

'It's time you saw a doctor. I know the right person for you to see, Doctor Miller. He looked after Kevin when he was ill and he was very good to him. I'll make an appointment for us to go and see him together.'

* * *

The next week, Annie met Bridie at Saint Vincent's hospital. Annie shivered, for she remembered Jane's tales of the work-house back in Galway. She was afraid this might be the same. But Bridie brought her through to a clean and airy building, with long, white-washed corridors. The doctor's office was in an annex so they didn't need to go near any wards. He had a friendly face and greeted Bridie, asked them both to sit down.

'Bridie, I glad to see you're looking well, and this is your niece, Annie?'

'Yes, Doctor. Annie's not been right lately, so I thought we'd come and get you to take a look at her.'

The physician turned to Anne. 'Tell me, Annie. What's been troubling you?'

'It's nothing serous, Doctor. But every so often I feel faint and my legs give way. I'm alright then, after a while.'

'Anything else, any aches and pains, coughs?'

'Only a bit of a cough. But ever since I had the fever last year, I don't have much of an appetite. Mostly, it's just the fainting. I can't seem to breathe, then everything goes black.'

'I think I'd better examine you. I'll have a listen to your chest and your heart, while you're here. Unbutton your blouse there.'

He put the end of the stethoscope against her chest and listened. 'Don't forget to breathe, Annie.' He smiled. 'Now, turn around and I'll listen to your back. Just slip off your blouse.'

Annie sat and faced Bridie, whose own expression seemed unreadable.

Bridie reached out and held Annie's hand, but she was watching the doctor, then she nodded to him.

The doctor moved the stethoscope across Annie's back and down to her waist. She felt his breath against her skin. He took his time, and paused for a moment. Then he tapped her shoulder. 'Get dressed now, Annie.' He sat back down at his desk and waited for Annie to finish buttoning her blouse.

'Well, your heart is fine and strong. That's a good thing.' He paused for a moment. 'But I'm not too sure about your lungs. The right lung, in particular, sounds a bit congested.'

Bridie looked from Annie to the doctor. 'In what way, congested, Doctor?'

'I can't say. I'd like to consult a colleague. Tell me, Annie, have you had any history of consumption in the family?'

'Consumption? No. Why? Do you think I've got that?'

'I can't be sure. And it's not a diagnosis I'd make on one examination. As I said, I'd like to get you seen by a chest specialist. Don't worry at the moment. It's probably what you think it is, a hangover from the fever you had on the journey here. Leave it with me and I'll get in touch with you and Bridie, when I've spoken to my colleague. For now, go home and be sure to rest. Are you working at the moment?'

'I've just finished work, at the Sisters of Mercy Orphanage. I've opened a refuge and I'll be helping young women and girls.'

'I suggest you take a week off, and rest. I'll let Bridie know about the appointment. It shouldn't take long. He works here at the hospital.'

They left and walked home together without speaking. At the door to the apartment building, Annie said. 'Don't mention this to Finn and Katty.'

She climbed the stairs to the apartment. No, she decided, her lungs were fine. She'd be fine.

* * *

One evening at the end of March, Annie and Colleen lit the oil lamps in the parlour and the upstairs bedrooms of the refuge. Bridie was busy in the kitchen preparing the tea and cake for their visitors. This was the formal blessing of the refuge.

They took it in turns to open the front door and check if their honoured guests were on the way. Annie looked out past the stone wall at the edge of the cemetery. 'They're not here yet. Sure, they wouldn't be late now would they?'

'Annie, it's still only early.' Bridie called from the kitchen. 'The Angelus bell only rang a short while ago. Sister Mary Angela and Sister Fidelma definitely won't be late.'

Annie sighed and waited by the door. 'Here they come!' She hurried over to greet the two nuns. Bishop Hughes and Pat Brady were a few yards behind them.

Dusk was falling, the sun had set half an hour before and Annie turned back to look at the cottage. The windows were lit with a warm honey glow from the lamps inside. She smiled.

Bridie and Finn stood together in the doorway. Katty and Colleen had stepped outside to wait.

The two nuns stopped to look at the house. 'Why, I had forgotten this was such a lovely spot, Annie.' Sister Mary Angela said.

By then the Bishop and Pat Brady had caught up with them and greeted Bridie and Finn at the door.

Bridie motioned to Annie. 'Annie will show you around. Then we'll have a cup of tea.'

Annie led the way upstairs to the two bedrooms. More lamps gleamed, their golden light refracted on the dark floorboards. The rooms were spartan, just the beds and a small chest of drawers beside each bed.

'Bishop Hughes,' Annie said. I want to introduce Colleen O'Brien, our first guest. She's been here for two weeks now and I'm helping her look for work.'

Colleen kissed the Bishop's ring. He put his other hand on her head and blessed her. 'God be with you, my child. May you have good fortune in your endeavours.'

He had brought along a narrow purple stole and he kissed it before placing it around his neck. 'I'll bless this part of the house, while we're here.' The Bishop blessed himself and Annie and the rest of them did the same. They all bowed their heads.

'Dear Lord, we thank you for Annie's determination to set up this refuge for Irish girls and women. We pray that this dwelling will become a place of safety and happiness for all who sleep under its roof.' Sister Mary Angela handed a small silver container with a wooden handle to the Bishop. He held it up and shook it. Drops of holy water scattered in the air. 'In the name of the Father and the Son and the Holy Ghost.'

All joined in the 'Amen!'

They trooped downstairs and the bishop repeated his blessing in the kitchen and the parlour.

Sister Mary Angela, put her hand on the bookshelves. 'Ah, this is where you keep your books.' She put her hand into her bag and pulled out the book she had borrowed from Annie.

'I brought it back. I'll put it just here, right next to the Bible.' The nun turned to Colleen. 'Have you read any of Annie's books yet?'

Colleen nodded. 'I'm working through the primers. I missed the last few years of school, so it's given me a chance to catch up, Sister.'

Bridie called them through to the kitchen. 'There's a nice piece of cake and a cup of tea waiting for you.'

When everyone had eaten and drank their fill, Annie stood to speak.

'I want to say thank you. First, to Bishop Hughes for lending me this beautiful cottage. Then to Sister Mary Angela and Sister Fidelma. Your support has helped me no end. Thank you to Mr Brady, for the donation from the Aid for Ireland Committee. That'll keep us fed for a few months. And Finn and Katty, thank you both. Finn, the bookshelves are beautiful. Katty, for helping me clean the house. Then there's Bridie. Thank you for giving us a home. I'd not have been able to do this without all of your help.' Annie smiled and nodded, hearing the clapping and congratulations.

Annie held her hand up. 'And one more. Thank you, Colleen, for trusting me. You're my first guest and now my friend. Thank you.' They hugged.

Later, when everyone was leaving, Sister Fidelma stayed back to speak to Annie. 'I have a pair of twins at the orphanage and they need to move on. One of them, Niamh, is a cheeky madam. Will you take them and help them get work, Annie? I can't do any more for them.'

'If they want to come, they'll be welcome. Bring them tomorrow.' Annie said.

* * *

After her visitors had left, Annie locked the front and back doors. She joined Colleen in the kitchen and they washed and dried the cups and plates.

'You're so good, Annie. So clever and kind.' Colleen said.

Annie shook her head. 'No, I'm just determined. But thank you. It's a great feeling to have this place blessed and open. Now we just have to fill it and start finding jobs. Sister Fidelma has a couple of twins, they'll be along tomorrow. Will you help me?'

Colleen had finished the washing up and said. 'I'd love to help. I'm off to bed now. I'll see you in the morning. Good night, Annie, God bless.'

'God bless you, Colleen.'

Annie banked down the fire and closed the iron door of the stove to keep the heat in overnight. She walked through to the parlour and blew out the lamps. She picked the autobiography of Frederick Douglass off the shelf and took it upstairs with her to bed.

It had been a long time since she had felt so satisfied with her life. She put her finger in a few drops of holy water that lay on her bedside table and blessed herself. She knew that she would sleep well that night. The book lay unopened beside her bed.

230

23

Jane Keating: Mid-April 1847. Port Phillip Bay.

J ane liked to swim in the mornings before she started her shift in the afternoons. On Sundays she'd go to mass then walk to the beach for her swim. The weather had been good all that summer, but by now it was well into autumn.

On that Sunday, Owen had some free time and joined her for his first swimming lesson after mass. They walked to the beach together. After half an hour of walking, they had left behind the Sunday strollers and came to a deserted stretch of sand. The woods along the edge of the sand provided some shelter for the two to get changed out of their clothes.

Most days, when she was alone, she swam naked, but this morning, in company, she kept her drawers on and wore a cotton shift. Owen wore cream linen shorts to his knees. The top half of his body was naked. Pale skin showed through his dark chest hair, just his face and forearms were tanned. His slim body was muscled and she glanced sideways at him as they raced into the sea.

'My God, it's cold!' Owen said, and stopped when the water

reached his knees.

Jane kept going past him and dipped down into the water.

'Huh!' she gasped. 'Come on in!' Then she stood, waist deep in the water, and held her hand out to him.

Owen caught up with her. They turned, feet sinking into the sand underfoot, and looked out to where the blue water shelved away into deeper green water.

'Right. Lay back against my hands,' Jane said. 'I'll hold your shoulders, and you straighten your legs out and kick a little.' She put her hands against his shoulders. He leaned back and looked up into her eyes and smiled. 'Don't let me go.'

'I have you.' She held him while he learned to stay afloat. She felt his body relax as he gained confidence in the water. Only then did Jane let him go. She floated beside him in the water and moved her hands and feet to keep her level with Owen. Her hair moved around her face in the water and she looked up at the heavens. The sun was almost at its zenith and glowed a pale gold against the faded blue of the sky. She glanced at him, at his smiling face close to hers. 'You've done this before, Owen Doran.'

He laughed and almost choked on a mouthful of seawater. 'And tell me this, how was I to get your hands on me any other way?' Then he swam off out to deeper water and she chased him and splashed water at him. They swam together for a while, then Jane said.

'You go and dry off. I'll have another swim for a minute,' and kicked away into deeper water. She had enjoyed touching his skin in the water, the smooth muscle of his arms and shoulders, the fine hair on his back, but felt shy now that she knew he had tricked her.

He was the first man she had touched intimately. But he

wasn't the first who had touched her; she had been mauled by constables in Tipperary, assaulted by that crewman on the transportation ship and the worst, raped by her employer.

Instead, this was her touching another, and she liked the feel of his skin under her hand, his strength. She wondered what it would be like to kiss his lips and smiled to herself.

Owen was dried and dressed by the time she finished her swim and walked up the beach to the tree line. Her shift clung to her and showed off her round belly.

She saw him look at her and narrow his eyes, then he glanced away out towards the bay.

* * *

When she was dressed, she sat next to him in the sea-grass at the edge of the trees.

'You know, don't you?' She looked into his dark blue eyes and saw only compassion, then he nodded.

'How far gone are you?'

'Since the Colonel, the beginning of December. Nearly five months. I've only found out a few weeks ago. And I've not told anyone. Colonel Johns knows, I think.'

'How do you mean?'

'He saw me a while back, on the bridge. He said I'm getting fat, and that he's not done with me yet. I didn't know what he meant about getting fat. Then later, I found out.'

She thought she was past tears but they fell, hot against her cheeks, and she picked at the spiky sea-grass and twisted it with her fingers as if it had the answer to her problems. 'I need to get away from here, Owen.'

Owen reached over and took her hand in his. 'Have you

told anyone at all? What about Mrs Chisholm, or the women in the dormitory?'

'The only one who knows is the Colonel. Mrs Chisholm is away in England. She won't be back for months. And I can't tell anyone in the dormitory. I don't know anyone really. Besides, they have their own worries.' She wiped her eyes and looked at her only friend. 'Owen, do you think he'll take my baby?'

'I don't know. But I wouldn't put it past him, if he wants to punish you. Janey, I'll do what I can to help you.' Owen said. 'You know I've signed up for twenty years in the army and I go where I'm sent. But while I'm here, I'll help you.'

'Thank you.' She didn't repeat what she had said about not staying, but it was set in her mind.

He stood and stretched his hand out to Jane. 'Here, take my hand.'

They walked back to the bridge together. The joy of the swimming lesson had been tempered by Jane's realisation that the Colonel might very well take her baby. Then she would have to kill him. Then she would be hanged. She put her hand to her neck, and decided. 'I'll go and talk to Gerald. He'll know what to do.'

* * *

She was cautious. She knew not to go near the Colonel's house but knew also that Gerald bought supplies at a chandlers store in the centre of Melbourne. She called there and learned that he was due to collect an order the next day, and came back early the following morning to wait for him.

After an hour standing outside the store, wrapped in her

shawl, and with a chill breeze blowing through her hair and skirt, she saw him and waved as he jumped down from the cart.

'Gerald! *Dia dhuit!* God be with you!'

He looked over at her and smiled and waved. 'Jane, how are you? You're looking well.'

She held out her hand to shake his. 'I am well, thank you, and happy to see you. I hoped you'd be here, for I need some advice.'

'Well, I suppose now's as good a time as any. Wait while I load up my order. Hop up there and have a seat, then we'll go for a drive out of town.' She climbed up onto the cart, sat on the wooden seat, and waited for him to load the sacks of feed and close up the backboard. Then he got up beside her, clicked the reins and the horse set off at a steady trot.

Gerald glanced sideways at Jane when they were under way. She saw the lines in his face had deepened over the few months since the last time they had met, the day he helped her get away after the rape. His short hair was more grey than brown and he had lost some weight. He looked every minute of his age.

'I cleaned up the place after you'd gone,' he said. 'The Colonel was still unconscious and I left him there on the ground. I don't think he knows that I know what went on there.' Gerald took a deep breath. 'And you. How are you, Jane?'

'I reported him to the army. They won't do anything. And I told them about the other girl, Elsie Corcoran, who disappeared last year. Did you know her?'

'I did. But I said nothing about it. And she was only a bit of a girl. To this day, I'm sorry.'

Jane reached over and put her hand over Gerald's scarred hand. He held the reins and kept his eyes on the road out of town.

'There's another girl there now,' he said. 'I've been keeping an eye on her, but I can't be there the whole time.'

'Do your best by her, won't you?' She took her hand away and brushed her hair back from her face. 'He saw me in town a while ago. And somehow, he saw I was pregnant by him, even before I knew myself.'

'By Christ, he's a vile man! I'm sorry to hear that. What will you do? I know it's late, but I'm of a mind to tell the authorities what I do know. I can back up your account. And maybe put a stop to him.'

Jane nodded. 'That's a good idea, Gerald, and I thank you. But don't do it just yet.'

'Why's that?' Gerald turned to look at her, and she smiled.

'After I found out that I was pregnant, I decided. I'm going to get away from here. I was trying to think how, and I remembered what you told me about the convicts who escaped. Tell me exactly what I need to do to get on a whaling ship to America.'

Gerald nodded. By now they were out of the town, and he pulled the horse and cart over to stop at the side of the road. From there, they overlooked a wide swathe of pastureland that stretched for miles to the horizon. Hundreds of white sheep, their heads down, cropped the grass. The sky was full of pale clouds and Jane saw a couple of men on horseback in the far distance but no other humans, just flat land, wide sky and sheep, for miles and miles.

'I hate this place,' she said. She felt the baby turn in her womb and give a gentle kick. She made a silent promise to her child. You won't be born here, in this prison.

'I'll tell you what I know, girl. It's not much, but it'll maybe give you a chance.' Gerald stepped down from the cart, tethered the horse, and held his hand out to her. 'Let's go for a walk.'

They strolled along a lane leading away from the road. After the summer, the ground was dry, and red dust kicked up from the ruts along the track. Newly installed fencing ran along the edge of the pasture and several sheep pressed up against the wire; their heads poked through to get some of the grass on the edge of the ditch. Jane thought of her friend Jimmy, whose family and tribe had once roamed here. All this was their land, wasn't it? And there were no whaling ships for them to get away on.

'Sorry, Gerald, what did you say?'

'I said, the Americans usually stop at Phillip Island for about a week. At Cowes, on the north of the island. They boil up the whale blubber into oil and store it in barrels then stock up with fresh water. When they've finished, they head off, up the east coast to Queensland and more whaling.' Gerald stopped, bent down and picked up a stone and rubbed it between his fingers. 'Then they set off for home, most are out of Nantucket on the east coast of America. Be very careful though, girl. If you're unlucky, you'll find a British whaling ship, then you're done for. But you know that, don't you?'

Jane smiled and took the stone from him, threw it high into the air and watched it fall to the ground further along the lane. 'Yes. I'll be careful. I've good reason to be, haven't I?'

'That's about all I know. I don't know how you're going to get on one of the ships. They won't have a woman. I'd say. And then there's the timing. The island is busy with whaling ships up to May, then it slacks off in the winter months, so you want to get a move on. When the weather breaks, and it'll be soon, there's not much doing.'

Jane shrugged her shoulders. 'I'd leave tomorrow. But I have a job to finish, it won't take long, then we'll go.'

'We?' Gerald asked.

'Me and my baby.' She felt a big smile stretch her mouth wide and laughed. 'I'll get on a ship. I just need to get there. Someone will take me.'

Gerald shook his head. 'Ah, I see I'd better help you if your mind is made up. Travel at night. I can bring you round the coast to King's Creek. It'll only take a few hours with the horse and cart, and I'll be back before morning. You'll get a ferry across to the island from there.'

Jane was silent for a moment and closed her eyes. In her mind she heard her own voice. *Decide on the day, right now. Say when you're going. . . But I need to print the posters.'*

'A week on Saturday. I'll get off work early and I won't be missed on Sunday morning. Come to me at the Dormitory at midnight. We'll finish my job and go.' She explained the task and he agreed to help her. They hugged and walked back to the cart.

'I'm fine to walk back from here, Gerald. I have an hour before work,' she said. They embraced again.

Gerald got back on the cart and picked up the reins. He paused when Jane called to him.

'When I get to America, I'll send money for an advertisement in the Odyssey, from Jane Keating. That's my real name.'

'I'll look out for it. God bless you, Jane Keating. You're a brave woman. A week on Saturday.' He shook the leather reins and began to turn in the road. The cart creaked, the horse whinnied as the bridle pulled his head around. Gerald headed back to Melbourne.

Jane walked the road back into town and planned her job. She needed to get some time alone on the press, somehow.

24

Annie Power: April 1847. Second Street Docks

Sister Fidelma came to the cottage with the twins. They had a small bag each and were hopping with delight. The nun introduced Niamh and Deirdre.

When Sister Fidelma had left and the front door was closed, one turned to Annie. 'You've saved us, Miss.'

'What have I saved you from, exactly?' Annie asked. 'The nuns have been very kind to you. I know that.'

The red-haired twin, Niamh, laughed. 'Sure, they wanted us to be cleaners at the orphanage. They said t'was time we earned our keep.'

'That's true,' the other twin, Deirdre, said. She had red hair, too, but hers was a darker shade, and less frantic. 'But we'd only be earning our keep. Sure, that's no good. We need to earn money and buy nice clothes. And we'll never meet a man to marry in there.'

Annie laughed with them. 'Aren't you a bit young to be thinking of marrying?'

'Maybe so, but we can look, can't we? We won't find any

men in the convent!'

'Anyway,' Niamh said. 'What jobs have you got for us?'

Annie was silent for a moment. Then answered truthfully. 'None, at the moment. But I said I'd help you find work, and I will.'

She thought fast. If she wanted to keep the girls from walking out of the Refuge, she'd need to convince them that they'd be earning money soon.

'I tell you what. My brother has started a business and he's going to need some assistants to help him. So that is one idea. Don't worry, I've got lots more.'

She really didn't have any other ideas, but her aunt Bridie had helped her before. Maybe she could help again. Annie resolved to speak to both Finn and Bridie.

Colleen showed the girls to the bed they would be sharing. 'Tomorrow, we'll go shopping for some clothes for you.'

Niamh and Deirdre both clapped their hands. The two girls had on quite short dresses, halfway down their calves. They were dressed like children, for now.

Annie smiled to see them so happy and excited.

* * *

Annie and Colleen took the two girls shopping the next day, and they came back with bags of clothes and shoes. The twins tried on their dresses and were transformed into the young women they were, no longer children.

Finn was delighted to meet Niamh and Deirdre. They spent a morning with him to see his food stall in operation.

'But I only need one extra person, Annie,' Finn said later.

241

'I'll talk to Bridie, to see if there are any more jobs in the hospital. ' Annie said. She worried about what to do when she had a houseful of young women.

'I'll bring home a newspaper and we look on there,' Finn added. 'It's full of advertisements for jobs.'

Annie smiled at her brother. 'You have the best ideas!'

They arranged to meet later that evening and go through the newspaper together.

* * *

By the beginning of May, Annie was now familiar with the times of the barges arriving at Second Street Docks. After a week spent watching and waiting, she recognised her next girls the moment they stepped off the same vessel she had arrived on from Quebec.

There were three of them, Annie guessed they were about sixteen or seventeen years of age. They each carried a hold-all, and wore a shawl to cover their tattered dresses. Only one of them wore shoes. The other two were barefoot. Their feet were filthy and wet from the cold ground.

Annie waited to see if they were being met by a relative. The three girls stood on the quayside, while all around them, the rest of the passengers moved away, most with some sort of purposeful step.

The crowd soon cleared, leaving just the three weary travellers. Annie stood beside the wall of a warehouse set back from the quay and decided they must be alone and didn't appear to be waiting for anyone. In fact, they look quite undecided about what to do next. She moved towards them, left the hood of her cloak down to show her face and hair, even though it was drizzling rain. She smiled and greeted them in Irish. '*Dia dhuit*, God be with you.'

The three girls turned towards Annie. One, a skinny little thing with hair so fine, her scalp showed thorough the lank hair plastered to her skull, lifted her hand in greeting. '*Dhia is Mhuire dhuit*, God and Mary be with you.'

The other two girls held on tightly to their bags and nodded, then looked at each other. Annie could almost read their thoughts. '*Can we trust her? Sure, what else can we do?*'

'My name is Annie Power. I'm from Waterford. Where are you from?'

The skinny girl answered first. 'I'm Christina, and these are my cousins, Roisin and Clodagh. We're from Tipperary Town.'

Annie smiled again. 'Well, we could be neighbours. Have you somewhere to go? Family here?'

Christina narrowed her eyes and looked at her cousins, then back at Annie.

'No. We've come to find work. Our families are in trouble and we need to send money home.' Christina said she was nineteen. She'd left her mother and six younger siblings back at home. She was to be the saviour of her family.

'I can help you find work,' Annie said. 'I've opened a refuge, a lodging house for single Irish women. You're just what I'm looking for.'

The girls whispered to each other. They were right to be wary of her, Annie thought, and glanced around the quayside, now almost empty of passengers, but still busy and full of noise and movement.

The crew on the barge had begun unloading bales of grain onto wagons lined up at the edge of the quay, while another barge, loaded with immigrants, squeezed into a gap at the quay.

'Step over here by the wall,' she instructed the girls. 'That barge is about to disembark its passengers.' The girls moved towards Annie and lined up beside her. There was a small bit of shelter from the drizzle beneath an overhanging eaves. Together they watched the barge's gangway lowered to the quayside. Dozens of new arrivals; family groups, young and old, men and women and children, raced to set foot in New York.

Annie scanned the faces trying to identify solitary females. There were none, so she turned her attention back to the girls.

'Don't worry,' she smiled again. 'I was like you last year. But I have an aunt in New York. She took me and my brother and sister in. I understand what you want to do. I can help you.'

'How can you help us?' Roisin asked. She was the taller of the three girls, with a pinched face and a worried frown.

'I have a cottage in the grounds of Saint Patrick's Cathedral on Mott Street. You can stay with me, while I help you find work and lodgings. The Bishop loaned it to me. It's not too far. Come and see it. I'd say you could do with stretching your legs.'

The skinny girl, Christina, spoke up again. 'We'll take a look at it. But if we don't like it, we'll not stay. We'll find somewhere else.'

'You'll like it,' Annie promised. 'Come on. There's a stew on the pot.'

The mention of food did it. They followed her up off the quay, and half an hour later they were at the refuge, sitting in the warm kitchen, eating a bowl of stew and drinking tea.

Annie now had six residents. There was hardly room for

more, until some of these had found work and lodgings.

Yet still, every week-end she walked down around Battery Park searching. She found other girls, like Sinead, and spoke to them. She became a familiar sight, usually accompanied by Finn, sometimes alone. The girls she spoke to were afraid of their minders. Annie became known as a 'do-gooder'. But she was usually in Finn's company, so ignored the warning glances.

* * *

Annie came across the seventh resident of the Refuge when she was at mass. Jeannie Sullivan from Tralee, was living in a basement room in a tenement in Five Points. Annie found her begging outside the church, spoke to her, then she took her back to the Refuge. Annie borrowed a roll-up mattress from her aunt and put it down in the shared bedroom.

The refuge was full and it was now urgent that Annie started to help her residents find paying work and permanent lodgings. She didn't want to start turning away anyone. And she needed more money to feed them.

Every Sunday morning, she attended different masses in the Manhattan diocese. She found that some had become weary of seeing her. One of two of the congregation left early after the priest announced that Annie was to speak and take up a collection. She persisted.

25

Jane Keating: April 1847. Loss

Andrew was busy in the office and left Jane to work on the newspaper's other form of income - advertising leaflets. As soon as she was alone, she set up a frame for the poster she planned to print out. She typeset the message and hid the completed frame in the back of the type cupboard. Now she just had to get the opportunity, she only needed a few hours, to print off some posters in the next week. Her task was under way. She had ten days, plenty of time.

She leaned over the typesetting table and felt her belly against the hard wooden surface. She hadn't felt the baby move for a while, and rubbed her hand across her abdomen. 'Are you alright, *a chroí*, my heart? We're going home soon. We'll get on a whaling ship to America. You won't be born here. ' She stroked her belly again, but got no answering kick or turn. 'I want to see your face. Don't worry, you won't look like him, I'm sure.' In her dreams, though, the baby looked at her out of the Colonel's dark eyes.

'No, They'll be your eyes, *a chroí*, my heart. And you'll be *mo stoirín*, my little darling.'

Her head ached, so she got a drink of water, then started work again. She held on to the thought. Going home. 'I'll swim tomorrow, that'll make us both feel better.'

* * *

'That's another good job done,' Andrew said when he finished proofreading the new edition. He glanced at her as he spoke, then he looked again. 'Jane, are you sick? Your face is . . .' He seemed lost for words, but he frowned and peered at her. The freckles on his cheeks appeared darker against his pale skin and his fair hair gleamed in the light of the oil lamp on the desk. It was late evening, and the starched white shirt and striped cravat he wore under his woollen suit were crumpled after the day.

He was only twenty-two, but to Jane, the care of his father's business pressed down on him, and left him looking old for his years.

She touched her face, her skin felt cold. Her cheekbones and jawbones were sharp under her fingertips. 'I think I'm tired, Andrew. I don't feel right. I'll get a rest when this is finished.'

They worked together to finish the print run. When the work was completed, Jane wrapped her shawl around her shoulders and tucked the ends of the woven fabric into her waistband. An ache bloom behind her ribs, as her hand rested on her round belly. A thought came into her head. What will Andrew say when he finds out? She answered her own question. He'll sack you, what do you think? And if he doesn't, his father definitely will. She left Andrew to lock up.

Outside the newspaper building, the street was silent, with

no horses or mules hauling vehicles at this hour in the commercial district. A huge yellow moon hung low above the town and reflected along the length of the Yarra, sliding and moving with the water, gold on black, breaking here and there, when the oars from a silent boat broke the gleaming water, as if shattering a mirror.

A shiver ran up through her body and forced her to swallow hard. A slow wrenching ache spread from her belly right down to her legs. She bent over and leaned her hands on her knees. The ache, it felt like something inside had twisted into a knot, first pulled tight, then eased. It left her nauseous and she vomited right there on the road, just missing the hem of her skirt and the tips of her boots. Her knees gave way and she put her hands out to the wall of the building she had just left to stop her from falling onto the vomit, then she sat down hard on the ground.

'Jesus, Mary and Joseph! What is this?' She leaned back against the wall. 'Andrew, help me.' But she had closed the door when she left, and no-one heard her call. Jane sat there while the cold shudder ran through her body again and she gagged and retched. Somehow she knew that something was wrong with the baby. 'Get up, girl! You can't tell Andrew. Get back to the dormitory. There'll be women there to help.'

She rolled over onto her knees and put one hand against the wall, with the other hand she hauled her skirt up out of the way. She rested her forehead against the stone wall and darkness closed down her vision. She couldn't seem to hold her head up, and began to slide down the wall until the stinging on her forehead woke her. Get up! She tried again, pressed down on her knee and heaved herself upwards. Afraid to stop, she began to walk, her legs trembling, leaning one hand against the building wall to steady herself. Then she let go of the wall to cross Collins Street and turned right onto the side road towards the dormitory. There were people here, some took no notice of her, while others probably thought she'd had too much to drink and left her to stagger home.

She let herself in and collapsed onto the bottom step of the stairs. The wrenching pain had eased now, but her head hummed with a hot, red ache and she couldn't take another step. Her vision speckled and faded. She heard the housekeeper's voice from further along the hallway. 'Who's there?'

Mrs Smith found Jane. The housekeeper held an oil-lamp in one hand, the globe gleamed dully, and a heavy brass candlestick in the other. She knelt in front of Jane and put the candlestick down on the step.

'What happened? Are you sick? You've not been drinking, have you?' The housekeeper must have smelt the vomit on Jane's breath

'Mrs Smith, thank God. No, I've not been drinking. But I felt bad when I came out from work. Now I can't get up the stairs.' Jane's hair had come loose around her face and her mouth was dry and sour.

'Here, let me help you.' The housekeeper stood the lamp and the candlestick on a small table near the front door. Then she put an arm around Jane and half lifted her to her feet. The two of them went upstairs together. The dim light dwindled as they reached the upper floor. They were left with only the sweep of stars and moonlight through the window in the roof.

The dormitory bedroom was in darkness. The other women lodgers were asleep, and the silence was only broken by the rumble of low snores from a few of them.

Mrs Smith untied the laces in Jane's boots and slipped them off. Then she unbuttoned Jane's blouse and helped her out of her clothes down to her shift. Jane felt the woman's hands pause as they brushed against her belly.

Jane lay down on the bed and pulled a blanket over herself while Mrs Smith went to fetch a cup of water. The housekeeper came back and put the water on the locker beside the bed.

'You're exhausted. Will I sit with you for a while?'

'No, thank you, Mrs Smith. I'll rest, now.'

'Call me if you need anything, in the night, won't you?'

Jane just nodded. The pain had left an ache in her lower back and a heaviness where her baby lay in her womb. Her legs were still full of cramp, and she shifted around in the bed to try to get comfortable. Her head throbbed. She took a sip of water to cleanse her mouth.

She whispered to herself, not wanting to wake the other women in the bedroom. 'It's not over, I can feel it's not over. It's waiting to start again. Dear Lord, it can't be the baby, it's too soon. What is it? I mustn't be ill. Not now.' Tears filled her eyes. 'Mrs Smith saw my belly. Should I tell her? I don't know what to do. I'll talk to Owen, he might know.'

She remembered telling Owen about meeting the Colonel a few weeks ago. Somehow the Colonel had guessed she was having his baby. A voice in her head whispered, *"What if your rapist claims the baby?"* Can he do that? *"Yes"*, hissed through her brain. At that moment, Jane's need to leave surged into a brilliant flame that burned all other thoughts away. He would never get her baby. She'd kill him first.

She knelt up on the bed and pulled the curtain back to look

out of the window at the gleaming sweep of stars and the pale gold of the full moon in the southern sky. At first, back in February, when she had found out she was pregnant, she had seen this baby as something unnatural, a punishment she didn't deserve.

Watching the night sky, she knew that today, right now, she had fallen in love with the little being inside her. Never mind if he or she had the Colonel's eyes. The baby's light kicks had reminded Jane that she was no longer an orphan girl, alone in the world, but a mother carrying a precious child. A Keating baby.

Jane, the last surviving member of her family, had begun to look forward to a future she could make with her child. 'Not here, in Melbourne,' she vowed. 'Stay well, *mo stoirín*, my little darling.'

* * *

Jane waited through the long night for morning. Her pains eased for a while and she dozed. When dawn came, she got up, exhausted. She washed and dressed. It wasn't yet six o'clock, and Mrs Smith was still in bed. Jane decided to go to early mass first, then come back and confide in the housekeeper.

* * *

The edge of the sun just showed above the horizon, cold and pale, as she walked to the church of Saint Francis for first mass. She drew in deep breaths of air still chilled from the night and her head cleared as she walked. Her pains had subsided in the night, yet she felt strangely weak in her legs. There were

251

not many at this early mass and Jane knelt and prayed and joined in the Latin prayers. As the mass progressed, minute by minute, she came to an understanding. She remained kneeling, instead of going to receive holy communion from the priest.

Without a husband, there was no place here in this church for her or her baby. She was certain then that the priest would never baptise her baby, born to an unwed mother, a sinner, for sure; her child, a bastard.

Full of sorrow, she left before the mass ended and crossed the Yarra to walk on the beach for a few minutes to think. What would Mrs Smith say when Jane told her? She hardly knew the woman, even though she had lived at the dormitory for months now. Mrs Smith was not like Caroline Chisholm. Jane could have confided in Mrs Chisholm.

* * *

At the beach, Jane took her boots off and walked barefoot, her feet sank into the cool, damp sand. The tide was on the way in, the sea water washed up towards her, lacy froth frilled the tips of the waves with light. Small black seabirds skipped along the edge where the water met the sand, and pecked at tiny worms and insects. The shrill calls of the birds echoed into her head and through her body. Little by little, lightly at first, her pain crept into her back and her belly, then pulsed down her legs.

It was still early, the sun just rising, and the beach was deserted. Afraid for herself and her baby, she turned, intending to walk back to the dormitory. Suddenly, her knees gave way and she fell forward, saving herself with her outstretched hands. She knelt there for a moment until another, sharper pain rippled through her body. She gave into the pain, turned to sit, then lay back, and looked up at the sky. No clouds, just a great pale blue vastness with the sun, pale orange, just above the horizon to the east, over towards Phillip Island and the American whaling ships. One thought only, came to her. 'I must get out of here.'

After a few minutes, she got her breath back and eased herself up to rest on her elbows. The waves in the bay edged closer, filled the lower part of the beach, and were now just a few feet away from where she lay. Her pain receded as she watched the water roll in. She began to relax a little, and caught the sharp smell of smoke from a campfire in the woods behind her. Jimmy's family might be nearby.

She slipped on her boots and stumbled up the beach to the seagrass margin where the woods began, and moved into the shadowy interior. Trees here had been left untouched for hundreds of years and grew to enormous heights. Many were deciduous and kept their leaves, while others had golden, autumn crowns. The sea breeze hummed through the treetops. The air felt cool and damp against her feverish face.

* * *

Jane moved away from the sounds of the sea, and further into the deep woods. She disturbed a flock of yellow-tailed cockatoos, who fluttered and called out to each other as she passed under their tree. Her pain gave her a light reminder across her lower back, but she kept moving. There were people close by and the smell of the fire drew her on. If it was her friend Jimmy, she'd ask him to help her get back to the dormitory.

'Jimmy. Where are you? It's Jane.' She called again, but got no response, and walked further, slowing, then stopping to let a ripple of pain run through her. Suddenly, she saw him come running towards her, full of energy, smiling when he got closer.

'I'm here, Jane.'

'I need your help, Jimmy.'

Jimmy didn't ask any questions. He took Jane's hand and led her deeper into the forest, along an almost invisible path, soft with fallen leaves and twigs. The great trees that towered above them to heights of fifty feet or more, closed off the sky. Daylight turned from bright morning to a misty shadowland, as if they had stepped out of their everyday world. She kept pace with her friend. Her skirt caught on low, green shrubs, the tips of her fingers brushed through beads of dew on the leaves. Twigs cracked under foot and appeared to echo in the call of the unseen birds in the evergreen branches above her head. She held her breath, then exhaled. This magical place had helped ease her pains.

After walking for a few minutes, the two arrived at Jimmy's family camp-site. He brought Jane straight to his mother.

Two shelters were set up in a clearing next to a creek that meandered along the west edge of the campsite. A fire burned in a pit, and Jimmy's mother, Sally, sat on the ground beside it. She appeared to be weaving a basket out of pale grass or reeds, but put it down and stood when she heard her son.

Jimmy took Jane's hand and held it out to his mother. 'Do you remember my friend, Jane? She swims in the sea, too.'

Jimmy's mother nodded. They had met a while ago, at the

land that would become the Botanic Gardens.

Sally took Jane's hand in hers and shook it. Jane saw the likeness between mother and son. Jimmy had his mother's dark eyes and wide cheekbones, and her smile.

'Welcome, my son's friend,' Sally said.

Jane had been so driven by her physical distress that she now couldn't find the words to explain what she needed. Perhaps because she did not know what she needed.

Another pain started to ripple across her lower back and forced her to bend over. She put her hands on her thighs to steady herself as it swelled and raced around to her abdomen. She groaned and blew out a breath. 'I'm sorry,' she whispered. 'I need help.'

Jimmy's mother put her hands on her son's shoulder and lightly turned him around. 'Fetch Grandmother.' The boy ran to do her bidding.

The mother then put her arm around Jane and helped her over to a log to sit on. The Aboriginal woman knelt in front of Jane. 'Tell me.'

'It's my baby. I think it's going to be born. But it's too soon.' Tears overflowed her eyes. Finally, she had spoken aloud the words that had haunted her for the last two days. She felt a strange relief.

'Where is your mother?' Sally asked.

'She's dead.'

'Your husband, your family?'

'No husband, no family.' The words brought bright tears to her eyes. 'My family are all dead.'

'Where do you live?'

'At the women's dormitory, near the docks.'

The woman nodded and stood. 'I know it. Come, we'll take

you there.'

'No, no.' Jane almost shouted the words. 'I can't go there!'

'Then the father of your child must help you.' The woman appeared almost exasperated with Jane's stubborn denials.

'He raped me. He won't help. He wants to take my baby.' Jane was crouched on the log and bent over her knees. She looked up at Jimmy's mother.

It seemed then, that Sally finally understood, for she turned to the older woman who had come to investigate, and spoke quickly to her. The woman, grey-haired and in her old age, nodded, peered at Jane, and went back into the shelter.

'We'll help you. Me and my mother. She is Grandmother.'

Another fierce pain came over Jane. She shuddered, as it flared, then faded and left her weak. Sally waited for the pain to subside, then helped Jane to stand.

'Can I feel your belly?' Sally asked.

Jane nodded. The woman's touch was gentle as she felt the sides and top and bottom of Jane's belly through her skirt. Sally had an intent expression on her face. She pushed her black hair behind her ear, knelt and pressed the side of her head against Jane's abdomen.

Jane felt the soft pressure of the woman's head, then another pain came right across the middle of her belly. Jane groaned, but the woman stayed, and listened, then stood up. 'You are right, your child is borning. But it is too soon.'

'What does that mean?' Jane asked. In her heart, she knew it could only mean one thing. Neither of the women spoke.

Jimmy's mother shook her head and looked at her own mother who had come back with a bag slung over her shoulder. Jimmy followed, and carried several long strips of dark, knobbly tree bark across his shoulder.

Sally linked Jane's arm in hers and called out to her husband and children who all watched, as if fascinated. Then Sally and Jane, Jimmy and Grandmother, began to walk back along the trail towards the beach.

Sally led the way, still linking Jane's arm in hers. Grandmother helped Jimmy carry the lengths of bark, which were more than twice his height. It only took a few minutes until they reached the edge of the rainforest. She could hear, but not see, the waves crashing onto the beach a few yards ahead. The small group were still enclosed by the ancient trees.

They stopped beside a fifty-foot tall eucalyptus tree. She touched the bark of the tree. 'This one.' Sally led Jane over to a tree stump beside a small stream. 'Rest here,' then went back to show Jimmy where to lay the strips of bark, before sending him off home.

Now, only the three women remained. Jane watched, as the grandmother helped her daughter to position the strips of bark, they were about ten or twelve feet long, at an angle to the trunk of the tree. The two women anchored the base of the bark strips with broken branches. In minutes they had created a shelter, using the trunk of the great tree as one wall and the long strips of bark to create a covered space, open on one side.

The grandmother took a small shovel out of her bag and handed it to Sally before she began to gather up sticks and twigs into a pile beside the entrance to the shelter.

Meanwhile, Sally dug two shallow depressions inside the shelter. One was at the base of the tree trunk and she lined it with dried acacia leaves from Grandmother's bag. Sally then dug a second pit near to the opening of the shelter and in it, she set and lit a small fire with the twigs and leaves.

Grandmother used a wooden vessel to bring over some fresh water from the stream, she took some berries from her bag and crushed them into the water, and offered it to Jane. The cool, sweet drink refreshed Jane's mouth and settled her stomach, for she had not eaten or drunk for almost twenty-four hours.

The shelter was ready, and Sally held her hand out to Jane and brought her to sit on a fur skin laid out near the fire. The grandmother came back with a bark platter of mixed fruits and nuts and took her leave of Sally and Jane. The two sat together and sipped the fruit drink in the shelter of the ancient eucalyptus tree.

When the next pain came Jane leaned forward and put her head on her knees. She breathed in the scented smoke and tried to relax.

As the afternoon wore on, Sally collected a piece of soft paperbark from a nearby tree and scooped some cooled ashes from the edge of the fire into it.

Sally helped Jane to undress, and folded her skirt, blouse, her drawers and shift into a neat pile at the back of the shelter. Jane wrapped her shawl around herself to keep warm. She sipped the drink and ate a few berries and nuts. She didn't speak for she had no words.

Sally folded the warm paperbark and applied it like a poultice to Jane's back and around her ribs when the next contraction came. The warmth from the poultice eased her pain a little. After an hour or so, the pains began to come faster.

Jane watched, as if in a dream, as her guide used a stick to shuffle some more of the hot ashes to the edge of the fire, let them cool, then rubbed them between her hands. Sally knelt behind Jane and pressed her hands gently down the sides of Jane's body just as another contraction started. The firm, warm pressure helped to counteract some of the pain and Jane leaned back against the woman, and closed her eyes, just feeling the pain and the pressure of Sally's strong hands moving downwards over the pain, soothing it until it eased.

After a while, Sally whispered. 'Jane, stand and I will show you how to help your baby born.'

Jane stood and the two women moved into the centre of the shelter. Sally stood on one leg and gave a little hop, then put both feet on the ground and took a small jump. 'Do this with me. It will help your baby.' Together they did several small hops and jumps until another pain came. Jane sat and rested while Sally massaged the pain, then they hopped some more. They continued this in the quiet of the shelter with just the sounds of birdsong outside in the treetops and the crackle of the twigs on the fire.

They sipped the sweet drink and Jane ate a few more berries and nuts. Time passed and her pains became constant.

'My baby is dead, I think.' Jane whispered. No tears came, for she could hardly believe the words she spoke.

Sally nodded her head in agreement. 'She will born soon. You will see her face. You are her mother.'

'Is she a girl, then?' Jane asked.

'Or a boy,' Sally replied. 'We will find out soon.'

* * *

Jane's baby was born just as the sun dropped and darkness fell over the woods. Sally demonstrated how to crouch over the depression she had prepared in the ground beside the tree and showed Jane where to place her hands on the tree trunk. Jane knelt and leaned against the tree trunk and pushed down, while Sally massaged her back.

The next roil of pain forced the baby's head into the birth canal. Jane leaned forward and almost toppled into the side of the tree trunk. She felt Sally's strong hands around her waist, helping her to push. The pain increased, to a hot agony that forced a scream from Jane. She looked down and saw a tiny creature slide down between her legs, then caught and laid on the bed of soft paperbark held by Sally, her guide.

Sally then helped Jane to sit back and see her baby, as if asleep in a nest. Jane sighed deeply. Every atom of her being strained towards her daughter, for she was a girl. Sally twisted the umbilical cord, cut it with a sharpened flint and tied off the ends with lengths of fibre, then gestured to Jane to pick up her baby.

Her hands trembled as she lifted her daughter to her breast. The baby was tiny, but fully formed, about ten inches from head to heel and skinny with fine, dark hair. And her skin was dark-red in death. Her eyes were closed and her little body was smeared with blood, the skin wrinkled at the elbows and knees. Jane examined her daughter's hands, she had long fingers like her own.

Jane used a pad of soft moss to wipe her daughter's face clean and rocked her gently. 'Wake up, *mo chroi,* my heart,' she whispered. 'You can wake up now. Mammy's here for you.' In her heart she knew that her first-born child would never draw breath or suck milk, or cry to be comforted by her mother. She leaned over her baby and wept for what would never be, then blessed her child and kissed her cold face, pulled the shawl around herself and whispered to her daughter.

Grandmother had brought a carved wooden basket and Sally lined it with more of the creamy paperbark. After a few minutes, when Jane's pains started again, Sally indicated for Jane to place the baby in the basket. Sally showed Jane how to crouch over the birthing pit to deliver the placenta and massaged Jane's abdomen gently to help the process. Once the placenta had dropped into the pit, Sally covered it with earth.

* * *

Later, Jane sat with Sally and sipped a sweet drink of warm fruit-water. She cradled the body of her daughter in her arms.

Sally spoke in the near-dark of the evening. 'We are Wurundjeri people. We bury our dead near water. I can help you.'

Jane placed one hand on the small basket that held her daughter's body and put the other out to Sally, who took her hand. 'You have helped me to be strong and birth my daughter. I thought I might die alone with my baby, but for you. And Jimmy and Grandmother.' Jane smiled. 'Thank you.'

Jane paused to gather her thoughts. 'I'm leaving soon, going home to Ireland, far away. I won't leave her here on her own.' She took a deep breath that caught in her throat and her voice was hoarse when she spoke. 'I want to put her in the water, so she can go, too.'

'What is her name?'

'Margaret, after my own mother.'

'Come, we will send Margaret on her journey. First I will close up her basket.'

Jane kissed her daughter for the last time, and watched as

261

Sally wove lengths of twine around the basket, pulling the edges together to transform the small coffin into a tiny barque about to set sail.

Jane got dressed and used some of the moss and paperbark to line her drawers, while Sally threw sand on the fire and gathered up the bag with her digging tool and flint.

Jane carried the small coffin, and the two women walked to the beach near the edge of the bay. It was a moonless night, but the sky was ablaze with a swathe of silvery stars reflected in the water of the bay, with just the ebbing shush of the tide.

The tide was almost fully out. They had only a short while to do this before the sea turned and swept back to shore.

Sally held the coffin and waited while Jane took her boots off, then tucked the hem of her skirt up into her waistband. She put her hands out for her baby, encased in the wooden coffin, held it close and took two steps into the icy water. Her feet sank into the sand and she felt the pull of the tide at her ankles.

Jane kissed the basket containing her daughter's body, and laid it on top of the water. She pushed it to send it on its way, a small barque heading out to sea on an endless journey. The water supported the light wood of the coffin and its passenger, and drew it out into deeper water where it spun around for a few moments. It steadied itself, like a miniature ship about to set sail to the other side of the world. Jane strained her eyes to watch it move out into the bay, further and further until it disappeared into the darkness of the sea and sky.

'God bless you, *mo chroi,* my heart.' The icy water swirled around Jane's legs. She stepped forward and her feet sank into the sand. Now the water lapped at her skirt, she'd soon be out of her depth. She looked out into the darkness.

She felt Sally's arm around her shoulders and leaned against her. The two women turned and waded back to the beach. No more words were spoken.

They continued together as far as the bridge across the Yarra, where they hugged and parted.

'Thank you, Sally. Give my thanks to your mother and Jimmy. I'll come and say goodbye to you all, before I leave.'

* * *

Jane arrived back at the hostel. She went straight to her bed, pulled a blanket over her and collapsed into a deep sleep. She woke through the night with more pains and her eyes were swollen almost shut by morning. Mrs Smith looked in on her and sat with her for a while.

Jane finally felt able to confide in the housekeeper. Later that morning she washed and dressed herself. Somehow, she had to be ready to start her shift at one o'clock. Because she had to see through her plan. Her daughter, Margaret, would never be forgotten, and Jane would get revenge on her rapist, then she'd get out of this place. Soon.

26

Jane Keating: 17th April 1847. Escape

At one o'clock in the afternoon, Jane opened the door into the newspaper office. Andrew was at his desk and she saw the look of relief on his face. 'Jane, are you feeling better?' he asked.

'Yes, thank you. I must have eaten something to make me sick,' She made a show of taking of her shawl, so as not to look him, in the eye. She hated herself for lying about her daughter, as if she was denying her.

'Well, if you need to get off early, I can manage here.' Andrew followed Jane into the print room.

'I'll do the typesetting and leave then. I promise I'll be better tomorrow.' Another lie. Was there no end to them?

The rest of that day, Jane's belly was still full of pain and she had to stop and breathe hard to let waves of pain pass. Thankfully, Andrew was in the office for most of it and he didn't hear her stifled groans. She managed to get her work done and left early to get back to the hostel.

Her breasts were wet; liquid had seeped through her blouse. Her body seemed to belong to someone else, a stranger, who bled and leaked. She washed again, half-afraid to look at herself, at this body she no longer recognised. Her swollen breasts with darkened nipples, and her belly, still big from the pregnancy.

She got into bed and slept right through to Sunday morning.

* * *

Jane walked across the sand to meet Owen for their Sunday morning swim. She could feel winter was closing in. These swims were coming to an end. She must tell Owen about the birth of her baby, but her mind was a jumble of stray thoughts. One thing she was certain of, she wouldn't lie to her friend. She kicked the soft sand and felt tiny fan-shaped shells catch between her toes. She bent to brush them away and brushed her tears away at the same time.

Further along the beach, Owen was already in the water and waved to her to join him. She shook her head and sat down on the sand, a few feet away from the waterline, to watch him swim. In Ireland, at this time of year, mayflowers would be out in the hedgerows, and a soft summer lay ahead. Here in Melbourne she was facing into winter, if she failed to escape.

She looked out over the water that held her daughter's body. A cool breeze lifted her hair, and she felt a chill at the base of her neck. In her mind, baby Margaret was still floating in her basket bound with woven grasses, right to the end of the world and into the Southern Ocean. There, her baby would sail past icebergs, and, in time, grow an icy cover to her little craft and might even become part of a small iceberg herself. Yes, my little darling will go on forever.

After he had dried and dressed, Owen sat next to Jane. He

265

must have sensed something was wrong, for he took her hand and said. 'Tell me.'

'My baby died, two days ago. A daughter, still-born.'

'Ah, Jane, that's terrible. What happened?'

'I don't know. One day I was fine.The next, I couldn't feel her move. Then the pains came. Jimmy's mother helped me.' Jane scanned the horizon then she closed her swollen eyes. 'I named her, Margaret, after my mother. She's out there. In a basket Sally gave me, a little ship, sailing to the end of the world.' Her voice broke and she felt Owen's arm around her shoulders. 'I have you, Jane.'

She leaned his face against his shoulder and cried again.

After a while, she sat up and pushed her hair away from her face. 'I was going to take her with me.'

'Take her where?' Owen asked.

'You know, away from here.' Jane pushed his arm away, stood up, and began to walk back along the beach.

Owen followed her. He seemed stuck for words. Jane looked at her friend; the angles and planes of his face and the dark curls that framed his face. He had the dark Irish looks she knew from her own family. But he could have no understanding of her loss. Everything she had loved was lost to her. She felt old and afraid.

She looked out at the ocean. She shook off the fear and pushed her shoulders back.

'I met Gerald and he told me.' Jane stopped for a moment and her voice grew stronger as she spoke. 'He told me how to escape on an American whaling ship.'

Owen stopped in his tracks and held his hands out to her. 'Wait a minute, now. You've just had a terrible loss, Jane. You're not thinking straight.'

She seemed not to hear his words and walked on. Owen caught up with her.

'I've heard those tales, Jane, of escaping on whaling ships. And every single one of them escaped convicts was captured and sent back here.'

'Gerald said there's a small fishing village on the coast near Phillip Island The whaling ships stop there for water and supplies. It's only fifty miles away, and I can take a ferry from the village across to the island and get on board a ship. I'll be out of here in no time.'

'Jane, listen to me. First of all, no-one will take you on board. You'll just be caught and they'll send you to Norfolk Island. It'll be the death of you. I guarantee it. The death of you.'

Jane blinked and she shook her head. She clenched her hand in front of her, her nails bit into the palm of her hand. 'No, Owen, instead why don't you hear me? I can't stay here. Not here, where my baby was born too soon. Not living in the same town as my rapist. I'll get on a whaling ship, or I'll join Margaret in the bay. I swear it.'

'Wait, Janey. Hear me out. You know I have feelings for you, don't you? We could make a life together here.' Owen moved nearer and put his face close to hers, so close she could feel his breath on her cheek.

'What are you saying?' She began to walk again, but he caught her hand and held it in his.

'Owen, you can't have feelings for me. Look at me.' She stood in front of him; sixteen years old, her stomach still swollen from the pregnancy; her face, gaunt and full of sorrow for her lost child.

'Don't tell me what I can feel. You've had too much to deal with to see it. I've been waiting for you, Janey. Since I first set eyes on you on the ship last year.' He lifted her hand and kissed the palm where her nails had marked her skin, then let it go.

Jane felt his soft lips on her hand, knew he spoke the truth and smiled at him and reached out to touch his face. She felt his sideburns, soft and curling, the sharp cheekbones below his dark eyes and nodded. 'Yes, I see now.' Then she took her hand away.

'But I still can't stay here. This is a place of death for me, now. I have to go home and find Brendan's children and Aoife, his wife. They are my only living family. And I promised myself I'd put a marker on my father's grave. I'll put my mother and brothers' names on the headstone, along with my baby's name.' Hot tears spilled onto her cheeks. 'Maybe when I've done all that, I'll be able to love someone, Owen.'

He looked hard at her and blinked away his own tears, then his face cleared. He nodded and took a deep breath, as if he had come to a decision, or an understanding. 'Then I'll help you. If I go with you, the army would come after me, and they'd have you, too. But I have some savings. You can use them to buy a way out of here. And I'll come to Phillip Island with you. We'll say goodbye there.'

She leaned over and kissed him on the lips. 'Thank you. I'll pay you back, I promise,' she whispered. They stood together at the water's edge, arms around each other.

'Will you help me put out the posters before I go?' Jane asked.

'What posters? And when are you leaving?'

She told him about her plan for the following week, then went back to the newspaper offices and spent an hour printing off her posters. All was nearly ready.

268

* * *

It was Wednesday, the 21st April, 1847. Thanks to Sally's care, Jane had healed fast. Now, she had a final goodbye to say to her daughter.

The weather had turned colder, winter was close and the waves in the bay whipped into white spray, but Jane got into the water and swam out in the bay, until her feet could no longer touch the sand, then rolled over and floated. Her fingers and toes turned white, then blue, as the cold water worked on them.

'Sleep in peace, little Margaret. I have to go home. I wanted to bring you with me, but I'll keep you in my heart, *mo astór*, my darling.'

She swam back and ran up the beach to the shelter of the trees. The sharp breeze blew through the branches above her head and made the leaves flutter and crackle. She shivered as she dried herself and dressed. She was almost ready to leave, when she heard a sound from deep in the woods.

Jane instantly recognised the sound. It was a cry of pain and fear. Then silence. Even the birds in the trees fell silent, the wind dropped and the leaves stilled. Again, the sound. Now it was high pitched and angry.

Jane got her bearings. The sound came from near the Aboriginal people's campsite, where Jimmy's family had their shelter. She ran with light footsteps over towards the east until she saw a tangle of people just ahead through the trees.

At first, she couldn't make out what had happened. Then the scene made sense. She saw a boy; it was her friend Jimmy. He was lying on the ground with his face turned towards her, but his eyes were closed. A skinny man stood over him with a whip and raised his hand to lash the boy's back. Jimmy's black skin glistened with blood and he looked to be unconscious.

Jimmy's mother was closer to where Jane hid, and was held back by a large, stocky man. She struggled to reach her son. In all there was a total of four men, all of whom looked to be bushrangers. The one with the whip, the skinny younger man, followed through and whipped Jimmy's back. The stocky man, threw Sally to the ground and she screamed in rage.

The two others, both younger looking, scuttled over towards Sally. One kicked her as she tried to get away.

Jane couldn't hear what the men said, but she saw a movement in the trees at the edge of the clearing. It was Jimmy's father, and he signalled to Jane. He had weapons, a spear and a club, and he was about to throw the spear at the skinny man with the whip. Jane nodded to him and crouched down. What could she do to help? All the men had guns. The stocky man nearest Jane unbuckled his holster and threw it, with his pistol, to the ground. He loosened his trousers and stood over Sally.

The spear whispered through the air and plunged into the skinny man's chest. He fell to his knees, roaring in pain and clutched the shaft of the spear. The stocky man froze.

While the other men's attention turned to their mate, Jane reached over and pulled the holster towards her. She took out the pistol. It was loaded, she cocked the pistol and took aim. She didn't hesitate, she shot one of the younger men nearest to her. The bullet went through his knee and he fell to the ground screaming in surprise and pain. She darted over to him and pulled out his pistol, smelt his stench as she bent over him and her own fear almost stopped her breath. She shouted out loud to herself. 'Do it, hold the gun up. Up, up.

Now. Speak!'

'Who's next?' she yelled. She held the pistol, ready to shoot again. Jimmy's father ran swiftly and hauled his spear out of the skinny bushranger's chest, then he stood beside Jane, his spear in one hand and a club in the other.

'Get out of here, and take them with you,' she screamed at the two uninjured bushrangers, and pointed at the wounded men on the ground. The men scrambled for their friends and hauled them away into the trees, blundering through the woods towards Melbourne.

Only then did Jane uncock the pistol and kneel with Jimmy's father beside Sally. Jimmy's mother was shocked but otherwise unharmed. Their son was unconscious from the whipping.

Jimmy's father carried his son to the campsite nearby. The bushrangers had caught the mother and son as they were gathering food.

* * *

Later, Jane left the family at their shelter and retraced her steps back to the woods and the bay. It was getting on for nightfall and she hurried back to the hostel. She was startled by a bird who clattered off a branch above her head. She took this as her warning. 'If they come back, they'll kill me.' She began to run to the hostel, and safety. She kept the pistol with her and prayed Jimmy and his family were safe.

* * *

Early the next morning Jane washed and dressed and went

271

down to get some breakfast in the dining room. After she had eaten, she wrapped her shawl around her and left the hostel, intending to start work early to print off a few more posters before Andrew arrived to open the office.

She was surprised to see Sally at the front door of the lodgings. She had braved coming into the town and waited for Jane to come out.

'Jimmy?' Jane asked. Before she could say any more, Sally smiled.

'Safe and well. We leave Melbourne today. To the Protectorate. You must leave, too. You will be in danger.'

Relief swept through Jane and she put her hand to her heart, her eyes filled and overflowed. 'I'm leaving. In two days.'

Sally put a soft, weighty package into Jane's hand. 'Thank you, Jane, for my son.'

The two women embraced, Jane felt the bones in Sally's shoulders and arms. The Aboriginal woman must have known hunger, too, but Jane also felt her strength and determination. Then Sally turned and walked away.

Jane looked at the package. It was a woven bag, made of coiled, dried grasses, both pale and dark green strands, intricately woven to form a smaller version of the bag that Grandmother had carried just a few days ago. She put her hand into the opening at the top. The bag was stuffed with acacia leaves and the scent instantly brought her mind back to the shelter near the beach, and her daughter.

The tips of her fingers touched a small, cool rock. She pulled it out, and saw that it wasn't a rock. It was unmistakable, although she had never seen one before. It was heavy for its size, and it was solid gold. She almost dropped the bag in her surprise, but held on tight and covered it with her shawl. She went back into the dormitory and raced to the washroom, locked the door and knelt, and turned the bag upside-down. She shook the contents of the bag onto the floor. In among the leaves, she counted seven irregular shapes of glittering, gleaming gold nuggets. The smallest was the size of her thumbnail and the largest fit into the palm of her hand. She picked them all up and they filled her two hands. For something so beautiful and gleaming, they weighed heavy. Some of the gold had a red tint to it; others were bright, like holding a piece of the sun in her hand.

'Where did she get this?' Jane had no answer. She put the nuggets back into the bag and clutched it to her chest and sat back on her heels to think. Her mind raced. Was this a reward for helping the family? Jimmy's father had another weapon in his hand. He would have sent the men packing, even if Jane had not been there. She was sure of that. But he was only one man against that gang. Jane had certainly helped, even in small way.

Yet they had nothing, the Aboriginal family. Why would Sally give this wealth away? She whispered the answer. 'Because their precious son, is alive and they are still free. And maybe she has more of this gold. Or she knows where to find more.'

Whatever the reason, Jane was now equipped with the means to get herself out of Melbourne. She would not need to borrow money from Owen. Someone would accept gold in return for a passage to America. Surely. She wrapped the bag in the end of her shawl, held it close and headed for the newspaper office.

* * *

273

The posters were printed out. She now had fifty of them.

```
People of Melbourne.
Colonel Johns, British Army, (ret'd), is a criminal!

He is involved in the disappearance of a young
immigrant woman, Elsie Corcoran, in September, 1846.
He said that she left to marry a sheep farmer, but
she has vanished.
He raped a young woman employed at his home in
Melbourne in December of last year. She was
fortunate to escape with her life and laid a
complaint against him with the army. No charges were
brought.
Today, there is another girl working at his home. If
you have wives, daughters, or sisters, beware of
allowing them to work at this man's house.

Superintendent La Trobe, do your duty!
```

* * *

Midnight, Saturday, 24th April, 1847.

Owen and Gerald were waiting in the side alley next to the hostel, as they had arranged,

Jane packed her clothes into her bag. She had told no-one she was leaving and stowed her bag and the posters in a downstairs cupboard beside the washroom. She kept the gold on her person. She picked her bag up on the way out of the hostel and hurried to the meeting place. They were there!

It took the three of them an hour to paste up the posters around the town. By morning, there would be a hullabaloo about the accusations against the Colonel.

When they were all done, Gerald drove the wagon across the bridge and they left Melbourne. They followed a narrow track along the coast, then cut across country towards the fishing village facing Phillip Island.

The sky was a black shroud pierced with glimmering red and gold stars. A gibbous moon hung low by the time they arrived at the village of King's Creek and Star Point.

They stopped, and Gerald turned to Jane and Owen. 'I spoke to an emancipist I know here. He'll bring you across to the island. Wait on the quayside. He'll be here at first light.'

Jane kissed Gerald. 'Thank you, my friend. I'll not forget to send the advertisement in December. So you'll know I'm safe.'

Owen shook hands with Gerald. 'Don't wait for me, I'll make my own way back. '

* * *

Jane and Owen waited on the quay until dawn began to break. Gerald's emancipist friend met them in his skiff. He rowed them across the dark waters of the bay to Phillip Island. On the way there, he told them there was an American ship anchored in the harbour. The captain was intending to sail that same morning up to Sydney to find medical help for his wife who was with him on the ship.

27

Annie Power: May 1847: The Refuge

'Watch me.' Annie picked up a folded bed sheet and shook it out over the single bed in the attic bedroom. She laid it on the mattress and smoothed it flat with her hands, then tucked one corner of the sheet under the mattress.'

'Christina, come and tuck the other corners in.'

Her latest guest bent over the bed and copied the actions Annie demonstrated. 'Yes, that's nice and neat. Niamh, come and do the other corner. Wait, your hands!'

'What's wrong with my hands?' Niamh, the youngest of the three, held out her grubby hands.

'They're not clean. Hurry downstairs and wash them and scrub your nails. Deirdre, here, you have a turn.'

Annie picked up the pillow and put it into the pillow case. 'Now we just need the top sheet, like so. Leave it turned back.

Niamh came back and took her turn at making up a bed, then she stretched out on the bed, her red curls spilled over the pillow. 'It's a lot of work for a night's sleep, Annie.'

'It is, and you'll make up the beds every day, in the houses you'll work in.'

Annie had discovered a couple of employment agencies in the newspaper and they had offices on Broadway. They all had vacancies for domestic workers and housemaids. Most of her compatriots, like Annie herself, had lived in one roomed cabins and had no idea about housework. Annie had gotten a list of household tasks from Bridie, for the girls to learn, including bed-making. They were fast learners, desperate to get jobs and start their new lives.

'I'd say we can go and visit the employment agency this afternoon. Let's get some dinner, then we can all get ready.' Annie shook her head. Christina would find a job easily. The twins, Deirdre and Niamh, might need to calm down a bit, but there was plenty of work in the middle class houses of Manhattan, and or further afield in Jersey City or Brooklyn. As soon as they were earning money, Annie was sure they'd do well.

Christina proved Annie correct and was the first to get a job. She had spent three weeks with Annie at the refuge, then landed a job as a scullery maid with an American family living in Brooklyn.

'I'll be sending most of my earnings home, Annie,' Christina told her. They had walked together to the ferry that would take Christina across to Brooklyn. 'At least for the next few years. It'll pay the rent and keep my mother and brothers and sisters fed.'

'You know where we are, if you need anything.' Annie said.

Thank you, Annie.' They hugged and parted. Annie's job was done. Her first success.

* * *

When she had any free time, Annie continued writing in her Commonplace book. Over those few months in the spring and summer of 1847, she recorded the names of the girls and women she helped. She worked hard at raising the money she needed to feed and clothe them.

* * *

Bridie had made her an appointment to see another specialist. A chest specialist recommended by Doctor Miller.

'I'm not going. You may cancel the appointment,' Annie told her aunt.

'Annie, you've had this for months. if you catch this early, whatever it is, then you can get treatment.'

'No, there's nothing the matter with me, Bridie. Sure, aren't I bound to be a bit run down after the last year?'

'I don't think so, darling. Something is not right. You've lost weight, and I've heard you cough. Don't pretend that's not a nasty cough.'

'Cancel the appointment. I'm too busy.' Annie kissed her aunt and sister, and left the apartment.

Katty looked at Bridie. 'Why won't she go to the doctor, Bridie?'

'Because she's a stubborn woman, so she is.' Bridie muttered. 'I only hope she's right, that's all.'

28

Jane Keating: April 1847: The Nantucket whaling ship

J ane and Owen both saw the ship anchored out in open water. The chimney of the boiler on deck blew out smoke and confirmed that this was a whaling ship, the boiler used to boil up the whale blubber and extract the oil.

A small boat was anchored at the port quayside with men loading barrels and sacks down into the skiff.

'That's their supply boat, I'd guess,' Owen said. The day was beginning to lighten, and the man on the quay was shouting orders down to the other in the boat.

'Do you think he might be the captain?' Jane asked.

'If he is, you've found your ship out of here. That's not a British ship, so we might be in luck.

* * *

'We heard you're looking for help for your wife,' she told the captain.

'Where did you hear that?' the captain asked.

'On our way here.'

'And which of you is a doctor or a midwife?'

The captain's words confirmed Jane's thinking. There was a baby involved in this.

'I'm not a midwife. But I am a mother. I had a baby myself, just a month past, and I can help your wife,' Jane said.

'Where's your baby now, then?' The captain clearly didn't believe her story.

'My daughter never drew breath. She was born too soon.'

The captain paused and scratched his dark red beard. He looked over his shoulder at the ship in the bay. 'I need someone who knows what they're doing. This is for my wife and child. What would a slip of a girl know about birthing babies?'

The captain stomped away from them towards the edge of the quay. Seagulls wheeled and screeched above his head. Some dived into the water beside the skiff tied up at the quayside.

They followed him and Owen spoke up. 'She has money to pay for her passage.'

The Captain gestured with his hand as if to say no, and began to climb down into the supply boat tied up to the quay.

But luck was with them. Just then they heard a crashing bang from the ship anchored in the bay. It echoed around the sky. A crewman on the Alpha had climbed halfway up the mast and fired his musket into the air.

The captain stopped and took out his spy-glass and pointed it towards the ship. Even without the spy-glass, Jane observed two people on deck: a crewman holding a woman that could only have been the captain's wife. The crewman's arm was around her waist and she seemed to swoon against him.

280

'Quick, get in the boat,' the captain said. 'I'll take you as far as Sydney. If my child is not born by then, I'll dock there and find a proper midwife. And I'll offload you.'

Jane turned to Owen. 'I thought we'd have more time to talk, and say goodbye.'

Her friend put his arm around her shoulders and pulled her close to his chest. He bent and pressed his face against the side of her head and kissed her hair. She smelt sweat and salt air from his body and closed her eyes to savour the smell, leaned in against him, against the rough wool of his shirt, felt the smooth muscles of his chest.

'Go with God, Jane,' Owen whispered. 'Just remember that I love you.'

She climbed down the wooden steps into the skiff, and Owen handed her bag down. Then he stood and watched as the Captain gave the order to row.

The small boat was almost full with two crew on the oars and the barrels of water and provisions. Jane squeezed onto the bench behind the rowers and held on tightly as the tender bounced through the water to the ship. She was fairly drenched by the time she climbed on board the whaling ship.

* * *

Captain Clayton was correct; the child was about to be born, but it took a fifteen-hour, hard labour for his son to come into the world, born at sea.

All the while, Jane remembered her own labour and how Jimmy's mother, Sally, had cared for her. She worried Lydia's baby might be stillborn like her daughter, but Lydia was full-term, and the labour progressed differently. Jane felt this baby pushing to get out. She put her hands on Lydia's belly and felt the baby move, then held Lydia's hand for her to feel. The two young women smiled at each other, excited at what was to come. One longing to see the face of her baby, the other heartsick.

During the hours of early labour, on that first day out at sea, Jane and Lydia walked up on deck together, their arms linked. A wintry ocean surrounded the ship, and the decks had been scrubbed clean of whale blood. There would be no more whales caught on this journey. Three hundred barrels of whale oil were stored below decks and represented a fine profit for the owner, Master and crew.

As their first night at sea drew in, Lydia's pains strengthened and became more regular. The two women shut themselves away in the captain's cabin. They talked about Lydia's hopes for her child, how she longed to see its face and show it off to her family back in Nantucket; the first grandchild in the family.

In the early hours of the morning, the pains came faster. Jane called for the captain to walk with his wife while she organised a bucket of hot water, some cloths and a sharp knife and thread. She returned and held the cabin door open for the captain to leave. He kissed his wife and placed his hand on her belly, now only covered with a light cotton shift. Then he nodded to Jane and left. She saw his eyes were full of tears and felt his anxiety. Jane remembered how her Aboriginal friend, Sally, had warmed her hands with the ashes from the fire. She used the warm water in the bucket to wash and warm her hands, then began to massage Lydia's back and sides when her pains came. The two women passed the night alternately walking and Jane massaging Lydia to help ease her contractions.

As morning broke, the baby's head breached. Lydia knelt, as Jane had knelt, and the baby's head pushed out. Lydia screamed, a high-pitched sound that brought feet running down the gangway from the deck. No-one came in. Jane did as Sally had instructed her, showing Lydia how to guide her baby onto a bed of clean towels at the foot of the bed. After the long hours of labour, the birth itself was quick; the only sound, Lydia's cry of joy to see her baby. The boy's face was red and he opened his mouth and let out a roar.

Jane helped Lydia to sit with her back against the end of the bed, then cut the umbilical cord and tied it off. She held the child up in both hands to show to his mother. 'What a fine son you have, mother!'

Lydia took her son, now loosely wrapped in a cotton towel, and wiped and kissed his face. They waited for the afterbirth, then Lydia lay back while Jane cleaned her up.

Jane saw her work was almost done, as the new mother gazed, fixated, on the face of her baby. 'Jane, thank you. He is beautiful,' she whispered. 'Will you fetch Matthew to see his son?'

'He's been out there for the last hour.' Jane took the detritus of the birth and the bucket of bloody water and opened the cabin door. The captain caught Jane by the arms and kissed both cheeks. 'Thank you, Jane!' he said, then rushed in to see his wife and son.

* * *

Jane shut the door behind her and bent her head. Her baby

had never breathed or felt her mother's touch. She went up on deck and walked towards the mainmast in the waist of the ship. She leaned on the railing to look out across a never-ending Southern Ocean and the grey sky above, and held on tight as the whole body of the ship rolled over a huge wave. Sails flapped and banged as the wind blew through the rigging overhead. This ship could sink in a moment and everyone on it would be lost; herself, Lydia and the newborn, the captain and crew. Then she leaned over the rail and emptied the contents of the bucket overboard into the iron waves. So be it.

* * *

Later that day, the captain gave out brandy to the crew to celebrate the birth of his son. Jane took a tiny sip of the brandy when the entire crew raised a cheer for the day-old crewmember, Nathaniel Clayton, and his mother. Jane took a last sip, then went back to the cabin to check on Lydia and her son, whose face was now pink, with fine downy hair on his head. She heard a hoarse cry stifled as he latched onto his mother's breast.

Lydia beamed with pride in her achievement. She held out a hand to Jane. 'How do I thank you?' she asked.

'You did it yourself. You'll be a wonderful mother.'

They both watched as the baby snuffled against Lydia's breast and continued to suck. Jane felt her breasts sting at the sight and looked away.

'I have something for you,' Lydia said. She reached to the table beside the bed and picked up a gold coin, then held it out to Jane. 'It's a gold Eagle for you, with our grateful thanks.'

Jane took the coin and felt the weight of it. On one side there was the date 1846 and in the centre was the Liberty Head. She turned it over to see an engraved eagle with its wings outspread in the centre of the coin. The value of the coin, and the name, United States of America, was engraved around the outside edge. She looked at Lydia. 'Ten dollars! This is too much, I don't deserve this.'

At that moment, the captain came in and saw Jane with the gold piece. He must have heard her words. 'It is our gift to you, Jane. To thank you for looking after my family.' He sat on the bed next to his wife and son. 'We're going home. We need to bring our son home.'

Jane left them and went back to her bunk. She lay down and put the coin under her pillow and let the movement of the ship lull her to sleep. In the night she woke to feel her breasts were hot and heavy. She touched her shift, it was damp with milk, come through for the daughter she had lost, and she wept.

29

Annie Power: June 1847. The Fire

Towards the middle of June, Annie went on her regular visit to Battery Park. She'd had no luck in finding the girl she thought was the sister of Sinead, the drowned girl.

That evening, however, a young woman came over to speak to her.

'Are you Annie Power?' she asked. Annie nodded.

'I've heard about you. You help Irish girls, don't you?'

'Yes, I've got a cottage at the back of the Cathedral. and its open for homeless Irish girls and women. Why do you ask?'

The girl appeared undecided. 'My Name is Peig Sweeney. I'm from Skibbereen.'

'You! Get away from here!' The shouted command came from a man striding towards them, his hair flying around his head. Peig stepped back into the shadow of the wall. 'I can't talk to you. I'll be in trouble.'

Annie glanced at the man and knew him immediately. McGonigle.

'Come with me!' she urged Peig.

'I can't. He'll kill me, if he catches me. You spoke to Sinead last year, didn't you? He knows all about you.' Peig walked back to her minder.

* * *

Annie hurried away from the park, crossed the road and half-walked, half-ran towards the Broadway. Out of breath, she looked over her shoulder. No sign of him. She felt safe now on the crowded street, and slowed her pace. She should give up these visits, stepping into gang territory. Maybe she'd be better off meeting the young women as soon as they arrived on the ships and barges. It would be safer, the nuns were there, and plenty of dock workers and passengers. Then she remembered that McGonigle had taken Katty just moments after they had stepped off the ship last August. 'But we got her back, thank God.' She tried to still her breathing. She got back to the Refuge in twenty minutes, and checked the doors and windows were secured. Roisin and her sister, Clodagh, were studying the Primers in the parlour.

'What are you doing, Annie?' Colleen called through from the kitchen.

Annie joined her at the table. 'Pour me a cup of tea, and I'll tell you.' Annie looked at the uncurtained window above the sink and vowed to get all the windows covered before winter, and dark evenings set in. 'Where're the others?'

'They're upstairs. Why?'

'I don't want to frighten you, Colleen. But I saw that man again, on Battery Park. McGonigle, the one who took Katty last year. I ran away. I really thought he'd hit me!'

'Did he follow you?

'No, he didn't.' She was almost sure. 'But from now on, I want to be careful with the windows and doors.'

'Here, drink this.' Colleen put a cup of tea in front of Annie.

Annie sipped the stewed tea. 'I think I just got in a panic. I'll stay away from there for a while.'

'All the beds here are taken, Annie. So let's get these girls sorted into jobs, soon, please God. Then I'll come with you, and there'll be two of us. We'll stand up to him.'

Colleen earned her keep at the Refuge by helping Annie with the housekeeping and training up their house-guests for their future jobs. As well, she worked part-time on Finn's food stall. Colleen saved that wage to send for her brothers one day.

'Yes, we'll do that. *Go raibh maith agat,* thank you, Colleen.' Annie sighed with relief. They sat together in the quiet kitchen.

* * *

Unknown to Annie, McGonigle and his gang had followed her to the Refuge. There were three of them, they stayed at a distance, and waited until after midnight. The street lamps had been turned down a couple of hours before, and there were no sounds, apart from the rustle of night animals as they crept across silent graves. Tiny bats glided through a patch of moonlight. The men watched and waited until a church clock in the distance struck again. It was time.

McGonigle sneaked up to the front of the cottage. The other two men went around the back. They each had a fistful of rags and a bottle of paraffin. One of the pair soaked the rags in the liquid, while the other scraped a lucifer across sandpaper to ignite the match and set fire to the rags.

At the front of the house, McGonigle used a stone to crack the window. He pushed the broken glass into the parlour and then the burning rag. At the same time, the other two men broke a pane of glass in the back door and shoved their flaming rag through into the hall.

The men waited a moment or two, until the flames took hold of the parlour curtains and the rug in the hall. Then they ran off.

* * *

Annie and Colleen woke at the same time. Barefoot in just her shift, Annie looked through the window, saw the men race away, and smelt smoke from the stairwell. 'Colleen!'

'Yes, I'm up. What's happening?'

'There's a fire. Get the girls up. Come on, we have to get out! I think McGonigle must have followed me here.'

Colleen came onto the landing, she was followed by the others, all in their night shifts.

'We've got to get downstairs,' Annie said.

'But it's full of smoke!' Colleen coughed as the smoke reached the top landing.

'I don't think the stairs aren't burning, yet. Try not to breathe. We'll go straight down and unlock the front door. Then get out. Quick! Move.' Annie grabbed her shawl off her bed and slipped her boots on. She looked around her, at her bed. She remembered the dead woman in the cabin in Sligo. How simple it was to burn that little home, the corpse and the rats. How quick. 'Go, now.'

The girls were crying and shivering. No-one had moved.

'We're going to die here, Annie.' Roisin's face was covered in tears and she coughed.

'Here, we'll go first. Come on!' Annie grabbed Roisin by the hand and started down the stairs.

The rug on the floor and the cloaks and shawls on the stand at the back of the hall were burning with orange flames. Dark smoke billowed towards Annie. She put her arm around Roisin and pulled her close. 'Don't breathe!'

Using her free hand, she unbolted and opened the front door and pushed Roisin through, then held it for the other girls to get out. The cool night air flooded in as they left, and the fire whooshed into life. The side of the staircase crackled, and flames licked across the bottom step.

Annie paused at the door, before stepping outside. She glanced into the parlour. 'My books!' Her beautiful bookcase was just catching fire. Her whole body shook with rage. 'No, not my books. I won't let them burn.'

She took a breath of air, then slammed the front door shut and stepped through into the smoke-filled room. The curtains were in shreds, dripping flames.

'It'll only take a minute.' Annie said to herself, and spread her shawl on the floor. Her hands trembled, and she knew she had to save herself, but still, she grabbed as many books as she could and threw them onto her shawl: her Commonplace book, the Gothic horror stories, the poems, the Holy Bible, the Primers. The smoke brought tears to her eyes and she choked, afraid to breath.

One of the Primers was already alight when she picked it up and her hands stung. She patted the flames out, not feeling the heat, gathered up her shawl and dragged it to the parlour door. The hallway was now dense with black smoke and flames. She could see flames leaping up the front door. She was trapped. She had made a mistake, had taken too long. She would suffocate and then burn to death.

She closed the door between the parlour and the hall and looked around the room. Flames from the rag rug reached up the legs of the sofa to the horsehair stuffing underneath the seats. A small explosion puffed and banged and the sofa lit up with red and orange flashes as the fabric dissolved in the heat and flames.

'*A Dhia,* Dear God, don't let me die in here.' she prayed. The smoke lifted a little and she spotted a way through to the back window. She tightened her hold on the ends of her shawl and dragged the books behind her. She slid along the wall dividing the parlour from the hall, and felt the force of the heat coming through the timber cladding. The ends of her hair singed and curled. 'I must get out! *A Dhia,* help me!'

She screamed and coughed and tried to breathe in some air, but just drew in burning smoke. Her chest felt as if it, too, would dissolve into flames, like the curtains. The weight of the books pulled her backwards and she felt her knees giving way, but she took another step, and another. She was just two steps away from the window. Her sight spotted and darkened. 'Katty, Finn!'

She heard banging on the window. It was Colleen, who gestured to Annie to undo the lock on the sash. Annie's fingers burnt on the hot metal, and with a last effort, she took the bible out of her pack of books. She tried to hammer the wooden covers of the bible against the window, but couldn't hold the weight of it. Then Colleen cracked the glass with a stone and leaned in to grab Annie and drag her out through the window. Flames and black smoke belched out. Scarlet tongues of fire and thick smoke rose into the night sky. The books and the shawl burned.

Annie's clothes and hair were alight, her face was covered in soot. Colleen and Niamh tore off Annie's shift and used it to smothered the flames. Roisin came running with a bucket of water to douse Annie. They half-dragged, half-carried her away from the building.

By now, flames were shooting out through the windows in the roof, crackling and creaking as they devoured the dry, seasoned timbers. Every last thing that Annie had so carefully gathered to make a home was consumed in the inferno.

* * *

Soon after, help began to arrive. The fire service truck clattered in and fire-men hosed down the building. By that time, there wasn't much left to douse, just the corner uprights and the ceiling joists, and by the end, they were burnt to charcoal.

Annie lay a little distance away from the burning cottage. She had just her drawers and bodice on. She was drenched and cold, but she woke at the sound of one of the chimneys collapsing to the ground. Warning shouts from the firemen. It was over.

The cathedral bell tolled twice. She shivered and coughed and spat. She had breathed in the flames and her throat and chest burned. Her fingers and the palms of her hands stung. She coughed and felt hot pain jolt through her body.

'Colleen?' she whispered to Deirdre, who sat beside her.

'She's gone to fetch your aunt, and Finn and Katty.' Deirdre said. 'Don't move, Annie. They're coming.'

Annie lay back on the grass and looked up at the night sky, at thousands of stars as they glittered and twinkled above her head. 'Why would he do this?' she whispered in a hoarse voice. 'Why would he burn us all in our beds?' She had no answer. Tears streaked her face, she held on to Deirdre's hand, and wept for everything she had lost.

30

Jane Keating: May 1847. The Alpha

On the journey to Nantucket, Jane heard the story of Lydia's great adventure with her husband. Lydia, the captain's new wife, was just twenty years old, and this whaling trip on the Alpha was to be their honeymoon. She fell pregnant on her wedding night in Nantucket and found out about it when the ship, the Alpha, was in the Southern Ocean. By then, she was four months gone.

The daughter of a Nantucket chandler, Lydia had grown up around seafaring and loved the idea of going to sea. She found her sea-legs fast, even when she suffered both sea-sickness and morning sickness. After a few weeks, she recovered, and would stand on the quarter-deck at her husband's side, wrapped in one of his greatcoats, her head covered by a stout bonnet with a funnelled brim that allowed her to look out over the ocean.

As the ship ploughed its way east towards the Pacific Ocean, Lydia told Jane how she realised early on that the killing of whales was a dangerous and stinking business. The danger came when one particular whale, after being harpooned, refused to die. The animal, slick and massive, half as long again as the ship, raised its great tail, and pounded the surface of the sea, then began to haul the ship along behind it. The crew laughed and joked as the ship sped through the water.

Lydia had stood on deck to watch the whale, with five or six long harpoons attached to its body, haul the ship across the ocean for almost an hour. This was the first time she had been close to a live whale. The baby in her belly kicked as the whale blew out a spout of water into the air, and tried to descend into the depths of the ocean and take the ship with it. The whalers hauled on the ropes attached to the harpoons embedded in the whale's back to shorten the distance between the ship and the great animal.

The whale began to tire, then faltered. Small boats were launched to surround the whale and the whoops and cheers of the crew echoed through the air when they saw they were winning this battle. The ship hauled down the sails to manoeuvre close to the whale. The captain himself, Lydia's beloved husband, finished off the animal with a final shot of a harpoon in its head.

Later, Lydia put it down to her pregnancy, but she could have sworn the whale looked at her as it died. 'That was the last whale I watched in its death throes. From then on, I stayed in my cabin below decks while the whales were hunted, killed and boiled for their oil. Even there, I had to cover my nose and mouth with a scarf to keep out the smell.'

One time she had gone up on deck for some air, and the blood and body parts of the whale scattered all around had terrified her. The blood-covered hands and gleeful faces of the whalers had sent her racing back down to the cabin. She still had nightmares about the sight and her appetite for food gradually diminished as the hunt continued; she lived on pickled vegetables and hard tack, while the crew enjoyed fresh whale-meat steaks.

By the middle of April, she knew she was nearing the time to have the baby and had started to experience mild labour pains.

'Matthew decided to anchor at Phillip Island for a few days, to find a doctor or a midwife to help with the delivery of our child. He said he was desperate to ensure both me and the baby were safely delivered and he worried he had made a mistake in bringing me along on this journey.'

The only doctor in Port Phillip was an ex-convict. Matthew had brought him out to the ship to examine Lydia. She had taken one look at the man; his yellow teeth and grubby hands, dirt-encrusted nails and the stink of stale brandy off him, and refused to let him near her. The doctor was taken back to the port. Two days passed with no sign of another doctor or a midwife willing to help. The place seemed to be a male-only port with women represented by a gaggle of prostitutes for sale.

After searching in vain, it was agreed they would have to sail up the coast. Thankfully, Lydia's labour had been a false alarm. They would find a midwife or doctor in Sydney.

The captain then made preparations to get under way and was on his final trip to the dock to buy barrels of water and hard tack for the onward journey. Lydia watched from the quarterdeck of the ship as her husband supervised the loading of the tender.

'I saw him turn away from you,' Lydia said.

Jane looked at her. 'Did you pretend to swoon?'

Lydia smiled. 'I borrowed a spyglass from the Mate. As

soon as I saw you, I wanted you to come and help me. Please don't tell Matthew.'

Jane blew out a breath. 'I was glad to help you, and you saved my life.'

The baby thrived on the journey back to Nantucket. He was almost four months old by the time the ship approached New York.

31

Annie Power: Summer 1847, New York

Bridie made a hot water infusion of camphor oil for Annie to inhale. She brought it with her every day while Annie was in hospital, and helped Annie to breathe it in. By mid-July, the doctors said Annie could recuperate at home. Katty was off school for the summer and would help to look after her sister until she was better.

Annie's hands were on the mend but she had no energy to get dressed. She lay on the pillow and looked at the statue of the Virgin Mary on the dresser. She didn't recite her favourite prayer, for her mind was blank.

She thought of her father sometimes. Yes, she was heartbroken when he died, but she had been driven to stop the eviction. She'd had to get herself to Dublin to try to save their home; their little cabin on the Ashling Estate. Now, though, it seemed as if the fire had burned away her desire, and left behind just the shadow of Annie Power, like the charcoal remnants of the beams in the refuge. And they were good for nothing, too.

She looked again at the statue beside her bed. The Blessed Mother was portrayed holding her baby. Annie gazed at the statue. The Mother of God, looked to be about Annie's age and she wore a long white gown with a blue cloak around her shoulders. Her son, Jesus, would be crucified, and his mother had not been able to save him. 'Who will save me?' Annie closed her eyes and turned her head away.

* * *

One evening towards the end of July, Bridie, home from work, came into the bedroom carrying a jug of water and put it on the wash stand. She pulled the curtains back from the window and lifted the bottom sash to let light and air stream into the room. Voices, shouts, and sing-song calls from street vendors, melded with the sounds of rumbling carts and coach wheels and rose up from the street below.

'Come on, girl. You need to get out of that bed. Come into the kitchen and have something to eat for yourself. Katty is demented with worry about you.' Bridie leaned over to kiss Annie and folded back her blanket.

'I'll stay here. I'm not hungry.'

'*Acushla*, darling, I have some good news for you, but you must eat something first. There's warm water there. Get yourself washed and dressed and brush your hair. I'll tell Katty you're on your way.'

Annie lay on the bed in her shift. Then she rolled over, caught the side of the mattress with one hand, put her feet on the floor and pushed herself off the bed. She stumbled across to the wash stand and poured some water from the jug into the basin. Her hands had almost healed, and she rubbed a small piece of soap between her palms, then washed her face. Her fingers slid over the bones in her cheeks and jaw and the taut skin on her face. Her body smelt stale, but she got dressed anyway. The skirt and blouse hung loosely on her, so she rolled up the waistband. She pulled a brush through her hair and left it hanging down, lacking the energy to tie it back or pin it up. Then she went through into the kitchen, where Bridie watched her eat a few spoonfuls of porridge.

When she had finished eating, Bridie held Annie's hands in hers.

'Your story has been in the newspaper. I wasn't going to tell you this yet, but perhaps now is the right time. The Bishop and Sister Mary Angela are coming to see you tomorrow to talk to you. They set up a public subscription to raise money to rebuild the refuge. Everyone is talking about your bravery, Annie. And the work you've been doing to stop girls being caught by the criminal gangs. If I was a crying kind of woman, I might shed a few tears.' Instead, Bridie picked up the porridge bowl, washed it and the spoon, dried them both and put them in the cupboard. She looked over her shoulder at Annie. 'You've been long enough lying down under this, my girl. Make your mind up what you'll do from now on, *acushla.*'

Annie looked at her aunt, at her greying hair and narrow lined face. 'I don't know if I can, Bridie. Da always said I was brave, and I was, back then. But I think I lost it in the fire.'

'You didn't lose it, *a stor.* Your Da was right. You've been a bit knocked about lately. Now you're on the mend.' Bridie leaned over and put her arm around Annie's shoulders. 'You saved your girls, and the books. Sure, maybe you could write what happened? I'd say the newspaper'd be interested to print it.'

Annie tried to smile. Her aunt placed Annie's notebook and pencil on the table in front of her. 'You might as well make a start now.'

Annie picked up the pencil and wrote a sentence. *The Refuge for Irish Girls and Women.*

* * *

It took a couple of weeks and summer was well underway when the subscriptions reached two hundred dollars. The Aid for Ireland committee stepped up and offered to help rebuild Annie's Refuge.

32

Annie Power: 1st August, 1847. Her Journal

*I*t is Sunday, and almost dawn. There is some brightness in the sky over towards the cathedral. I pulled the curtain open next to the bed and saw I forgot to blow out the candle last night. It has burnt away to nothing. Now there are only thin lines of smoky wax stuck to the brass stem and pooled in the well of the holder. Such a waste, there was half a good candle there.

I used the chamber pot and crawled back into bed. I just don't understand why I'm still so weak. Surely, I should have more strength now, after all this time. I haven't been outside for weeks. Bridie bought me a writing slope that I can use in bed, and I'm writing this journal on it now. It's got a tiny steel inkwell in it. The sound it makes, when I dip and tap the nib, keeps me company.

That, and the birdsong outside the window are the only sounds this early. The birds must be in the eaves of the roof, for there's not a single tree around here. I can see grey-tiled rooftops from the window and the sky, of course. Today the heavens are a blue that reminds me of the Blessed Mother's cloak. I think they call it cerulean blue.

It's getting lighter now. I can hear Bridie in the kitchen, getting washed and dressed. She's been back at work for a while, but I have Katty to look after me for the next few weeks, before she starts school again. I'll be well by then. Please God.

I have to write about this. Jane's letter arrived yesterday. Holy Mother of God, bless me and keep me safe, and protect Jane on her journey here.

In her letter, she said she'd see me in September. I don't know how she will get here, but I can truly feel she's getting closer. I often think she must surely be angry with me. Why did I let her take my place and be transported all that way to New South Wales? I dream again and again of that moment in Kilmainham Gaol. But in my dream, things are different. I can hear myself saying, 'No, Jane. I won't allow it. It's my punishment. You can take care of Finn and Katty for me.'

But I was too selfish, and a coward. Afraid for myself, and afraid to leave Finn and Katty. I knew Jane was stronger than me, and she would survive. When she gets here, I'll tell her how sorry I am. Please God, she survives the journey.

* * *

Tuesday, 3rd August 1847.

I've just read again the newspaper account of the fire at the Refuge. I cut the newspaper report out and pasted it here. It sounds as if it happened to someone else. But when I look at my poor scarred hands, I believe it is true. Here I am sitting up in Bridie's bed, like a queen, being waited on hand and foot for the last month or more.

Now Katty sleeps on my roll-up mattress in the parlour next to Finn. Bridie bought another small mattress, so she can sleep on the floor, at the foot of her own bed.

Only for Bridie came into the hospital ward every day to check on me, I'd have died of loneliness. Then they said I'm getting better, so I came home.

But even now, I still can't take a full breath. It's wearing to try and get enough air in. I have such a hunger in me, not for food, for air. The window beside me is open and I can see the curtains move when there's a breeze. I just want to open my mouth wide and swallow big gulps of air, but none will go in.

Strangely, it's only now I can understand what starvation does to a person. Back home, we were hungry because we didn't have much food when the potatoes rotted. Somehow, Da always managed to get hold of a handful of oats or barley to boil up for a pot of soup. In that regard, we were fortunate. It's those who had nothing left, after they had boiled up and ate the nettles, the rats and the dogs. We never had to do that, thank God. And we got out in time. That was Jane's gift to us. We're alive. And the others, left behind. What of them? They come to me in my dreams. Every night.

* * *

Thursday 12th August 1847.

Bishop Hughes called in to see me after the blessing of the new Refuge. I'll see it soon. Aunt Bridie brought me the newspaper to read about the Refuge.

Newspaper article pasted into Annie's journal.

```
The Sun, New York. 12th August, 1847.
Today is a fortunate day for Miss Annie Power after
```

her travails of recent months. As readers will be aware, Miss Power set up the Refuge for Young Irish Females, to help newly arrived young women emigrants from her famine-stricken homeland of Ireland.

Readers would also think the Refuge, situated in the grounds of St Patrick's Cathedral, would be a place of safety.

Tragically, last June, the entire building was destroyed in an arson attack. It is believed that a gang of felons set fire to the house in revenge for Miss Power offering succour to their girls and women. The arsonists have not been found.

Thanks to the stirling efforts of a band of Miss Power's supporters, a Public Subscription raised the funds needed to rebuild the Refuge. Earlier this week, Bishop Hughes officiated at the reopening ceremony and praised Miss Power's devotion to the Blessed Mother. It will be known forthwith as Annie Power's Refuge.

Miss Power was unable to attend the reopening as she is still recovering at home from the injuries she sustained during the arson attack.

All readers of this newspaper will join the Editor in wishing Miss Power a speedy recovery.

* * *

Journal entry. Sunday, 15th August 1847.

I read a poem by Speranza and copied it here. I saw this take place with my own eyes, in Dungarvan. The best of the country's food being loaded onto ships for England, while our poor people starved.

"The Famine Year
 by Speranza
Weary men, what reap ye?--Golden corn for the
stranger.
What sow ye?--Human corses that wait for the avenger.
Fainting forms, hunger-stricken, what see you in the
offing?
Stately ships to bear our food away, amid the
stranger's scoffing.
There's a proud array of soldiers--what do they
round your door?
They guard our masters' granaries from the thin
hands of the poor.
Pale mothers, wherefore weeping? - Would to God that
we were dead -
Our children swoon before us, and we cannot give
them bread."

I read what the English politicians say in the newspapers. They think we are deserving of our fate. "It is the will of God." But sure, they have no love for our island or the people on it. They won't let their horses or hunting dogs go hungry, but will close their hearts to hundreds and thousands of Irish men, women and children starving and dying by the side of the road. They won't even look at them, and disbelieve all the reports they get.

I still do not understand how the Irishmen in the British army and the Irish farmers and the Irish businessmen, the men and women who buy and sell butter, cheese and grain; corn, barley and oats; bacon, beef and lamb; apples, cabbages and carrots; beer and whiskey. The men who load the ships with all that food. Send it off to England, to feed English people. How could Irishmen and women do this? Why are they still doing it? I read they have armed guards at the ports and I saw that for myself in Dungarvan. But still, after two years of hunger and disease. And what are the priests saying? I suppose no-one will listen to a Catholic priest in London, but there are plenty of them to speak out.

Bridie tells me not to fret. It will stop me from getting well. Yet I'm still here in her bed, with no sign of me improving. The doctor comes and listens to my lungs. They both know I have the consumption. He says it is of long-standing. Perhaps I caught it on my travels with Speranza. That was more than a year ago now. Is that long-standing enough? I've not told Finn or Katty.

My dream was to go back to Ireland, yet I can hardly get out of the bed.

Today, I'll try and sit out of the bed, then stand. Soon I will move back to the Refuge. Very soon.

'Remember, Oh most Blessed Virgin Mary,
that never was it known . . .'

* * *

Annie's poem

My Promise
I pledged to go back to Ireland.
My heart is broken for my beautiful homeland.
A land of corpses and those who watch them starve
Even now I see it in the faces of my countrywomen
Hear it in their tales of devastation.
We must wait a while longer for the Avenger.
'Vengeance is mine,' sayeth the Lord. When this is over,
vengeance will be wreaked on those who stood and watched
the suffering people of Ireland.

My dreams for Finn and Katty.
I will write this later. I have such grand dreams for them.

* * *

Newspaper article pasted into Annie's journal.

The Sun Newspaper. Monday, 16th August, 1847.

It is with great sadness that we report the death of
Miss Annie Power of Princes Street, Manhattan.
Miss Power, aged seventeen, died peacefully in her
bed. She was surrounded by her family; her aunt, Mrs
Bridie Foley, her brother, Finn, and sister, Katty.
Miss Power was injured in the arson attack on the
refuge she had set up earlier this year.
Unfortunately, she did not recover from her injuries.
The funeral will be held at St Patrick's Cathedral
on Thursday, the 19th August at 11 a.m. His Grace,
the Bishop of New York, will officiate at the
funeral.

33

Jane Keating: Wednesday, 18th August 1847. New York

Lydia had urged her husband to make a quick stop in New York harbour to put Jane ashore, before continuing the journey home to Nantucket. It took an hour to manoeuvre the whaling ship past the throng of three and four masted ships and the Alpha anchored around midnight, just off South Street Dock.

Jane stood on deck with Lydia and looked over at the crowded quays. They both agreed that the new gas lighting all along the quays was an amazing new technology. It provided illumination as if on a stage. Even at this time of night, the roadway was filled with horse-drawn trams and trucks, all moving at speed, stopping, starting, loading and unloading; with workmen pushing and pulling sacks and crates of goods, shouting orders and instructions, servicing the ships in the harbour. The din rebounded off the walls of the brick built warehouses, businesses, hotels and shops that lined the waterfront and echoed in the night sky above Manhattan.

The cutter was launched, and the crewman waited for Jane and the Captain to climb down into it. Jane hugged Lydia, having earlier kissed baby Nathaniel in his crib. Then she tucked the hem of her skirt into her waistband, leaving two hands free to hold onto the rope ladder and climbed down into the boat. The captain threw Jane's bag down and followed her. He grabbed an oar and rowed with the crewman the few hundred yards across the harbour towards the quayside.

Jane held on tight to the side of the cutter. She looked back and waved to Lydia, then turned to look at Manhattan, bustling even at midnight.

'Annie is near, I can feel it.' She smiled and shook her head, then laughed out loud, for the first time in more than a year. She wanted to jump up and shout out her joy, but kept hold of the side of the boat as it pulled and rocked over the choppy waves in the harbour.

Captain Clayton walked Jane to a hotel on the quayside and waited while she paid for a room. She placed the gold Eagle on the counter and watched as the clerk looked twice at it. 'I need to get the manager to change this for you, Miss Keating.'

Then it was time to say goodbye. She held her hand out to shake hands. 'You did a good deed that day, when you took me on board, Captain. I'll always be thankful.'

'You and I know it worked well for both of us. You've been a friend to Lydia and helped her take care of my son these last few months. Now then, I must get away while the tide is right.' He tipped his hat to her. 'There's banks and booking offices along this seafront. I know you'll be careful. Good luck to you, Jane.'

She stood in the doorway of the hotel while he crossed the muddy street back towards the cutter and the whaling ship and the last leg of his journey home.

In bed that night she hardly slept. The bed itself seemed to move under her as if she were still at sea. She got up and paced the floor in the dark and thought of the next day when she would finally see her best friend. She had dreamed of this day for so long, and now it was almost upon her. She waited impatiently for morning. How would she tell Annie about her lost daughter? She shook her head. She'd find the words, somehow.

* * *

Thursday, 19th August, 1847.

The first thing Jane did the next morning, was go to a bank on South Street to change one of her gold nuggets into dollars. She stopped off at a pawn shop and bought some clothes to replace her shabby skirts and blouses. Then she called in to one of the ticket offices lined along the quay to enquire about a passage to Ireland. Ships sailed for Liverpool and Dublin almost every day of the week. Very few passengers travelled outwards, so she would have no difficulty getting a ticket on the day of departure. Jane decided that she'd spend some time with Annie, then make up her mind when to go. There was no hurry.

She went back to the hotel and changed into her new clothes. Her image in the mirror looked nothing like the girl who had buried her daughter in the Southern Ocean just months before. Her face had lost the grim, watchful look she had developed in Melbourne and her cheeks had filled out. And she looked more her age, almost seventeen.

The skirt was tight at the waist, Jane had never worn a

corset and she wasn't about to start now, so she left the top two buttons open and pulled on the matching jacket. The navy blue flounces of the skirt felt ridiculously wide. She recalled the slim trousers she had worn on her travels in Ireland, when she had passed as Jack Keating. For a moment, she was tempted to go back to the pawn shop and exchange her outfit for some trousers. It was too late now, she had to find Annie. Besides, she smiled when she remembered that Owen had said no-one would take her for a boy now.

* * *

She hailed a cab outside the hotel to take her to Princes Street. She sat in the small cab and clutched Annie's prayer book tightly. The small prayer book had Annie's Manhattan address inside the cover. The half hour journey to Princes Street brought Jane deeper into Manhattan and streets criss-crossed each other in an almost haphazard manner. Pedestrians risked their lives dodging the speeding horse-drawn carriages and trams. The cab then turned onto a wide street with four and five storey buildings on either side.

'The going will be easier along Broadway,' the cab driver explained.

Here, pedestrians had smooth, stone pavements on either side of the road to walk on. Awnings reached over the walkways to provide shelter for street markets and stall-holders along the route.

* * *

She paid the cab driver and crossed the road towards the

building on the corner. A crowd of people lined the sidewalk, young and old, men and women.

Yes, she had found the right address, the number thirteen was on the pillar at the side of the entrance. There must be some business going on here, with all these people, she thought. The front door stood open, although none of the onlookers entered. Jane passed by them and heard soft Irish murmurs. 'They say t'was the fire. Sure, God help them.'

She walked down the hall and started up the stairs to apartment twelve. Her legs were still unsteady, from the ship maybe, or her foot had gotten caught in the folds of her skirt. She swayed and grabbed onto the bannister to steady herself. It was as if the staircase had tilted, was fixed neither to the ground nor the wall, but suspended in the air. At the top of the first flight of stairs she counted the apartment numbers. 'Five, six, seven, eight.' All the doors were closed against a dim silence in the hallway. And the crowd outside? What fire?

She turned to set her foot on the next row of steps upwards and heard voices. 'Let it not be them.' Her bag weighed her down, as if to anchor her to the step. Light came from above and glimmered through dust motes in the air. 'I've come twelve thousand miles across half the world, and here I am like a ship run aground on this one step. Can go neither forward nor backward.'

Footsteps clattered up behind her and she was overtaken by two black-clad nuns. 'Thank God, we're in time,' one said, and glanced back at Jane. 'Are you here for the funeral? You need to hurry.' And Jane's feet unmoored themselves from the step and moved her upwards.

On the top floor, the staircase opened onto a lobby and the door to apartment number twelve was open. Inside was

313

a narrow space, filled with too many people to count, and overflowing out onto the landing.

Jane followed the nuns, and pushed through into the kitchen at the end of the hallway, where all the air seemed to have been sucked away. She stood at the threshold, saw the cast iron stove. The black kettle steamed. Light glinted through the lace curtain at the window and fell on the teapot and the whiskey bottle on the table. The men had whiskey glasses in their hands and the women sipped tea. All were dressed in mourning black, despite the summer day that was in it.

'I'm here for Annie Power,' she said in a half-whisper. Then louder. 'Annie! Annie Power? Are you here?'

The voices fell silent. She looked back at the faces of strangers turned towards her. Then a young man stepped forward and she knew him, instantly. The darling boy, Finn. No longer a boy, a man now, but she recognised him all the same. He wore a black arm-band around his jacket sleeve. Jane closed her eyes at the sight of the armband, and heard his low voice.

'Jane. We've been waiting for you. We prayed you'd get here in time.' Finn put his hand out to the woman beside him. She was thin and bird-like, dressed in black, with round wire-rimmed spectacles on her lined face. The woman kept hold of Finn's hand. A space opened up around Jane, Finn and the woman. Silenced whispers susurrated.

'Not for Annie?' Say not, she prayed. Dear Lord if there's an ounce of mercy left in heaven, then say not.

Finn nodded, with his lips pressed tightly together and tears on his cheeks. He looked young again, like the boy he had been, when she knew him back in Waterford.

The woman beside Finn, she must be the aunt, moved closer

and caught Jane's hand in hers. She led the two of them, Jane and Finn, out of the kitchen. 'Come and see her. She's in the parlour.' The aunt drew Jane on through the now silent crowd. Jane resisted, she wanted to catch her breath, take a minute to understand, but the woman drew her on.

The coffin was placed on two trestles in the middle of the room next to the kitchen. And a body lay in it. Not Annie, for this corpse looked nothing like her. The woman lay as if asleep, her head rested on a pillow and she was dressed in a white shroud. What is this, some cruel trick? Dread churned in Jane's stomach. Then she saw Katty.

There were just a few people in the room; a large priest, who was speaking to men in the corner, and a girl, all in black. It was Katty, sitting on a stool next to the coffin. Katty's face and eyes were swollen from crying, and she cried again when she saw Jane.

'You came.'

Jane bent down and kissed Katty, put her arm around her, and looked again, and saw it was indeed her friend's body laid out in the coffin.

Annie's long hair was plaited and lay across her shoulder. Not the lustrous copper that Jane remembered. Instead, dun-coloured threads. Annie's eyes were closed and her lips parted a little to show her teeth. Her skin was waxy in death and her bandaged hands were crossed on her breast; a pale, wooden rosary beads linked between her fingers. Jane touched one of the smooth beads, then Annie's cold fingers. 'So, it's come to this, my friend.'

She heard the aunt whisper to the priest, who had joined them around the coffin.

'This is Jane Keating, Annie's friend. She's come all the way from New South Wales, expecting to see Annie alive and well. This has come as a great shock to her, your Grace.'

The priest, or Bishop, spoke to Jane. 'You have my heartfelt condolences, on the loss of your friend.'

Jane didn't hear, just kept looking at Annie's face, then she turned to Finn. 'Is there somewhere I can sit down?' She touched the side of the coffin, to prove this was real. It's not a dream. Don't fall, she urged herself, as tears tracked down her cheeks.

'Come with me,' Finn said. 'Here, take my hand.'

There was a bedroom off the hallway, and she sat on the edge of an iron bedstead. 'Dear God, what happened, Finn? The last letter I got, she had great plans for a hostel. She wasn't sick. I don't understand.'

'She opened the refuge in March. We'll go over and see it after the funeral. But she hadn't been well, Jane. She told no-one, but it turned out she had consumption for months, and it wore her down. Then there was the fire. Criminals set fire to the refuge, and the smoke damaged her lungs even more, and burned her poor hands.' Finn shook his head and wiped his eyes. 'She tried so hard, but in the end she just couldn't breathe. She left us, Jane.'

Jane wanted to ask about the fire, but at that moment, Bridie looked in around the doorway. 'It's time to go. Come and say your goodbyes.'

Jane stood beside Finn and Katty as they kissed their sister's face, then she stepped forward, bent and kissed the cold grey lips of a corpse.

Annie was long gone. The open window in the parlour had let her soul escape, leaving behind just the shell of Annie Power, who had no further need of her mortal body. Jane blessed herself. 'Rest in peace my friend. Between us we saved Katty and Finn. That's enough for one lifetime.'

The Bishop began to pray over the body. The pallbearers screwed the coffin lid down, then hoisted the coffin onto their strong shoulders and manoeuvred down the stairs onto the waiting hearse. It was just a short walk behind the carriage to the cathedral.

There must have been more than a hundred people in the pews. Jane stood with Bridie, Finn and Katty. She knelt and prayed with the others, inhaled the incense, received the Blessed Host, and wept for her beautiful friend.

* * *

Afterwards, Annie was laid to rest in the grave that held Bridie's late husband, Kevin Foley. Then, when everyone had left, all was quiet, just Finn and Katty, Bridie and one of the nuns stood beside the grave. It was over.

The two older women nodded to each other and the nun spoke. 'Jane, I'm Sister Mary Angela. We want to show you the new Refuge. It's only a few steps away. Annie would want you to see it.'

They walked along a narrow path through the graveyard to the far wall surrounding the graves. Jane saw a two-storey cottage with a gleaming slate roof. The newly whitewashed walls reflected the noon sun. There was no sign of a fire, all had been rebuilt.

The nun walked beside Jane. 'It's such a tragedy. I was very fond of Annie. She was a good soul and we became friends. She'll be missed. My order, the Sisters of Charity, have taken over the Refuge. We'll continue Annie's work with young

Irish women and girls. The only change we've made is in the name. It'll be known from now on as Annie's Refuge.' They stopped in front of the door to the cottage. 'Will you come and visit for a while? I'll show you around. And you must see Annie's books.'

Katty took Jane's hand in hers. 'Stay for a while, Jane.'

* * *

Sister Mary Angela showed her around the new refuge and introduced her to Colleen, who had come back to help run the Refuge. Jane sat and talked with Finn and Katty. They drank tea, and reminisced about their time together in Ireland. She looked at her young friends.

'I could stay here,' she thought. 'Make a life with Finn and Katty. Maybe one day I'll come back. But not yet.'

Then it was time to go. She embraced her friends and Sister Mary Angela. Then she walked back through the graveyard and made her way to the hotel at the docks. She wiped her face with a handkerchief as she walked. Not one of the passersby took a second look at all, at the smart young woman in her new, second-hand navy twill jacket and skirt.

* * *

Friday, 20th August, 1847.

Early the next morning, Jane bought a ticket to Dublin, on a ship leaving that day. There were very few passengers travelling back to Ireland, for human passengers were all one way. The ship was already loaded with timber, bound for Liverpool, then would sail on to Dublin to pick up more migrants to North America.

She had a couple of hours before she needed to board the ship, but she didn't go back to Princes Street. They had said their goodbyes. Instead, she got a cab back to the cemetery and knelt beside the newly-filled grave.

'I'll never forget you, Annie. I wanted to tell you about Margaret. Maybe you'll meet in heaven? Maybe you already have? Tell her about me, won't you? And about the day you and I first met.'

It felt like a lifetime, when Jane had first seen Annie, a year and a half ago in the market in Waterford town. After spending days alone travelling the road from Galway to Waterford, Jane had been starving and destitute. It had seemed then, that the Hunger was at its worst when, in hindsight, it was only getting started.

Jane had been looking for a friendly face in the market, someone to ask about her relatives in Waterford. She had watched as Annie packed away the few items left on her stall. Annie's copper hair hung down her back, she wore a pale blue dress and seemed to shimmer in the evening air, like Onagh, the fairy queen from the old legends of the Sidhe race.

'I promised we'd meet again, my friend,' Jane said. 'I'm heartbroken not to see you alive and well. I'm going back to Ireland, Annie. I hoped you might come with me.'

After a while, Jane stood and brushed the dirt from her skirt. She picked up her bag and turned away and walked towards the gate. Just beside the entrance to the cemetery she stopped beside a large stone cross. It stood on a wide, red-brick plinth, and reached high into the sunlit sky.

A snow-white swan, sculpted out of pure marble, lay the

foot of the speckled, granite cross. The swan's neck lay curled along its back, as if asleep. Its wings were raised around a tiny cygnet, carved out of the same white stone, asleep and safe in its mother's alabaster embrace. Jane touched the cold stone, and ran her fingers along the soft lines of the cygnet's feathers.

She spoke to the stillborn daughter she had buried in the Antarctic Ocean. 'I love you, *mo stór beag,* my little darling, and I'll never forget you. If, one day, I have more children, I'll tell them all about you. Your auntie Annie is in heaven, she'll look after you.'

34

Jane Keating: August 1847. Going home

Jane stood on deck as the ship moved away from the pier. It was now midday. The tide was on the turn, and the ship was ready for the journey to Dublin. In June, over a year ago, she had been locked in a prison below deck on a convict transportation ship to Melbourne. Now, on this journey, Jane had a cabin and would eat at the captain's table.

'Weigh anchor!' The shout rang across the deck to a team of crew who raced to obey the captain's order. They turned the winch to haul up the anchor and the ship began to move. Jane put her hand on the rail to steady herself as the ship jolted awake. The sails flapped and unfurled and each heavy sheet of canvas thrummed as it filled with air. The ship made its way out past dozens of other vessels anchored in the harbour. Jane looked back towards New York for a moment. 'Goodbye, Finn and Katty. Please God, we'll meet again, one day.'

'Why, just look at that!' A man spoke beside her. Jane followed his pointing finger up to where a great bird, an albatross, soared high above the top-mast of the ship. 'It's a wandering Albatross. Must have been blown off course,' the stranger said.

She squinted in the sun and watched the lost bird silently swoop, to almost touch the top-mast. She recalled Owen telling her that those huge birds never set down on land. They lived always in the air, on their journey across the oceans, alone.

The albatross swooped down along the length of the deck and dipped out over the water to within a couple of feet of the waves, its yellow beak, glinted.

Then it turned and flew back over Jane's head. Its white body and black-tipped wings came so close that the air trembled against her cheek. It seemed as if the great bird wanted to wish her well on her next journey.

After a final turn around the top-mast, the albatross soared into the air and flew off, away to the east and out to sea, to spend its years and years alone, skimming over the waves for thousands of miles.

Jane took a deep breath of the salty air, and lifted her hand in farewell, but also in greeting. She, Jane Keating, was going home to Ireland.

The End

Author's Note

I have researched my character, Jane Keating's, time in Melbourne in 1846-47. During her stay there, she comes into contact with a family of Wurundjeri people and is helped by them, and then helps them in return. As the novel progressed, Jane would seek help from her friend's mother, who would step in and guide Jane through her sad loss.

I spent some time researching traditional Aboriginal birthing practices. The main resource I found was a research article about Traditional Aboriginal birthing practices (referenced below). I also tried to contact an adviser on Aboriginal culture, particularly for the birthing scenes and also characters' names. However, I was unsuccessful in my endeavours.

I am aware of the need for cultural sensitivity when referring to the First Nations peoples of Victoria and Australia. I hope that I have respectfully represented the interactions between my main character and the Aboriginal family she meets while in Melbourne.

* * *

As an Indie writer and self-publisher, I am happy to correct any mistakes in my representation of Jane's experiences in forthcoming editions of this novel.

References:

Melbourne Museum. https://museumsvictoria.com.au/wom injeka-welcome/ Accessed August 2021.

Traditional Aboriginal birthing practices in Australia, past and present.
   https://www.researchgate.net/publication/215781043_T raditional_Aboriginal_birthing_practices_in_Australia_Pa st_and_present
   Helen Callaghan. 2001. Accessed August 2021.

The Fatal Shore, Robert Hughes, 2003, London, Vintage

The Founding of Melbourne & the Conquest of Australia, James Boyce, 2012, Victoria, Black Inc.

The Famine Year by Speranza. (1847). Accessed on Project Gutenberg's Poems by Speranza, by Jane Francesca Agnes Wilde

https://www.gutenberg.org/files/61742/61742-h/61742-h. htm#THE_FAMINE_YEAR/

About the Author

I was born in England, of Irish emigrant parents. I have always had a deep interest in Irish history, particularly in relation to British colonialism, the fight for independence and emigration.

An Indie writer and publisher, I am working on an Irish Famine Trilogy.

"Daughters of the Famine Road", Book 1, follows the two protagonists, Annie and Jane, as they navigate the dangers of the potato famine in Ireland 1845-46. Published in March 2022, in paperback and Kindle ebook. **https://rotf.lol/Famine-Road**

"Daughters in Exile" out now, is the second novel in the series, and traces the experiences of young women who were forced to leave their homeland to survive.

"Home - 1847" (draft title) will be published by the end of this year, 2022.

Find my books on www.Amazon.com

Together with writing novels, I blog about 19th and 20th century Irish history, emigration, women, writers, poetry and art.

You can connect with me on:

🌐 https://www.bridgetsjournal.com

🐦 https://twitter.com/bridgetw1807

Subscribe to my newsletter:

✉ https://www.bridgetsjournal.com/contact

SD JST

Printed in Great Britain
by Amazon

44502479R00185